Hounds of the Basket Stitch

A Black Sheep & Company Mystery:

Knit to Kill

Purls and Poison

Hounds of the Basket Stitch

Hounds of the Basket Stitch

Anne Canadeo

KENSINGTON BOOKS
www.kensingtonbooks.com

KENSINGTON BOOKS are published by

Kensington Publishing Corp.
119 West 40th Street
New York, NY 10018

All Kensington titles, imprints and distributed lines are available at special quantity discounts for bulk purchases for sales promotion, premiums, fund-raising, educational or institutional use. Special book excerpts or customized printings can also be created to fit specific needs. For details, write or phone the office of the Kensington Special Sales Manager: Kensington Publishing Corp., 119 West 40th Street, New York, NY, 10018. Attn. Special Sales Department. Phone: 1-800-221-2647.

Kensington and the K logo Reg. U.S. Pat. & TM Off.

Library of Congress Card Catalogue Number: 2019944523

ISBN-13: 978-1-4967-0865-6
ISBN-10: 1-4967-0865-2
First Kensington Hardcover Edition: November 2019

ISBN-13: 978-1-4967-0866-3 (ebook)
ISBN-10: 1-4967-0866-0 (ebook)

10 9 8 7 6 5 4 3 2 1

Printed in the United States of America

To the clever, faithful, sweet, and funny dogs who have given me unshakeable, unconditional love: Loozy, Daisy, Rose, Abby and Lily.
And to everyone who treasures their own beautiful, wise dogs.

"The world is full of obvious things which nobody by any chance observes."

Sherlock Holmes
The Hound of the Baskervilles, Arthur Conan Doyle

Chapter 1

"We're *almost* there. I promise." Dana turned and offered an apologetic smile to the rest of the group, who sat shoulder to shoulder in the backseat of Suzanne's huge SUV.

Like birds on a wire, Maggie thought. Birds with knitting bags on their laps.

"No need to apologize. We're fine. Aren't we?" Maggie glanced at Lucy and Phoebe. "I come this way all the time in the summer for the farm stands. It just seems longer in the dark."

"Said the woman who would cheerfully drive to Antarctica to teach penguins how to knit." Lucy had been watching out her window but now turned to catch Maggie's eye.

Maggie shrugged. "I guess I would, if they invited me."

"Sign me up for that trip." Phoebe sounded as if she thought it could actually happen. And as if she'd much prefer that adventure to their present one. "Did you see that video on the internet with this cute old guy who knits sweaters for penguins? It was unbelievably sweet."

"No wonder they haven't called me yet," Maggie said.

Penguins had not asked for a knitting lesson, just the Piper sisters, Holly and Rose. Or rather, Dana had asked

Maggie if she would teach the young women some basic stitches. Dana was Holly's godmother, and both sisters were as dear to her as family.

Holly and Rose had been set to join the group's usual Thursday night meeting, but just before seven, Holly had called. One of Rose's dogs had given birth to eight puppies about two weeks ago. The new mother was not feeling well today, and Rose couldn't leave her.

Maggie had heard a bit about Rose's pack of rescued hounds. She didn't know how many dogs there were in all, but as of two weeks ago, you'd have to add eight more.

Without much debate, the group had decided to pack their knitting gear, along with the dinner they'd prepared, and bring their weekly meeting to the Pipers, who lived in a far corner of Plum Harbor.

Maggie was not sure which consideration had weighed heavier in each member of the group: sympathy for their fearless leader, who had put together a special lesson for the night, or the lure of puppies. The end result was the same. Here they were, driving down a black ribbon of a road that cut through thick woods on either side, with houses few and far between.

The calendar had announced the first day of spring, but you'd never know it from the weather, just more of the raw, ragged edge of a New England winter. A brisk wind tossed bare branches that arched above their path, and low gray clouds gathered in the night sky. Heavy rain was coming, and Maggie hoped the storm would hold off until they were safely back in town. The puffs of frosty mist that floated out between the trees made Maggie think of wandering ghosts who had lost their way.

But we're not lost, Maggie reminded herself, though they had fallen behind the usual schedule.

Usually, by this time of night, they'd be seated around

the big oak table at the back of her knitting shop, snug and warm, sharing a good dinner, juicy gossip, and showing off their knitting projects and discussing their stitching predicaments.

"At the risk of sounding like a five-year-old," Lucy said, "when we arrive there, we'll get to see the puppies."

"Personally, I'd prefer kittens, as you already know." Phoebe, the youngest in their group and the most expert stitcher except for Maggie, had pulled out a project and was managing the needles well, despite the moving car and dim light.

"At the risk of *also* sounding like a five-year-old, I'm really hungry and definitely need a bathroom," Suzanne said, her gaze fixed on her driving.

"Come on, Suzanne," Maggie coaxed. "We haven't even left Plum Harbor. Not the town limit, I mean."

"Not officially." Suzanne knew about such things. Maggie would trust Suzanne, a real estate professional who had just opened her own office, Cavanaugh Fine Homes, to find the town line blindfolded and also recite the zip code for every neighborhood on the way.

Lucy watched out her window again, though there was little to see. "Holly and Rose must feel isolated out here. Don't you think?"

"Holly never complains," Dana said, "but I'm sure she must be lonely at times with only her younger sister for company."

"It is very rural out here, compared to town," Suzanne agreed. "But the zoning has been tweaked, and pretty soon new houses will be popping up like mushrooms. I'd say those Piper sisters are sitting on a gold mine."

"They've already had offers," Dana confided. "Holly said she'll never sell their property. Moving away would be too upsetting for Rose."

Phoebe held a needle up to her nose to examine a row. "You said Rose had a head injury a long time ago. How did it happen . . . if you don't mind telling us?"

Maggie was also curious to hear more about Rose, without breaching her privacy, of course. When Dana had asked if Maggie would give the sisters a lesson or two, Maggie had gathered there was some special reason Dana thought Rose should learn, but she hadn't asked too many questions.

Dana turned to answer Phoebe. "It's okay. I can tell you a bit about her. I should explain so that you know what to expect. About fifteen years ago, Rose and Holly were in a car accident. Holly ended up with only a few cuts and bruises, but Rose emerged with a serious brain trauma. At first, you probably won't notice anything different about her. She's bright, charming, and very warmhearted. Very trusting, too," Dana added, sounding as if that trait was a mixed blessing.

"But a large part of her personality is frozen in adolescence," Dana continued. "She hasn't matured much since the accident, which happened when she was just fourteen. Which is why Holly is so protective of her and devoted to her care."

"Admirable. But sad," Lucy said. "Sad for Rose and the whole family."

"They don't have much family left. Their parents passed away not long after the accident, within a few years of each other, and there aren't any relatives in the area," Dana continued. "When the accident happened, Holly was about to leave for college, but she decided to stay home so she could watch over Rose. She learned the family business and has been running it on her own for at least ten years now. She and Rose are very close. And very much alone."

"But they have you, Dana. An unofficial aunt and guardian angel rolled into one," Maggie reminded her.

Dana laughed. "I'm not sure about the angel title, but I am Holly's godmother, and I try to help them as much as I can."

"You knew their mother, right?" Lucy asked.

"She lived right next door when I was growing up." Dana's voice softened with the memory. "Ava was a few years older than me, but we were very close friends. She got married after high school and moved to Vermont. The marriage didn't last long, and she came back to Plum Harbor with a son. We reconnected, and when she married George Piper, I watched the girls grow up. They still call me Aunt Dana," she added with a smile.

Phoebe turned her work over and started a row. "I bet you've been a very good aunt. You understand Rose's condition and can really help her. Is it just that she's stuck in adolescence, or are there other things going on, too?"

"There are other issues," Dana said. "Mood swings and problems concentrating. She can act impulsively or even black out if she's overwhelmed. Trauma can derail the timekeeping part of the brain, and there's sometimes memory loss. But she's been doing very well lately. Most of those problems have disappeared, with the help of the new therapies and her comfort dogs."

"Comfort dogs?" Lucy sat up, suddenly alert. Maggie had a feeling the term would catch the attention of Lucy, a dedicated dog lover who had recently married a veterinarian.

"She calls them comfort dogs," Dana explained. "Most people would call them therapy dogs. They're specially trained to offer their owners comfort and emotional support in stressful situations. The dogs can even short-circuit a stress reaction. Rose has three special pets of her own and is training some of her rescues as therapy companions. The work has made her much more responsible and has definitely boosted her self-esteem."

Everyone needed a sense of purpose, a reason to get up in the morning. Maggie thought it was the key to a happy life, and it was wonderful that a person with Rose's challenges had found a meaningful role for herself. Still, it sounded like a lot to handle for Holly.

"Is there any hope Rose will recover someday?" she asked.

"Head injuries are still mysterious. But there have been some amazing discoveries recently. Treatments for this type of injury, and for post-traumatic stress, which often results, have really advanced. Rose is very lucky that an expert in this field, Dr. Timothy Riley, opened a center right in Plum Harbor. She's made so much progress there the past few months. It's remarkable."

"Isn't that where you're working now? To get that new certification?" Suzanne asked.

"Yes, it's the same place. I can't work with Rose directly. It wouldn't be professional. But I keep an eye on her and hear how she's coming along in meetings. It's inspiring to work with Dr. Riley. He has degrees in both neuroscience and psychology. He's making real breakthroughs with innovative treatments that go way beyond talk therapy. I'm learning a lot from his partner, Dr. Curtis too. She's the unsung hero there, I'd say. Tim is an innovator, but Emily is a fine doctor in her own right and keeps everything running smoothly. They've known each other since early college days and make a dynamic pair."

Dana was very dedicated to her patients and was an excellent therapist, too. Maggie would easily say that. She already had several degrees hanging on her office wall, but she had decided last fall to work toward this new certification and somehow managed to juggle several days a week at Dr. Riley's center, along with private appointments at her office on Main Street. Which was not far from Maggie's shop and convenient for frequent knitting breaks, which, Dana said, were her favorite therapy.

Maggie wasn't sure how Dana kept her schedule straight, or where all that energy came from. Dana chalked it up to green smoothies and her yoga routine. She loved helping her patients and was very inspired by this step in a new career direction, coming in her midfifties.

"Dr. Riley likes the idea of teaching Rose how to knit. It's such an enjoyable way to improve concentration and focus. We've tried traditional sitting meditation with some patients, but it's difficult for them to master," Dana added. "Knitting is active, and you feel so good creating something, which really boosts those good brain chemicals."

And it was probably for the best that Rose had her first lesson in her own home, Maggie thought. The shop may have been too distracting for her.

"I love those good brain chemicals," Suzanne said. "But my drug of choice is chocolate . . . or shopping. It's works a little faster than knitting, for me."

Everyone knew Suzanne was the slowest knitter in the group, and no one debated her declaration.

"There might be some challenges teaching her, but I know it will help her. I'd like to teach other patients, too." Dana met Maggie's glance, silently recruiting her for the next stage of the experiment.

Maggie didn't mind. It was a great compliment that Dana thought so well of her teaching skills.

"And Maggie will make it seem easy as pie," Lucy said.

Phoebe shook her head, needles clicking in the dark. "I never understood that expression. Pie is *not* easy for some people." Phoebe paused to pull out a length of yarn from the ball in her lap. "The crust can fall apart or stick to the pan. A lot of things can go wrong with pie. 'Easy as toast' or . . . 'easy as a hard-boiled egg.' That would make a lot more sense to me."

Icy cold butter was the trick, but Maggie didn't want to digress into the fine points of mixing pie dough.

"I see your point. I'll go with toast. It's just knots and sticks. Not much more than that. I've prepared a lesson on a special technique. Very simple but fun, and I hope it will pique her interest." Maggie's knitting bag, well stocked for the evening, shifted on her lap.

"Now you've caught my interest. Do we already know how to do this stitch?" Lucy asked.

"It's not a stitch exactly . . . It's a surprise, and don't try wheedle it out of me. I think you'll all enjoy it."

"I'm up for simple and fun," Suzanne said. "I've been knitting for years, and I'm still waiting for that Zen-flow thing to kick in."

Lucy leaned forward and whispered in Suzanne's ear. "Maybe if you put down your cell phone and iPad? It's easier to handle the needles."

They all heard Lucy's advice and had to laugh.

"Come on, I'm not that bad. Maybe sometimes. I can't help it. I'm in demand."

Maggie heard a pout in Suzanne's tone but knew she'd soon recover. "Everyone thinks they get more done if they multitask, but it's really just the opposite. 'One tangle at a time.' That's my motto. "

Phoebe sat up like a meerkat popping out of a tunnel. "I love that, Maggie. Can I use it on my website? I'll give you full credit."

"Oh, it's all yours, dear. Plenty of fiber wisdom where that came from."

An intersection came into view. Maggie noticed a gas station with a convenience store, which had to be a busy spot out here.

"Here's the turn, finally." Dana said to Suzanne. "Take a left. The nursery comes up quickly."

A collective sigh of relief rose, along with appetizing aromas from covered dishes stowed in the hatch. Maggie realized she was hungry, too.

The roadside sign for Piper Nursery was reminiscent of the 1960s and looked like it had not been painted since. Suzanne drove through wooden gates, and gravel crunched under their wheels. The vehicle bounced along the rutted drive as a large old house appeared in the headlights.

They pulled up beside a battered green pickup truck, and Suzanne shut off the engine. Raindrops splattered the car windows, and Maggie gathered her belongings in a rush. She wanted to get inside before the rain fell any harder. They all had the same idea and quickly took hold of their totes and food containers and ran up a bumpy brick path that led to the front door.

A yellow lamp glowed above a small portico but did not cast much light. Maggie tried to make out the outline of the house, a shadowy silhouette against the cloudy dark sky.

She could see it had started as a conventional colonial or saltbox but over the years had been extended many times, in many random directions. The result was that now the house looked like a collection of different-sized boxes taped together for a school project. One that would not win a very good grade, Maggie decided, falling back on her schoolteacher standards.

Thick, rough shingles had been painted dark green; the trim painted white, though probably not since the roadside sign had gone up. Huge old oaks on both sides of the house stood guard, their thick boughs dipping down like strong arms, ready to protect the occupants from unseen dangers.

The drive extended into the property and curved around

the back of the house. She'd caught sight of a large garage, one that could hold at least three vehicles; there was also a greenhouse and what looked like a potting shed.

The rest of the land was shrouded in darkness, but she could discern open fields that stretched in all directions, bordered by thick woods. The Essex River ran through this area, she recalled, maybe even right behind this property. No wonder the lot was worth money, though from the looks of it, the Pipers were land rich and cash poor.

Running a seasonal business like a garden nursery would be challenging for anyone, no less a young woman like Holly, who also had to care for her sister. Now that they'd arrived, Maggie recalled visiting once or twice in search of plants for her garden but could not remember meeting either of the sisters.

She did know Piper's was not the place to find pumpkin festivals or flower-arranging classes. It was a no-frills operation that offered plants and garden design at decent prices, the sort known to dedicated gardeners and attracting a loyal, if not large, patronage. Still, it looked a bit run down and not very successful.

But it was a dormant season for the business, and best not to judge from first impressions. Maggie had learned that lesson more times than she wanted to admit.

The sound of barking dogs grew louder as they approached the front door. Not just two or three, but a chorus of canines worthy of any Wagnerian opera. One soloist let out a long, echoing howl, and others quickly joined in. A lonesome, eerie sound that lifted into the night sky.

Maggie and her friends clustered on the front steps, and Dana knocked. Maggie wasn't sure if it was the howling that gave her a chill, or a sharp wind that swept across the countryside, seeping under her jacket and rattling dead leaves.

"I know you said she has *some* dogs . . . How many are

there, do you think? Approximately?" Phoebe sounded nervous.

"Oh, a dozen or so. Maybe a few more than that," Dana said. "Not counting the puppies, of course."

"So it's maybe like . . . a hundred?" Phoebe asked in a small voice.

It wasn't that Phoebe disliked dogs. Maggie knew she loved all furred and feathered creatures. But the barking and howling was intimidating, even for a genuine dog lover.

Suzanne gripped Phoebe's arm on one side and Lucy's on the other. "Isn't this the scene in a horror flick when you start shouting at the characters? 'Go back! Go back! Don't go in there! Are you crazy?' "

Maggie didn't know much about horror movies, but she did know Suzanne had a flair for drama. "You're just being silly. I hope the Pipers didn't hear you."

"The dogs are all gentle and well behaved. Rose is amazingly good at keeping them under control," Dana promised.

Before she could say more, the front door swung open. A tall, slim woman greeted them with a smile. She had to be Holly, Maggie decided.

"Did it start to rain already? I hope you didn't get wet. We're so happy you could come. Can I help carry anything?"

Dana kissed her godchild on the cheek and stepped aside to let everyone enter.

"I can't believe you came all this way and brought dinner, too. I'm sorry to have put you through all this trouble," their hostess added.

"No trouble at all," Maggie insisted.

"We always eat well at our meetings. It helps you knit better," Suzanne said.

Maggie silently agreed. What had Virginia Woolf once

said? *One cannot think well, love well, sleep well, if one has not dined well.* Maggie would definitely add knitting to that list.

Introductions were exchanged as they moved into the center hall, which opened onto large rooms on either side. They dropped their tote bags and pocketbooks on a wooden bench and shed their jackets.

Holly looked very much as Maggie had pictured. With dark, wavy hair pulled back in a loose braid, a long oval face, and dark eyes that reminded Maggie of portraits by Modigliani. She was not beautiful in the conventional sense, but there was a unique loveliness to her features, and she possessed a distinct air of intelligence and independence. Her work outdoors clearly kept her fit. She stood straight and strong, dressed in a big brown sweater and jeans, her smooth skin bare of makeup.

"Just leave your things in here. I'll help you take the food into the kitchen," Holly told them. "The dogs won't bother you. Don't worry."

The dogs weren't barking anymore. Maggie wondered how that could be. But Dana had promised that Rose had control over them.

Another young woman hung back near the staircase. This had to be Rose. The similarity between the sisters was striking, yet they looked like different versions of the same person.

Rose was a little younger than Holly—in her late twenties, Maggie recalled—though her wide gaze and curious expression made her seem younger. While her older sister had dark eyes, her eyes were bright blue, her hair the same wavy texture but golden blond, hanging loose past her shoulders. She was not as tall as Holly and didn't look nearly as strong. Her face was round and softer, with rosy apple cheeks. Holly appeared confident and open, but Rose seemed cautious and far more vulnerable.

Yet in total control of her canine charges, Maggie noticed. Three dogs lay obediently at Rose's feet, making her look like a Greek goddess. Diana of the Hunt? Though the dogs were far from celestial ideals—a motley group that ranged from a large shaggy specimen with pale white fur and a wolfish grin, which displayed an impressive row of teeth, to a small barrel-shaped dog with stubby legs and pointed ears.

Maggie didn't know much about breeds, but in the big dog she could see German shepherd or husky mixed with . . . coyote? The stout tan-and-white one was a corgi, the favorite breed of Queen Elizabeth. Its quick gaze darted between its mistress and the visitors.

There was also a medium-sized dog, with black-and-white markings and long fur. Its body was lithe, with floppy ears and a pointed nose, like a collie. The dog leaned into Rose's leg, and Rose had her hand set on the dog's soft head.

Maggie heard more panting and followed the sound. The entrance to a room off the foyer—a parlor or dining room, she guessed—was blocked with a wooden gate, the type used to corral children. Behind it, many other dogs huddled together, tails wagging, as they sniffed the air and stared curiously at the guests.

The room appeared to be a large front parlor. A dog parlor, she'd have to call it, filled with dog beds of various shapes and sizes, chew toys, and a line of silver bowls along one wall. There was some furniture for humans and even a TV. But the seating was covered with sheets and blankets, available for dog lounging, and the TV was tuned to a nature show.

How many dogs were there? More than a dozen, that was for sure. Before Maggie could manage a wet-nose count, she heard Rose greet Dana, enveloping her in a warm embrace, which her aunt heartily returned.

Dana stood with her arm around Rose's shoulder as she introduced each member of the knitting group. "And this is Maggie. She owns the shop in town that I told you about."

"How nice to meet you, Rose." Maggie took the young woman's hand.

Rose offered a shy smile. "I'm glad to see you, too . . . Did you bring us something good to eat?"

Maggie managed not to laugh out loud at her refreshingly honest question. "I think so. But I guess that depends on what you like to eat."

"Oh, I'm not fussy. Holly's not a very good cook. But I'm even worse. I clean up and set the table. Holly made me use the good china tonight," Rose confided, sounding as if she didn't understand the fuss. "Bella and her puppies are in the mudroom. We made a cozy spot. Want to see them?"

"Absolutely," Maggie replied. "That's why we came."

"And to do some knitting," Dana reminded them.

Maggie had not forgotten the fundamental purpose of the visit, of course, but she knew her answer would please Rose. And was also true.

Maggie wondered if the dogs would join them for dinner, and had a fleeting thought of so many sniffing noses under the table. Rose's special trio did follow them into the kitchen but immediately lay down in a corner near the stove at Rose's command.

While the food warmed in the oven, Rose led them to the mudroom, a small space off the kitchen that doubled as a storage area and pantry. She turned and stopped them before they could enter en masse.

"Just peek in a few at a time, please. Bella might get nervous. She's very protective."

Maggie understood. Poor Bella was watching over a

large brood. She didn't need a crowd of strangers hovering over her.

Maggie took her turn with Lucy, who had seen plenty of puppies by now. Or one would assume. But she oohed and aahed as if she'd never seen a one before.

"I forgot how small they are," Maggie whispered, careful not to upset their mother.

"Me too," Lucy replied. "They look like little balls of fur."

Maggie thought so, too. Though her mind made the analogy to balls of soft, fuzzy yarn. Maybe angora?

Most of the pups were reddish brown, with thick fur. A few, however, were a golden color. Most were also asleep, flopped this way and that on top of each other. Others were cuddled next to Bella, eagerly nursing. Rose leaned over and stroked her head.

"They are adorable," Maggie remarked. "How long do they stay with their mother?"

"They'll be with Bella four more weeks. They can't be separated until they are six weeks old," Rose replied.

"Can we have our turn?" Phoebe poked her head around the doorway before Maggie could ask Rose any more questions.

Maggie and Lucy left, and Suzanne and Phoebe stepped in, and everyone was soon seated at the table.

Maggie took a moment to admire the china, cream-colored plates with a pattern of pink roses. Perhaps a wedding gift to Ava Piper or a family heirloom passed down? Maggie knew her own good china would go to her daughter, Julie, a long time from now, she hoped.

Holly and Rose were so young when they'd lost their mother. Maggie felt sad to think of it. They'd lost both parents close together, Dana had mentioned, barely past their teenage years, a time when young women really need guidance and support. At least they'd had Dana to fill the gap. She was still doing her best to help them.

Holly took a seat at the head of the table. She had opened a bottle of white wine and had also set down a large pitcher of ice water. "Everything looks delicious. I don't know where to start."

"I'll start," Rose cheerfully volunteered. She scooped up a large portion of the dish Dana had made—a cheesy mix of vegetables and brown rice, oven baked. Dana had mentioned that the sisters enjoyed it, especially Rose.

Maggie liked it, too, and served herself a scoop.

Lucy had made roast chicken with lemon and herbs, and Maggie had brought a green salad and crusty bread. Phoebe had baked a dessert she called Blackout Brownies. Maggie fully expected a chocolate hangover but never doubted it would be worth it.

As they ate and chatted, Maggie noticed the rain was coming down harder. Heavy drops spattered on the windows and struck the roof with a dull, steady rhythm. Suzanne had passed on the wine, Maggie was glad to see. If the rain kept up, the drive back to the village would be even more difficult than the one out here.

But she didn't want to worry about that now. She wanted to get to know the Pipers and teach them some knitting.

Everyone's appetite was keen, and they made short work of dinner. Holly and Rose began clearing the dishes, and Maggie's friends jumped up to help.

"Just leave it all in the sink. We'll take care of it later," Holly said.

Rose drifted off to check on Bella. She had saved scraps from dinner for the dogs and gave some to the three pets who had lain patiently near her seat and the rest to the new mother, who needed all the good food and energy she could get.

While she was gone, Holly quietly confided, "Is it okay

if we knit in here, too? I let Rose have the parlor for the dogs. She's rarely in her room upstairs anymore. She basically lives down here with them now, even sleeps on one of the couches. It's obviously inconvenient at times. But we hardly ever have guests, and the responsibility has been very good for her."

"No need to explain. We're happy to knit anywhere," Maggie assured her.

"Is it time to hear about your surprise lesson, Maggie?" Lucy asked.

"I'm more interested to find out what this lesson is than what's for dessert. That's saying something," Suzanne clarified.

"It is," Maggie agreed. "The lesson is quick, so we'll get to dessert soon enough."

She unpacked her supplies, medium-weight balls of soft yarn in many colors, and set them in the middle of the table. "Pick some yarn, everyone. I have printed instructions, but I'll just demonstrate first."

Everyone at the table chose a ball of yarn.

"What size needles should we use?" Phoebe asked, glancing through her bag.

"No needles necessary. We're going to use our fingers." Maggie glanced around the table, enjoying their surprised expressions.

"Fingers?" Phoebe, the most skillful in the group, after Maggie, seemed the most incredulous.

"That's right. This is an interesting stitching technique, and you can make some very nice projects quickly with just yarn and your fingers." Maggie took her own yarn in her right hand and extended her left on the table so everyone could see. "I'll show you first, and then everyone can try it."

She let the strand of yarn dangle down her palm about six inches and turned it toward the outside of her hand.

"You drape the yarn like so and then just wind it in and out of your fingers. We'll start with two fingers for now," she said, showing them, "but you can use all four. You need to wind the yarn two times to make stitches." She slowly wove the yarn between her index and middle finger, trying to show everyone the easy technique. "When that's done, you just slip the bottom loops over the top loops and slide them off your fingers."

She completed that step and showed them the back of her hand. "See how the stitches are forming? You can't see much yet, but I'll do a few more rounds." She quickly did two more turns on the winding and lifting of the yarn.

Before she could show them the growing chain of stitches, Lucy and Phoebe were starting off for themselves. Rose sat between Maggie and Dana and seemed very pleased by the process, which Maggie thought a good sign.

Maggie glanced around the table. "Ready to start, everyone? Just give a shout if you have any questions."

She turned to Rose, who had put the yarn in the right position on her hand and now carefully pulled it around the base of her fingers. "Like this?" she asked Maggie.

"Perfect." Maggie nodded, watching her. She found it was best to let students make their mistakes. They remembered much better for the next time.

But Rose carried out the procedure easily and pulled the first stitches over her fingers. She looked over at Maggie and smiled. "I like this. I was sort of nervous about working the needles," she admitted. "I'm not even very good with chopsticks."

Maggie smiled. "I think knitting needles are a little easier than chopsticks. You'll get to that in time."

She took out a fringed scarf, finger stitched with thick yarn, and showed it around the table. "Some people might call this more of a weaving technique. But you get fast results, and the projects can be really lovely."

Dana stretched the scarf out on the table. "That is very pretty. Why didn't you ever teach us this before?"

Maggie shrugged. "I wanted to do something a little different than my usual Knitting one-oh-one."

Even her basic beginner knitting lesson took some will and focus, but finger knitting seemed the perfect starting point for Rose. Maggie silently gave herself a pat on the back for thinking of it.

Suzanne was delighted and perhaps had finally found a project she would not abandon. "Maggie, I so love this. I'm never going to knit with needles again."

Maggie wondered about that. Anything was possible.

"I'm going to make a dog collar," Rose announced.

Maggie leaned over to check her work. She was doing very well and working at the same pace as the others, too.

"Good idea. You can make all your dogs new collars this way. I'll leave you extra yarn."

Holly caught her gaze and smiled. Maggie thought she appreciated the way the evening was going, how everyone was not simply nice to Rose but was treating her with respect. Maggie imagined that was not always the case once people knew about Rose's disability.

Holly brought a pot of coffee and a teapot to the table, along with mugs and Phoebe's brownies. While they quietly worked, a harsh wind whistled in the big trees outside the house.

"The storm is getting worse," Phoebe remarked.

"Maybe it will pass by the time we're ready to go." Lucy was the eternal optimist. Maggie loved that about her pal. The skies above answered with a huge rumble of thunder and a clap of lightning.

The dogs in the kitchen jumped up, alert and on edge, and the gang in the parlor began barking again.

"Guess it's going to get worse before it gets better," Suzanne said. Maggie had to agree.

Rose put her work down. "I'd better check the dogs. Most of them hate thunderstorms."

Holly met her gaze and nodded. "Let me know if you need help."

Rose left the kitchen, and her four-legged squad followed, looking all business.

Holly stood up and began to serve the coffee and tea. "Some dogs are fine with the bad weather. But many get very nervous. Rose gives them a herbal medication, and a few will tolerate a thunder jacket."

"Thunder jacket? What's that?"

"It's a tight-fitting garment that makes the dog feel secure. The pressure soothes anxiety. The technique helps humans, too," Dana explained.

"I think I'll try that for Kevin. He has a meltdown in a thunderstorm. He's worse than the kids," Suzanne said, mentioning her big, burly construction worker husband.

Lucy took a brownie and set it on her plate. "You'd think with Matt being a vet, we'd have the storm thing figured out. But it's still mayhem. Tink jumps on the bed, shivering, and we have to hug her under the covers, and Wally digs all the shoes out of Matt's closet, then hides in the back."

"Van Gogh doesn't like storms, either, but he's much more sensible than that." Phoebe sounded a bit smug describing her cat. But she was clearly outnumbered by dog lovers tonight. Then she asked everyone, "Hey, isn't anyone going to try the brownies? I made up the recipe myself."

Phoebe picked one up and took a big bite. Lightning flashed in the kitchen windows, along with a boom so loud, it sounded like a bomb falling on the house.

The fixture above the table flickered a moment and went out.

"I have my phone right here. I'll put the flashlight on."

Dana quickly lit the space with the light from her cell phone.

Lucy and Suzanne had their phones handy, too, and did the same.

"I was afraid this would happen. We lose power a lot out here. I meant to take out the flashlights when I heard it was going to rain." Holly rose from her seat and headed into the mudroom.

Rose was alone in the front of the house with the dogs. Was she scared? Maggie didn't have time to voice the question.

Rose burst through the swinging door into the kitchen. "Holly? Where are you?"

Dana jumped up and quickly hugged Rose. "It's all right, honey. We're right here. The rain will pass in a few minutes."

Rose looked up, about to speak. Then laid her head on Dana's shoulder when another rumble and bolt of lightning shook the house.

As the din subsided, Maggie realized she heard another sound. Someone was knocking on the front door. A sharp, brisk knock and then a hard, closed-fist pounding. Someone was intent on being heard above the thunder and the dogs, who had burst into another chorus of barks.

Holly returned from the mudroom with flashlights. Dana turned to her. "Are you expecting anyone?"

"No." Holly shook her head. "Maybe a driver got stuck on the road and walked up for help?"

Maggie thought that was possible but was still wary of the unexpected visitor. She glanced at Dana, who seemed to share her concern.

Of course, the dogs—by sheer number—would make anyone bearing ill will stop and think. But at the risk of seeming overly cautious, Maggie said, "I'll go with you, Holly. I'll hold the flashlight."

"I'll go, too." Lucy rose and quickly followed.

"Why don't we all go? No sense waiting here in the dark." Dana slipped her arm around Rose's shoulder. "Let's go see who's there."

In the cover of darkness, Maggie pulled the largest, fattest needle from her knitting bag. She'd never used a knitting needle as a weapon, but there was a first time for everything, wasn't there?

You're letting your imagination run away with you, she told herself as she followed her friends through the pitch-black house.

She could hear but not see the vigilant pack of dogs behind the gate, their loud barks and low growls. A beam of light swept over the pack, and their eyes glowed.

Holly was at the entranceway when the knocking stopped. Had the visitor given up? She pulled the door open as Dana stood nearby with a light.

A tall, gaunt figure filled the space—an old man with a sweatshirt hood pulled over his head, his shoulders hunched and hands hidden deep in his pockets. He looked half drowned from the rain and stared at Holly with a bright, dark gaze and a hungry expression.

Before Holly could speak, a lightning bolt crackled across the sky. The dogs barked even louder, but the stranger didn't flinch.

A logical voice in Maggie's head insisted it was just a trick of the light and shadows. Still, his hollow cheeks and long nose made his face look like a floating skull. It was only slightly softened by a long, scraggly gray beard, the type you'd see on a homeless person or an island castaway.

Maggie took a breath and gripped the thick needle in a tight fist. Where had this man come from? Why was he here?

Chapter 2

"Sorry to disturb you, ladies." His voice was low and gravelly. A smoker, two packs a day, Maggie guessed. His broken, stained teeth supported the theory. "I skidded in a puddle and plowed through the fence on your property. Knocked down a section or two. It's hard to say in the dark."

Holly sighed and crossed her arms over her chest. She seemed annoyed about the damage but didn't appear rattled by the man's off-putting appearance.

"Thanks for owning up to it. Did you come by just to tell me, or will you cover the damage?"

Maggie had wondered the same thing. She assumed there was property insurance, but by the time a deductible was satisfied, it usually wasn't worth making a claim.

"I can't pay you out of pocket, miss. But I can fix it. I'll come back tomorrow, first thing. I'll do a good job, too." He nodded; the tip of his beard briefly brushed his chest. Then he lifted his chin and stared straight at Holly, waiting for a reply.

Dana glanced at Holly, waiting for her answer, as well. Maggie sensed Dana was not in favor of Holly taking up the offer. After all, who was he? Where had he come from? This whole situation could be part of a scam—though

Maggie couldn't figure out what the stranger might have to gain by knocking down a fence and fixing it. Then again, grifters went to elaborate lengths to gain access to a person's home and their private information.

"Maybe you should take the gentleman's phone number and think about it, Holly?" Dana suggested.

"Good idea. Can you give me a number, Mr. . . ."

"Thornton. Carl Thornton," he said, quickly filling in the blank. "Should I talk with your husband or a boyfriend?"

Classic sexist attitude, to assume a man was needed to manage the situation. But Mr. Thornton was clearly from a distant generation. Maggie had to cut him slack on that count. And maybe he knew that he did not cut the most reassuring figure; in fact, he looked like someone a young woman might—and probably should—be wary of.

Holly took out her cell phone. "Type your number in my phone. I'll let you know if you should come back."

He did as she asked, and handed the phone back. "I'll do the job right and for free. You won't be sorry. Good night, ladies."

He stepped back into the rainy night and vanished like an apparition.

Holly shut the door, snapped both locks, then turned to face them. "Drivers have hit our fence from time to time, but he's the first to admit it."

"It was decent of him. But I have to say, something about the guy gave me the shivers," Maggie admitted.

Lucy smiled, her gaze drifting down to the knitting needle, which Maggie now tried to hide behind her back. "I noticed you're packing heat, Mag. Don't you need a permit to carry that thing?"

"Don't make fun. Maggie had the right idea," Suzanne said before Maggie could answer. "That dude has *jailbird* written all over him."

"I hate to judge, but I don't think it's a good idea to let him come back, Holly." No matter what a person looked like, Dana always gave a stranger the benefit of the doubt. But Maggie could see her protective feelings had pushed aside her fair-minded standards.

Holly smiled and touched Dana's arm. "He didn't scare me, Aunt Dana. But if it makes you feel better, I'll tell him not to return."

Dana thanked her with a smile.

Rose had been standing back by the staircase, the canine trio at her side. She walked toward Holly, the dogs softly padding behind her. "Do we know that man?"

"No, Rose. He was driving by and knocked down part of the fence by accident. He came to tell us, that's all."

Rose looked away, her expression confused. "Oh . . . I thought we knew him from somewhere."

"I can't imagine where, if we do," Holly replied. "Though I doubt he means any harm."

Perhaps he was not a scam artist, or a jailbird, Maggie thought. Just a hardworking man trying to do the right thing. Nonetheless, it was wise for Holly to steer clear of him. Especially since she and Rose were alone out here.

As the group stumbled back to the kitchen, the lights suddenly flashed on. Everyone laughed at the sight.

"That's no fun. I thought we were going to pretend there was a campfire and tell spooky stories," Suzanne said.

"Maybe next time," Lucy replied. "I bet you know a lot of them."

"We'll have a meeting on the beach one night, when the weather gets warm," Maggie suggested. "We can build a bonfire. Toast marshmallows, tell ghost stories, and knit. How does that sound?"

"Marshmallows and yarn could be a problem," Phoebe said.

"I think it sounds fun. Can I come?" Maggie met Rose's

eager expression with a smile. She wanted to hug the girl for her sweet, open nature.

"Of course you can. Dogs will be invited, too," she added.

Back in the warm, well-lit kitchen, they returned to their knitting and Phoebe's brownies.

"Brownies always calm me down in a thunderstorm," Suzanne said. "In any weather, to tell the truth."

"These look yummy. What did you call them, Phoebe?" Lucy asked.

"Blackout Brownies. What else? There's a secret ingredient. I'm not sure I'm going to tell you."

"As long as the lights stay while we eat them, I'm not sure I care," Maggie said.

The lights did stay on as the evening continued, with a few more knitting tips but mostly more conversation. Maggie was glad to get to know Holly and Rose and genuinely sorry when it was time to go.

As they gathered their belongings, Holly said, "Don't worry about your platters and pans. I'll drop them off at the shop sometime." Holly turned to Rose, who stood by her at the door. "Please thank Aunt Dana and her friends."

"Thank you for coming. I liked knitting, and I'm really glad there are a lot of leftovers," Rose said in a matter-of-fact tone.

Maggie could not wish for higher compliments. "You're both very welcome. Come to the shop next Thursday night. I'll cook something special," she promised Rose.

"Dogs allowed?" Rose asked.

"Your three musketeers? Absolutely. They're so well behaved. How can I refuse? I bet they lie down under the table all night and are no trouble at all."

She also guessed that Rose would enjoy the visit much more with at least one of her comfort dogs at her side.

Lucy gave her a look; Maggie knew what she was think-ing, but ignored her. Maggie had often told Lucy she was free to bring her golden retriever, Tink, and her chocolate Lab, Wally, into the shop when she stopped by on their morning walk. But Lucy knew her dogs were not well be-haved and could cause plenty of trouble, given the oppor-tunity. Hadn't Tink once jumped into the window display, chasing down Phoebe's cat?

Lucy wisely preferred to keep the dogs on the porch, leashes tied to the railing. Maggie appreciated her courtesy and good judgment. Still, she had never banned Tink and Wally from coming in the shop, if customers were not about, and she didn't think she deserved such a look now that Rose's dogs were invited to the next meeting.

"I think I'll invite all the dogs for next week's meet-ing," Maggie said as she slipped on her jacket. "Tink and Wally . . . and Barkly, too," she added, glancing at Suzanne.

"Barkly is a typical guy. No interest in knitting, except to snack on the yarn. Which always leaves me with a big vet bill."

With harmony restored and the next meeting planned, Maggie and her friends headed to Suzanne's SUV. The storm had cleared, revealing a deep blue velvet sky stud-ded with stars and a shiny crescent moon. Maggie looked forward to clear weather the next day and hoped it was warmer, too.

The ride back to the village seemed faster than the ride going, but the group had a lot to discuss, especially about the bearded stranger.

"I'm glad Holly decided not to take the man up on his offer. Chances are he's perfectly sincere and harmless—" Lucy said, but Phoebe cut in.

"But he could easily be a serial killer."

"I wouldn't go that far," Lucy countered. "Though there was definitely something off about him."

"I thought so, too," Dana admitted. "I know Holly has been feeling financially pinched lately. If she has a problem with the insurance, I'll pay for the fence. I'll tell her tomorrow."

"That's generous of you," Maggie said.

"No big deal. She says it's just the winter. There's no revenue from the business this time of year. But it might be something more. I worry about them."

"Of course you do. You care about them very much. And they love you, too," Maggie added, knowing that was true.

Dana thought about Holly and Rose as often as she did her own children. She had two boys, her oldest son, from her first marriage, and a second son with her husband, Jack, who was an attorney with an office in town. Holly and Rose were surrogate daughters, and Maggie could see Dana enjoyed that aspect of their relationship, too.

Small children, small problem. Big children, big problems. Who had told her that years ago? *A more experienced mother*, Maggie recalled. She knew now it was true. She had fretted over the most trivial questions when her own daughter was a baby and a toddler, and all through elementary school.

Little had she known what lay ahead, the trials of navigating Julie's teen years and young adulthood. The challenges were even greater once Julie had graduated college and had begun living her own life, forging new relationships with whoever she pleased and making her own decisions—good, bad, or otherwise.

Maggie knew she'd been greatly blessed as a mother. She and Bill had faced no significant problems with Julie. But she worried now about Dana. Holly and Rose were alone, without family or close friends to advise or help them, except for Dana and Jack. Maggie wondered if she could help in some way.

If she saw a chance to support Dana and help the Pipers, she must try, she decided. And not just by teaching them how to knit, as wonderful a gift as that was.

As usual, the next morning, Lucy was the first to drop by Maggie's shop on her daily jaunt to town with her dogs. The panting duo had yanked Lucy down to the harbor and were now pointed back toward the Marshes, a modest neighborhood near the beach, where Lucy and Matt lived. Maggie's shop on Main Street was the perfect resting point midway on the trek.

Lucy had spent summers in Plum Harbor while growing up, visiting her Aunt Claire, and when her aunt had passed on, she had inherited the cottage where she and Matt now lived. It was a small but charming home, decorated in Lucy's quirky, unique taste: part IKEA, part thrift shop, and part semi-antique leftovers from Aunt Claire. It was not a large house, but it had adequate room for a baby . . . or two.

When the time came, Maggie reflected as she watched her pal and furry friends make their way down the path. Maggie opened the shop door and found Lucy tying the dogs' leashes to the porch rail, as she usually did.

"I thought we set new rules last night. Canines welcome, as long as there are no customers around," Maggie said.

Lucy stood up and smoothed down her jacket. "The dogs think that's very gracious, and they might come to the meeting next week. But even they can see the wisdom of staying out here, clear of temptation."

"Smart pups. And they love watching other dogs pass on Main Street, and the squirrels and birds hopping around the garden."

"And they're tired enough not to try to chase them." Lucy set up and filled a portable water bowl and tossed a few biscuits from her pocket, then followed Maggie into the shop.

Maggie felt she'd done the right thing, offering to let Lucy's dogs come in. But she was relieved that Lucy had left them on the porch. Phoebe had made a lovely display of new stock yesterday, soft spring-colored skeins cascading from one basket to another. *A masterpiece*, Maggie thought. But it would easily be turned to a shambles by curious sniffing.

As if reading her mind, Lucy said, "I had a thought last night. You'd better make the shop dog proof for next week's meeting."

Maggie laughed. "I like the term. As if I'll be hosting a convention of hyperactive toddlers."

"Almost." Lucy sounded serious. "I didn't know you liked dogs that much. I was surprised that you offered."

"In the light of day, so am I. Something in the air at the Pipers—dog hair, most likely—carried me away. But it occurred to me that Rose might not come here without a comfort dog. Didn't Dana say she's rarely without Oreo?"

Lucy looked surprised that Maggie even remembered the dog's name. "I do remember, now that you mentioned it. But all dogs are sort of therapy dogs, when you think about it. Maybe even all pets."

She had followed Maggie to the back of the shop and took a seat at the oak worktable. Maggie went into the storeroom, which doubled as a kitchen, and poured two mugs of coffee. She didn't even ask Lucy if she wanted coffee or how she liked it. She knew the answer to both questions. Lucy took her coffee black, and Maggie fixed her own with a dash of milk.

She carried the mugs back to the table and set Lucy's down in front of her.

"That smells good. I could use some more caffeine today." Lucy took a sip. "I've been thinking, Maggie. You and Charles should get a dog. You should surprise him with a puppy. A belated retirement present. He's home all day, all alone, while you're here, working. He'd love the company. I bet he'd love walking the dog into town, too. It's perfect exercise."

Lucy was a prime example. But even though Maggie liked dogs and was even willing to allow dogs into the shop, under certain circumstances, she had no intention of owning one.

"Charles finds plenty to do without a pet. Is that why you stopped this morning? To talk me into adopting one of Rose's rescues?"

Lucy shrugged. "I was just thinking about it."

"Obviously," Maggie replied.

"I don't think you should dismiss the idea so quickly. I'd be happy to dog-sit when you go on vacation. And when you take a trip on the boat, you can bring the dog with you. They love boats. Did you know that?"

"I've noticed." Maggie had seen plenty of furry sailors, large and small, gazing out from the deck of a boat or even standing out on the bow, fluffy ears and tails flying in the wind. One could even find canine life jackets and other dog boating equipment at the marine supply store. "Can't say I've ever felt the one accessory missing from Charles's sailboat is a canine passenger. He would like a new ship-to-shore radio. I don't think he ever mentioned a sea-worthy hound."

Lucy looked ready to debate the point further.

Like a dog with a bone, Maggie thought, though she decided to keep that witty observation to herself.

Before Lucy could continue her case, the shop door opened, and Dana walked in.

"Thank goodness. Saved in the nick of time," Maggie greeted her.

Dana answered with a puzzle look.

"Lucy wants me to get a dog. She's absolutely . . . hounding me. Pun intended."

"A puppy, for Charles. It would make their little home complete, don't you think?" Lucy asked Dana.

"Please don't gang up on me," Maggie cut in.

Dana set her large leather tote on the table. It doubled as a purse, computer tote, and briefcase for her professional files and, often even carried knitting. She searched around the top and took out a white paper bag.

"How is Charles? How does he like retired life?"

"He'd like it a lot better with a sweet little dog, I'll tell you that much," Lucy muttered.

"Charles is fine. Everything is fine. Just as it is," Maggie insisted.

Dana smiled and took a container out of the white paper bag. Her breakfast, Maggie gathered, wondering which healthy choice Dana had chosen today.

"So, as much as you worried about Charles moving in, it all worked out. And I'd bet there are some unexpected pluses?"

"Quite a few. He's happy. I'm happy. It's all good." Maggie felt herself blush and pulled open a carton that was sitting on the table, suddenly fascinated to see what was inside.

Dana opened her breakfast container, then fished a plastic fork and a napkin from the bag. Avocado toast, Maggie noticed, a recent favorite.

"But no wedding date yet?" Lucy asked. "Are you any closer? I don't mean to push, but Matt and I are thinking about summer vacation, and you know we'd never miss your big event."

"Nothing grand," Maggie insisted. "Just our nearest

and dearest. That's all we've decided so far. Don't worry. We'll give you all fair warning."

Dana looked satisfied by the answer and took a bite. "I'm happy to hear it's going so well. I knew it would."

The carton contained another order of spring inventory. Maggie checked the invoice and counted the pastel-hued skeins. "That makes one of us."

She was partly joking and partly not. She and Charles Mossbacher had moved in together about six months ago, soon after it seemed they'd broken off for good. Charles had not only apologized in order to get them back together but had also proposed.

He'd found a solution to their bickering over her amateur sleuthing and interference with police business; he'd decided to retire from his long career as a detective for the Essex County Police Department.

Maggie had been shocked. She'd always known he was a man of solid character, but this step had gone above and beyond, and had also shown her how important their relationship was to him. Her heart had been won over before then, but his bold gesture had made his proposal all the more sweet.

Six months later, she still wasn't totally accustomed to calling him her fiancé, and they hadn't yet set a wedding date. It was no secret that she'd been anxious about giving up her independence. Especially since Charles no longer went out to a job every day, one that often kept him busy around the clock. But he had many interests—working on his sailboat, classes at a local university, volunteer work— and she could always hide out in her shop when she needed a break from domestic bliss.

She had to admit their lives had blended almost seamlessly, and they were, so far, very content together. Over ten years a widow, and with her daughter gone from the house for almost that long, as well, Maggie had forgotten what it was like to share her life and her home—to talk over her little problems and triumphs, to make plans with someone special, and look forward to returning to that person at the end of the day.

As she'd often told her daughter, there were pluses and minuses to every relationship. That was just a fact. But when you found someone who loved and accepted you, just as yourself, and you loved them the same way, that was a rare gift. One you should hang on to with both hands.

She had nearly ignored her own advice and had even sent Charles away for a while. Fortunately, his cooler head had prevailed.

"It was a big change, but definitely the right one for me. I've been alone for so long, I forgot what it's like to share my life with someone. Someone special, like Charles," she added.

"Charles is special. And so are you. You're both very lucky to have found each other." Dana's expression turned wistful. "I wish Holly would meet someone. The right person, whom she can rely on, someone who can help her run the business and help take care of Rose. Not that she needs protecting, but someone who's there, watching over her. As much as I try, it's no substitute for a life partner."

Maggie was surprised to see Dana so emotional. Her calm temperament was rarely rattled. Maggie felt certain there was something more to her reaction. Some button that had been pushed this morning or last night?

"Very true. No substitute at all," she agreed.

"Is something wrong, Dana?" Lucy asked. "Did something happen that got you thinking about all this?"

Dana shrugged. "I'm not sure. Maybe you can tell me if I'm getting worked up over nothing. I called Holly this morning to see if she'd called the insurance company about the fence, and she told me that strange man, Carl

Thornton, had already finished the repair. He must have come back at the crack of dawn."

Maggie was surprised. "Holly said last night she was going to tell him not to come."

"She said she sent him a text right after we left. But he never answered it. Obviously, he was determined to do the work, whether she wanted him there or not."

Maggie wanted to laugh at the irony—it was practically impossible to find a reliable handyman even halfway as dedicated. No less one that would come at the crack of dawn and work for free. Of course, she couldn't point that out. Dana was truly concerned.

"How did he get the supplies so quickly?" Lucy asked. "It's not even nine o'clock."

"Builder's Warehouse, up on the turnpike. It's open twenty-four hours a day," Maggie reminded them. "Maybe he bought what he needed last night and went back to the nursery at first light."

"On one hand, to be so intent on repairing something he'd broken shows good character," Dana said. "But I can't help feeling this is some sort of trick. Or maybe he's just . . . well, a nutjob."

Lucy's eyes grew wide. "Tell me I didn't hear that. A psychologist with about twenty diplomas just used the term *nutjob*?"

Color rushed to Dana's fair complexion, but she had to smile. "His behavior is inappropriate, I mean."

Maggie shrugged and closed the carton flaps. "You're allowed to slip up here and there. It's just us."

"It does seem as if he was obsessed. Or has some other agenda," Lucy added. "Trying to make Holly think he's honest and helpful?"

Dana wiped her fingers on the paper napkin. "That's what I'm worried about. This morning he knocked on the door quite early and told her that the repair was done.

Which I found unsettling enough. But instead of just accepting her thanks and heading on his way, he talked Holly into hiring him."

That was a twist. Maggie understood Dana's distress. "How did he manage that? Holly wasn't frightened of him, but she did agree that sending him on his way was the smart thing to do."

"I thought so, too," Dana said. "The storm last night knocked down some big branches on her property, and he offered to clear them. It is heavy work that would be hard for her alone. She hires a few helpers this time of year, but none have started yet. Mr. Thornton does seem very . . ."

"Enterprising? Manipulative? Working the angles?" Lucy offered.

"Something like that." Dana sighed. "I asked, in a respectful way, of course, if he gave her any references, that sort of thing. But she brushed off the question and said it's just for the day."

"The next thing you'll hear is that he talked his way into a permanent job," Lucy said.

"Exactly," Dana said. "Her busy season is about to hit, and he knocked on the door at the perfect moment."

Maggie could see Dana's distress but wasn't sure what to do or say. "I know Carl Thornton wouldn't be your first choice, and the circumstances are odd. But we're probably fretting for no reason. Out of mother hen instincts or something." Maggie hoped Dana would smile at the accusation, but she didn't. "I think you have to trust that she knows what she's doing. No matter what we thought of the man last night. Anyone would have looked scary standing at the door in the middle of that storm."

Dana still didn't seem convinced.

"What if we'd met him on a bright sunny day, without a black hood over his head? Presumably, cleaned up a bit—which I assume he did, to ask Holly for a job," Lucy added, her imagination embellishing the scene. "He definitely would have made a better impression."

"Lucy's right," Maggie said. "And she wouldn't keep him on without some references, would she?"

"I don't think so." Dana's frown softened. "But I plan to do just that—get another look at him. I told Holly I would give Rose a lift to Dr. Riley's center this afternoon. Rose knows how to drive, but she actually doesn't. It's too stressful for her. I can save Holly a trip, and while I'm at the nursery, I can size up Mr. Thornton. Maybe get a better impression?" She sighed, her head tilted to one side, as she nibbled a crust of the toast.

"Good plan." Maggie recalled how the old man had looked positively ghoulish backlit by the lightning flash. Any other impression would be a good one, she thought.

"I don't know that it will make any difference. But it might give me some peace of mind. Holly has been running the business on her own for a long time. It's definitely not my place to comment on who she hires to help her."

"I'm sure you respect her boundaries. But, on the other hand, I think Holly counts on your opinion and your advice. I don't see any harm in checking out Thornton," Lucy told her.

"If you want a *second*, second opinion on Carl Thornton, I'm happy to tag along. I'd like to see where you've been working, too. It will help me figure out what sort of knitting lessons I should plan for a larger group there."

Dana's expression brightened, and Maggie knew she'd said the right thing. "Are you sure it's no problem to leave the shop?"

"My able assistant manager will be here, holding down the fiber fort."

"That's why I get the big bucks, ladies." Phoebe's voice proceeded her, as did the clunking sound from her heavy black boots as she descended the staircase that led down from her apartment. "Though I'd call this place more of a fiber castle . . . a magical fiber castle. And I'm like the assistant magical fiber fairy."

She appeared at the bottom of the steps—looking very much the part of an assistant fairy, Maggie thought— wearing black leggings and suede boots that reached above her knees and a flowing white peasant blouse with a long lavender vest on top. The fuzzy fringe border looked like Fun Fur. Maggie knew Phoebe had designed the piece herself, and it was a very popular pattern on her website.

Phoebe's thick hair was gathered at the back of her head in a hairstyle she called "a sloppy bun," and it certainly fit that description. The punky blue streak contrasted vividly with her dark tresses. Her dark eyes were lined with kohl, and large hoop earrings, the circumference easily as wide as Phoebe's slim waist, hung nearly to her shoulders.

Hula-Hoops, Maggie called them. "You can slip those off anytime and get some exercise," Maggie had once suggested. Phoebe, who was a good sport, had laughed at the possibility.

The Hula-Hoops were worn in addition to the many and varied piercings on her ears and nose. Maggie did not approve of pierced body parts and tattoos, but she could see how it helped some express their identity, mark themselves as unique and unconventional, in case there was any doubt.

Phoebe was all of that and more. And young enough to get away with her style choices. For now anyway.

Phoebe's design specialty was socks—unique footwear that was actually too eye catching and amazing to be hidden under shoes and boots. A corner of the shop displayed Phoebe's socks and other handmade items, and she also sold her wares at outdoor markets and on her website, Sox by Phoebe. But she still filled all the orders herself and was wary of spreading herself too thin and diluting her brand.

She experimented with all types of knitwear and fibers, often combining textures, colors, and stitches that Maggie would not dare to blend in her wildest dreams. And yet in Phoebe's talented hands, the combination was practically always a great success. Maggie had long ago realized that Phoebe was far too talented to remain her assistant forever. Someday, she would spread her fiber fairy wings and move on to great heights. But for now, it was a pleasure to have the little punky sprite around, for countless reasons, the least of which was her refreshing personality and perspective.

"So that makes me the *head* fiber fairy?" Maggie asked.

Phoebe had ducked into the storeroom a moment ago and now emerged with a mug of mint tea. "How about queen of the fiber fairies? I like that much better."

Lucy laughed. "You've always seemed majestic to me, Maggie. You just have that dignified air. I'm leaving before Phoebe decides what my title should be."

"Ditto here." Dana also rose from her chair, then gathered her trash and her tote bag.

"Fiber fairy friends. What else could it be?" Maggie decided. "What time should I be ready?"

"How about noon?" Dana replied. "Is that a good time for you?"

"Perfect. I have a class today that ends at noon—Spring Garden of Felt Flowers. I'll need just a minute or two to clean up after they go."

Dana had followed Lucy toward the door. She turned and waved. Or was that a royal flourish? "As you wish, Your Majesty," she said.

Maggie smiled in answer. At least Dana looked more cheerful leaving than she had when she'd arrived. *Even if the joke is at my expense.*

She closed the door behind her friends and recalled the

silent promise she'd made last night, that she would try to find some way to help the Pipers, too.

She hadn't expected an opportunity to present itself this quickly but was glad now that she'd seized the chance. Would she and Dana be able to discern if the stranger posed any threat?

And would Holly heed a warning?

Chapter 3

There was a little traffic on Main Street at noon, but Dana easily maneuvered around it and headed for Beach Road, which led out of town and toward the nursery.

"Thanks for coming with me, Maggie. Part of me feels as if I'm being intrusive and second-guessing Holly. Another part feels as if I'm racing to her rescue."

Maggie was amused to hear her friend admit the conflict. She usually seemed so clear and settled about things. "Maybe it's a little of both. But safety always wins out over remaining silent, in my mind."

"That's a good rule. I'll remember it . . . And I didn't mean to broadcast Holly's private matters, either. About dating and all that. But I know you and Lucy won't tell anyone."

"Of course not. I think it must be hard for Holly to get out and socialize with so many responsibilities. I can see why that concerns you, too."

"It does," Dana admitted. "She claims she has no time to date. But sometimes I wonder if she was traumatized by her first real relationship, with a boy she dated in high school."

"Was it a bad breakup? That can be very hard when you're young."

"It was more involved than that. He was driving the night Rose was injured. A motorcycle rider was killed in the accident. George and Ava wouldn't allow Holly to have any contact with him after that. The boy was eventually arrested and went to jail."

"Holly's been through a lot in her young life, hasn't she?"

"Yes, she has," Dana said quietly. "Enough to make her feel it might be safer to remain alone and unattached. Despite being lonely."

Maggie understood why Dana hoped Holly would find someone to share her life. It would certainly set Dana's mind at rest, but these things had to come in their own time, in their own way.

The passing scenery looked much different today than it had the night before. A bright, warm sun bathed the fields and woods with golden light, and a clear blue sky arched above. The heavy rain had washed the air clean, and the countryside looked refreshed and eager for spring.

They arrived at the Pipers, and Maggie had a clear view of the land behind the house. There were mostly acres of planting beds, with tufts of bright green leaves just starting to push through the dark soil.

"Holly said they're working behind the house. That's where most of the branches fell. I don't want to be too obvious, though she'll probably guess what I'm up to," Dana added. "I just want to get another look at the guy. A good look. And exchange a word or two. But if I seem too nosy, Holly might be offended."

Maggie met her glance. "It's tricky. Let's just play it by ear."

Dana walked toward the back of the house, and Maggie fell into step beside her, glad she had stuck with her trusty weatherproof walkers this morning as they marched across the wet grass. The ground was muddy from the rain, but an avid gardener herself, Maggie loved the smell of damp earth, and it definitely felt good to be walking in the brisk air.

Maggie heard dogs barking outside the house this time, and the sound of wood being sawed, a sharp metal edge grating in a steady rhythm.

As they followed a path and came around to the back of the house, she saw a large square of white picket fencing and Rose's dogs romping within. The dogs chased each other and tugged on balls and toys, generally making the most of their time outdoors. Dogs did love to play, didn't they? It brought a smile just to watch them.

Rose stood in the center of the space, her back toward Maggie and Dana, focused on a small, sleek terrier who ran an agility course. The little white-and-brown dog climbed up and down ladders, zigzagged through traffic cones, then raced through a cloth tunnel. The dog emerged at one end to meet Rose by jumping right into her arms.

A few more sedate and serious souls stared through the fence and barked at them. Somebody had to protect the place, Maggie thought.

"I think they're working on the other side of the house. Let's just follow the sound," Dana said.

They walked farther, toward a stand of big trees on the far side of the house. There was little grass, mostly muddy ground and some mulch on a path.

They soon saw Holly's new helper up on a ladder that was tilted against an old tree. He wielded a jagged saw as he cut through a thick branch. Holly stood at the bottom, directing him.

"The one above looks weak, too. May as well take it off now, before it falls."

Focused on his task, Carl Thornton did not answer. The

branch seemed a better match for a power tool, Maggie thought. But he was determined to bring it down with slow, sure strokes.

His head was uncovered today, except for a thick red bandanna tied around his forehead. A Willie Nelson look, she'd call it. She liked Willie Nelson, and Thornton certainly seemed less ominous than he had last night in his hooded goblin attire.

Despite a chill in the air, he wore only a gray thermal shirt and a thin fleece vest, the long sleeves of his shirt rolled over his elbows. Maggie was not surprised to see that tattoos, a tangle of images she couldn't decipher, covered both arms.

She was surprised at the muscles in his upper arms and shoulders. She'd wondered if a man his age was fit enough for such heavy outdoor work. But, for better or worse, Carl Thornton could not be ruled out on those grounds.

Holly turned to greet them. She picked up a long branch and tossed it on a pile in the back of her truck. She looked all business, Maggie thought—outdoor business—wearing a tan barn jacket, heavy leather work boots, and a baseball cap.

"Rose needs to clean up and change her clothes. I hope she remembered the appointments. She's been working with the dogs all morning."

"We just saw her," Maggie said.

"The frisky ones need a lot of exercise. And she gives all the dogs basic training—sit, stay, heel. It's always easier to find a home for a dog with manners than a misbehaving one," Holly added with a patient smile.

"Better stand clear down there," Thornton shouted from his perch.

Maggie had noticed a rope tied to the branch, rigged so the branch would not come crashing down when it was finally cut through. But she definitely saw his point and quickly stepped away, as did Holly.

Dana followed. "How's Mr. Thornton working out?"

"No complaints so far. He did a good job on the fence and seems to know his way around a nursery and a lot about horticulture, too," Holly replied.

"So his references were good, I guess." Dana was trying to sound casual, but Maggie caught a note of concern. Holly didn't seem to mind the prodding.

"He gave the names and numbers for former employers. I haven't checked yet. But I will if he works here any longer, Aunt Dana. You needn't worry."

Maggie felt certain that Dana had more questions, but she left it at that. Maybe because Thornton had descended the ladder and was walking toward them. Maggie noticed the side-to-side gait of a man who had done manual labor all his life and had paid the cost in his back and knees.

Here's a chance, Maggie thought. Though she doubted he'd reply to any queries with more than a syllable or two.

"Hello, Mr. Thornton. I'm Holly's aunt, Dana Haeger. We met when you stopped by last night." Dana offered a gracious smile, as if they were at a garden party.

Carl Thornton looked confused, his shaggy brows drawing together at the edge of his bandanna. "I remember you. Hello, ma'am."

Holly looked impatient. They did have work to do.

Before Dana could engage him in small talk, Holly dug into her pocket and pulled out a key ring. "There's a wood shredder behind the greenhouse, Carl. Mulch those branches and add it to the pile."

"Will do." He took the keys and headed to the truck.

Holly turned and called after him. "That ignition is getting stuck today. I'd better show you."

Dana looked disappointed as she watched them walk

away. Her quarry was disappearing, and she hadn't learned any more about him.

But he did seem less threatening in the daylight, Maggie thought. Maybe some of her worries would be laid to rest?

The crackle of splintering wood filled the air—a frightening sound that made Maggie's head spin as she tried to figure out where it came from. Dana grabbed her arm, her eyes wide with alarm.

Thornton and Holly stood at the back of the truck. Without a word, he grabbed Holly's shoulders and pushed her so hard, she stumbled a few steps and fell to the ground.

"Get back!" he shouted, then jumped to one side as a huge branch crashed down. Smaller branches, twigs, and dry leaves rained from the sky as the heavy limb landed and bounced with dull thud.

Maggie and Dana were far enough away to be clear of any danger, but close enough for Maggie to see that the branch had landed right where Holly stood moments before. On the very prints her heavy boots had made in the ground.

If Thornton had not acted so quickly, she would have been struck and seriously injured or worse.

Dana ran to her side, and Maggie followed. "Holly . . . are you all right? Are you hurt?"

"I'm fine . . . I think." Holly lifted herself onto one elbow. She looked dazed and tried to stand.

"Easy does it," Thornton said quietly. He took hold of her arm on one side.

Dana took the other. "Let us help you. Are you sure nothing hurts? You might be in shock."

Holly didn't reply but looked grateful for their support. She took a few shaky steps, Dana and Thornton hovering close by, ready to catch her if she fell.

"That branch could have hurt you very badly." Dana was trying not to sound hysterical, Maggie thought, but the moment had been truly frightening. If it had hit Holly with full force, the branch could have killed her. But Maggie didn't want to voice the worst possible scenario.

"Lucky for me, almost doesn't matter." Holly offered a small smile. Her sense of humor was intact. That was a good sign.

"I should have seen that one was loose when I was up there." Thornton shook his head, sorry for his lapse.

"It's hard to spot every bad branch. I didn't see it, either." Holly took a breath and brushed some grit from her clothes, then looked over at the truck. "A few more scratches and dents in the fender, not that anyone will notice. It could have been worse."

"Much worse," Dana said. Maggie knew she was talking about Holly being hurt, not her truck. "Carl acted very quickly. He may have saved your life."

Thornton shook his head, his expression hidden in his beard. "I was lucky to hear it breaking off. It's a big one." He looked down at the thick, knarled branch, taking its measure. "I'll need the power saw to chop it. I'd better dump this load and come back."

"The power saw is in the shed behind the greenhouse. The gasoline is stored on the shelf below. I'm going inside for a few minutes," Holly told him. "Let me know when you're finished."

They headed toward the house, and Dana softly brushed away some leaves that still clung to Holly's jacket. Maggie could see her resisting an urge to fuss over Holly more. The young woman gave every sign that she wanted to move on from the incident quickly. Holly was definitely not the hysterical type. Far from it.

They turned toward the backyard. Holly seemed relieved. "Good. Rose went inside. I bet she didn't even hear the branch fall. She would have come to see what was going on."

The dog park was empty, Maggie noticed. Rose and her pack were gone.

Holly turned to Maggie and Dana. "Please don't mention it. It's no big deal, and you know how she worries about me."

Maggie had already noticed, and how Holly was ever mindful of cushioning Rose's world.

"We won't say a word, right, Maggie?" Dana met Maggie's glance as she answered for both of them.

Holly seemed calmer. "I reminded Rose this morning that you were picking her up. I hope she's ready. She can get distracted if I don't keep her on track."

"Don't worry. We have plenty of time." Dana walked with her arm circling Holly's shoulders in a comforting embrace.

Dana and Maggie followed Holly into the house through the back door. It took Maggie's eyes a moment to adjust from the bright sunlight outdoors. She soon focused on Bella and her pack of squirming, softly yipping puppies.

She could not resist crouching down for a closer look. She hadn't gotten a very long look at Bella the night before. Now she admired her shiny, thick coat. Not tightly curled like a poodle's, but soft swirls of fur. She had floppy ears and a long muzzle and dark brown eyes. And curiously large paws for her size, Maggie noticed.

Maggie slowly extended her hand, careful not to startle her. When it seemed safe, she pet Bella's head. The dog wagged her short tail, appreciating the attention.

"Bella is so pretty. What breed is she?"

"A Portuguese water dog mostly, Rose says." Holly leaned over and picked up the water dish, which was almost empty. "Bred to help fishermen. They love to swim. Her toes are webbed, if you look closely at her paws."

"How interesting." Maggie stood up again. She didn't know much about breeds beyond the names of the most popular. "What sort of dog was the father? Do you know?"

"Bella hasn't said much about him," Holly offered with a wry smile. "Rose thinks the father was a golden retriever. The puppies will have a good temperament with that mix. They're both gentle, friendly breeds."

Bella seemed to sense she was being discussed. She met Maggie's gaze and seemed to smile, then resumed licking one of her babies.

"The puppies look bigger. They must have grown an inch overnight." Maggie watched as a few tested wobbly legs and tumbled on top of each other.

Dana was entranced with them, too. "They'll outgrow this nursery in no time. What will you do when they're old enough to leave Bella? Will you keep all of them?"

Maggie could imagine the sight. An adorable but a marauding pack of mischief.

Holly had filled the water dish at the kitchen sink and returned it to Bella's lair. "Rose would love to keep them. But if she's wants to take in all these stray, needy dogs, we agreed that she has to find good homes for most and ask for some fee or donations. We don't get all this dog food for free. The dogs she trains for therapy are easy to place, and so are puppies. It's the older dogs that are hard to find homes for. But she's doing very well getting the word out. She's placed three this month. Then again, she's taken in five. You do the dog math," she added with a wry smile.

Maggie couldn't tell if Holly was happy about that equation, though she was definitely proud of the way her sister was running her home-based shelter.

Maggie had more questions, but Rose came into the kitchen, her trio of loyal companions—Wolf, Oreo, and Queenie—following on her heels like personal bodyguards. She walked straight to the mudroom, and quickly peered in to check on Bella and her puppies, before acknowledging anyone in the kitchen. She had changed from her dog-training outfit into jeans and a white sweater, free of paw prints, Maggie noticed. Her hair was brushed into a low ponytail.

Dana greeted her. "Hi, honey. Ready to go?"

"I remembered. I set an alarm on my phone." She waved the phone in her hand at her older sister, as if to say, "I can remember things on my own sometimes, too."

Then she walked over to Holly and lifted a leaf from her hair. One Dana had missed. "You're all dirty. Did you fall down?"

Holly smiled and shrugged. "Some branches fell during the storm. We were just taking them away. You know how muddy it is out there."

Dana and Maggie stood in silence, remembering Holly's request. Rose seemed concerned but didn't say more.

She glanced at Maggie but didn't seem surprised to see her again. "I've been working on my project. It's halfway done."

"That was fast. I'd love to see it." Maggie was sincerely pleased, but had thought Rose would take to it quickly. She left the scientific jargon to Dana but did know that even fumbling first attempts at knitting activated the reward centers of the brain, which was why beginners would stick with it, even if they stumbled along stitch by stitch.

Maggie took pride not only in her knitting skills and talents but in her abilities as a teacher of the art, too. She could see she'd taken the right approach with Rose by starting on a simple project, like a dog collar, that could be completed quickly. Rose would get good practice making more of them.

"Do the dogs need any care while you're out?" Holly asked.

"Everyone is in the parlor. You can check their water bowls later. You're coming to pick me up, right?"

"I'll be there at three, after your appointment with Dr. Riley. He wants to meet with me."

"I'll bet he does. He always finds some excuse." Rose rolled her eyes.

"Rose . . ." Holly looked embarrassed. Maggie could see Rose's teasing had a pushed a button. "Tim and I are just friends. You know that."

"He'd like to be more than your friend, Holly. Anyone can see that." Rose sighed, as if she were the older sister. She kissed Holly's cheek.

A *sweet gesture*, Maggie thought. She did seem like a little girl at times, but in a touching way.

"Don't work too hard," Rose added.

"That's why I hired Thornton. He's been a huge help."

An understatement, Maggie would say. She was sure that his quick action to keep Holly from being hit by the branch now weighed heavily in his favor.

"Mr. Scary, you mean?" Rose murmured.

"Rose, that's not nice." Holly paused. "But I'm not sure if you're kidding. I told you this morning, if you really don't like him, he doesn't have to work here. I don't want you to feel uneasy about any of the helpers. You know that."

Rose chose an apple from a bowl on the table and took a bite. "He's not so scary in the daylight. I can give him a chance. And Wolf will check him out. He's a foolproof judge of character."

Rose headed for the side door; her dogs walked in her shadow. She turned to them and clipped a lead to Oreo.

"You guys stay," she said to the other two. "I'll be back in a little while."

Wolf and Queenie stopped in their tracks and watched Rose as she grabbed a down vest and a small purse from a row of hooks near the door. The black-and-white sheep-herding dog, Oreo, pranced with excitement, happy to be the chosen one.

Maggie was still amused as they left the house and headed for Dana's car. "Do your dogs understand every word you say?"

"Not every word. But more than you think possible. A dog can have a very large vocabulary. Some can understand over one hundred words. But you need to know how to talk to them, too."

"You seem to know exactly how," Maggie said.

"I've read books about it, and there's loads of information on the internet. I love dogs. That helps the most in learning how to understand them. I like them better than people," Rose said. "Dogs love you, no matter what. Most dogs are nicer than some people, too."

Even with her limited canine experience, Maggie thought that might be true.

As they drove to the center, Maggie wanted to ask Dana if this second meeting had changed her impression of Thornton. But she didn't want to bring the subject up in front of Rose. It might lead to them mentioning Holly's close call with the crashing branch.

The center was a short distance from the Pipers' nursery, and as they drove through tall wrought-iron gates, Dana explained that the building and property had been bought at a bank auction and had been quite a good deal.

"This beautiful old house was going to be knocked down. Can you imagine? It needed a lot of renovation, but the space has been transformed very efficiently," Dana explained as they pulled up the long drive.

The building was beautiful, a classic brick colonial with a slate roof, white columns, and long windows in front. It was surrounded by thick shrubs and a manicured lawn that was already green. A small, tasteful sign read RILEY-CURTIS WELLNESS CENTER.

To the right side of the house, Maggie noticed a smaller building that looked like new construction, also brick with white trim, its traditional design blending well with the surroundings.

Dana parked near the entrance, where a few stone steps led to glossy black doors.

"I'd better find my group. I'm late," Rose said. She hopped out of the car with Oreo and headed down a shrub-lined path to the new building.

"See you later, honey," Dana called after them.

"Rose seems very cooperative about her treatment. That must make it easier for Holly," Maggie said as they walked toward the main building.

"She knows what she has to do to stay on course, and takes responsibility for her care. She wasn't always that way," Dana added. "She likes Tim and Emily and trusts them. That helps enormously."

They entered the building and stepped into a long open space with a glossy wooden floor and walls the color of fresh butter or maybe vanilla pudding. Maggie knew it was a medical facility, but it looked more like the lobby of a fancy hotel.

A round antique table in the middle of the space held a spring arrangement in a china bowl—branches of forsythia and pussy willow, the buds just starting to peek open. Upholstered armchairs and benches lined the walls, with small wooden side tables set in between.

A few people sat waiting—a middle-aged man in a suit and tie, reading his phone, and a young woman who had a little girl about ten years old with her. The woman looked nervous but forced a smile as she held the child's hand. Maggie wished them well. Nobody came here without a serious problem, that was for sure.

Framed prints were hung at intervals along the walls, and an elaborately carved wooden staircase led the way to a second floor.

"This is a big place," Maggie said. "Treatment here must be costly."

"It is, but it costs a lot to run a health center like this, believe me." Dana's voice was nearly a whisper as she added, "Rose is treated by both Dr. Curtis and Dr. Riley. Luckily, they've taken her on practically for free. Partly as a favor to me, and partly because Dr. Riley is interested in her case. If his treatment protocol can turn her condition around such a long time after the injury, it will be truly groundbreaking."

"I see," Maggie replied. So Rose was sort of a guinea pig for Dr. Riley? Maggie could see the benefit and also the downside of that arrangement. But Dana seemed fine with it, she noticed. Dana understood these advanced treatments, and Maggie knew she wouldn't allow a hair on Rose's head to be harmed. Maggie was sure of that.

At the far end of the space, near the staircase, she saw a small reception desk. A young man in a white lab coat sat typing on a keyboard. He looked up and smiled at Dana as she signed a ledger.

When Dana was done, she said, "Let's go upstairs. I hope Tim and Emily are around. I want to introduce you."

Maggie followed her to the staircase, thick carpet muffling their steps. They soon arrived at the second floor, and Maggie stared down a long hall.

The walls were painted the same soothing shade, with nubby brown carpet covering the floor. Instead of framed prints, black plastic bins that held folders hung beside each of the dark wooden doors.

More like it, she thought. *Definitely more medical looking.*

"Offices and exam rooms are on this floor," Dana explained. "The new building has a few multipurpose rooms, where we hold group sessions, and there's a special gym for physical therapy. We'll go over there later. You can decide which room might be best for a class. I need to pick up some files from a colleague. Can you wait here a minute? He might be with a patient."

"Take your time. I have my knitting."

Dana smiled. "Of course you do."

Dana disappeared through the first door on the left. Maggie spotted a bench about halfway down the hall and took a seat. She took out her knitting and started to work. She was making a lightweight pullover for Charles in a basket-stitch pattern. She'd knit Charles some small gifts, a scarf or two and heavy socks. But this was the first large-scale knitting project she'd ever started for him, and she wanted it to come out perfectly. She'd chosen a slate-blue shade of yarn, medium weight, mostly cotton with some stretch, which she knew would be a good thickness for the spring weather or even a cool summer night on the boat.

The basket stitch was very useful and created a wonderful texture. She intended to teach her friends the stitch sooner or later. She would have shown them at the last meeting, except for the Pipers needing a beginner lesson. But the right time would come to fit it in. For every stitch there is a season, she mused.

She heard quick footsteps approaching and looked up, but it was not Dana. A young woman wearing a white lab coat strode purposefully down the hall, a sheaf of file folders tucked under one arm.

Maggie looked back at her knitting. She didn't think she had even been noticed, until the woman stopped abruptly just before passing her by.

She looked down at Maggie. Bright blue eyes framed by round tortoiseshell glasses gave her an owlish look. Her blond hair was parted in the middle and pulled back in a clip.

"Can I help you?" Her tone did not sound helpful exactly, more like she wanted to know what Maggie was doing there.

Maggie smiled and took a moment to read the name tag clipped to the pocket of the young woman's lab coat. BETH DUNCAN, PH.D., RESEARCH ASSISTANT.

"I'm waiting for a friend, Dr. Haeger. She just ducked into her office for a moment."

Beth Duncan leaned back, seeming satisfied with the explanation. Without saying more, she continued on her way, then stopped at a door a short distance beyond the bench. The door was partly open, Maggie noticed, but she knocked on the trim anyway.

"Can you go over the staffing schedule now, Dr. Curtis? I know you need to leave soon."

"Not now, Beth. I'll catch up with you before I go." The voice was curt and dismissive.

Maggie saw Beth's frown, but she turned on her heel and proceeded to the end of the hall, then disappeared down the stairs.

Maggie began knitting again. Voices drifted out of the open door. A man and a woman talking in casual, intimate tones. Maggie focused on her stitching but couldn't help overhearing their conversation.

"I'd wish you luck, but I know you never need it. When will you be back?"

"Wednesday night," the woman said.

"With a big, fat check, I hope. Or the promise of one," the man countered.

"I'll do my best. We can't count on it. I hope you know

that, Tim. If the grant had been renewed, we wouldn't be in this position." The woman's tone was accusatory. She had called the man Tim. Was Dr. Riley in that room?

"Back to that again? It's so unfair to blame me. You know that." He suddenly sounded angry. "Come on. Admit it. You love to be the rainmaker around here. The super-hero," he added in a warmer, cajoling tone.

"And I do it so well, don't I?"

"Absolutely. I know how persuasive you can be, Emily. Believe me."

It was Emily Curtis and Tim Riley, the partners of the health center, Maggie decided. She heard Dr. Curtis sigh, but she didn't answer.

"Call me when you get to the hotel. Let me know you're okay."

"Will you pick up the phone?"

"What's that supposed to mean?"

"You have a meeting with Holly Piper this afternoon. What's that about?"

"I do? Oh, right . . . How did you know about that?"

Dr. Curtis sounded amused. "Is it a secret?"

"Not at all. She has some questions about Rose's med-ication."

"Questions she can't ask over the phone?"

"I don't know. She's picking up Rose later and asked if I had a few minutes to see her." His tone was matter of fact. "Is that a problem?"

Maggie recalled Holly had told them she had a meeting at three with Dr. Riley . . . but hadn't she said that he had initiated the appointment?

"Not at all. Unless you're lying to me. Again. That would definitely be a problem. I've told you before, Tim. Don't take me for a fool. This place wouldn't last five min-utes without me. I think you know that."

Dr. Curtis sounded angry. The sort of pent-up anger that could explode without warning. Maggie held her breath, waiting to hear his reaction.

"You give me too much credit, Emily. We wouldn't last *two* minutes without you." Surprisingly, his voice was calm and affectionate, the tone one might use to soothe a child who's had a bad dream. "As for Holly Piper . . . Okay, maybe she has a little crush on me. That 'doctor thing' women get sometimes? It's flattering. I'll admit it. But you have no reason at all to feel threatened by her."

When she didn't answer, he said, "If it makes you feel better, I'll text her right now and cancel." Maggie heard the sound of tapping on a phone keyboard. "Here's the message, see? I'm hitting SEND."

Maggie waited again to hear Dr. Curtis's response. He was obviously trying to placate her. Was she persuaded?

"Do whatever you like. If I find out you're lying, I'm done. I'm not kidding this time."

Maggie heard the sound of footsteps, and Dr. Curtis swept out of the room.

Dr. Riley followed, rushing to keep up. "Emily . . . for goodness' sakes. Don't leave like this. Let me walk you to your car."

Maggie was eager to match faces to the voices but didn't want to stare. She did manage to peer up as Dr. Curtis swept by, her gaze fixed straight ahead.

Emily Curtis was petite but looked charged with power and energy—or was it simply the fury of a woman often scorned? She marched down the long hall, the strap of a black briefcase slung over one shoulder, as she tugged along a compact silver suitcase, the expensive high-tech kind Maggie had often eyed in catalogs, though she had had no plans to travel lately.

Her thick, dark hair was cut to her chin in a sleek bob and parted on the side. She brushed it back impatiently, then adjusted large, stylish glasses. Her tailored outfit was deceptively simple and unmistakably expensive—a black blazer with a pale blue silk blouse underneath, charcoal-gray pants with short black boots. Pearl earrings and a dash of red lipstick were finishing touches to a sophisticated professional look.

Dr. Curtis glanced at Maggie, surprised to find a woman on the bench outside her office, knitting no less. Maggie thought she was going to say something, but she paused only a moment to hitch the strap of her shoulder bag, then rushed forward again.

Dr. Riley had caught up, matching her pace, but Dr. Curtis did not acknowledge him.

"Let me take your bag. That looks heavy," he said.

Dr. Riley was tall and lean, with broad shoulders and dark red hair. Thick brows emphasized large brown eyes, fixed on Emily with a humble, obsequious gaze.

Maggie guessed he was somewhere in his early forties but was the type of man who would always have a boyish look and dressed the part, as well, in a brown tweed sports jacket over a blue oxford cloth shirt and jeans.

A door down the hall opened, and Dana appeared and walked towards Maggie. "I'm so sorry. That took much longer than I expected."

Before Maggie could reply, Dana had turned to look at the two doctors. "Emily . . . Tim . . . do you have a minute?"

The bickering pair had almost reached the staircase. Dr. Curtis turned to answer.

"I'm just on my way out. But sure . . . What's up?"

"This is my good friend Maggie Messina," Dana said as she and Maggie walked toward them. "I wanted to introduce you. She's going to assist with my knitting idea. She gave Rose her first lesson last night."

"Nice to meet you, Maggie," Dr. Curtis said.

Dr. Riley met Maggie's gaze with a warm smile. "How did Rose like knitting?"

"She didn't have much trouble at all. Maggie started her on a very simple technique," Dana said.

"She's doing very well," Maggie added. "She's almost finished a small project. A dog collar."

"That sounds promising." Dr. Curtis looked pleased. "I'll be in Boston the next few days, Dana. But we can talk more when I get back next week."

"Another conference?" Dana asked.

"Not exactly. I have appointments with foundations that might fund our work."

Maggie assumed that much from what she'd overheard, but it was interesting to hear the point clarified.

"An important mission. Have a good trip," Dana said.

"Thanks. I hope it is a good trip. I'll be in touch when I get back." Dr. Curtis looked at Maggie. "Nice to meet you, Maggie."

"Same here, Dr. Curtis. Safe travels." She had lovely eyes, Maggie noticed, with an unexpected softness in their gray-blue light.

As Dr. Curtis and Dr. Riley started down the steps, Beth Duncan met them on her way up. She seemed even more stressed than the first time Maggie had seen her.

"Dr. Curtis, I'm glad I caught you. I still have a few questions about the schedule."

"Oh, right. I'm sorry, it slipped my mind. Walk me to my car, Beth. We'll sort it out." Dr. Curtis glanced at her business partner. "I'll see you next week," she said over her shoulder.

"Right." He didn't try to follow them, and once the two women were out of sight, he walked back up the steps toward Dana and Maggie. "It's always an emergency with Beth. Sometimes I think it's just attention-seeking behavior."

Dana frowned. Maggie could tell the criticism didn't sit well with her. "Beth has a lot of responsibilities and she's still working on her degree. I think she's doing a good job."

"You're right. That was unfair . . . and unkind. She's very conscientious. We should encourage more of that." He smiled and nodded, looking admonished. He glanced at his watch. "Sorry, I have to run. It was nice to meet you, Maggie. Hope to see you again soon."

"I look forward to it," Maggie replied.

She and Dana headed downstairs and, once outside, started off toward the new building. Dana started to tell her more about the center and the cutting-edge therapies offered to clients. But Maggie's head was filled with questions about the conversation she'd overheard between the two doctors. Should she tell Dana? Not just to gossip but because Holly's name had come up?

Who had really asked for the meeting this afternoon? Tim Riley or Holly? Dr. Riley had claimed Holly had asked to see him, and he had sounded very sure of that. But Holly had stated very clearly that Dr. Riley had asked for the appointment. What did she have to gain by lying? Unless what Dr. Riley had said was true—that Holly had a crush on him—and she didn't want anyone to know.

They had arrived at the new building, and Dana pulled open a heavy glass door. "Let's go in. I'll show you some of the meeting rooms."

They walked into a sunlit foyer with a very high domed ceiling, long windows, and a tile floor. It was filled with large green plants and upholstered benches, where people sat quietly talking or working on laptops. In the middle of the space, water flowed through a stone fountain, the gentle splashing sounds creating a soothing backdrop.

Maggie barely noticed. "Dana, I want to tell you something."

Dana turned to her with a curious look.

"It's probably not important, and I hate to gossip. But . . ."

"Aunt Dana?" Rose walked toward them, leading Oreo. Maggie wasn't sure where she'd come from. Perhaps from one of the corridors that led off lobby? "Holly said to look for you. She said you're giving me a lift home?"

"That's right," Dana replied. "She sent me a text. Her appointment with Dr. Riley was canceled. I guess something came up."

Maggie knew what it was, too. But now that Rose was with them, she didn't feel free to tell Dana. She'd find a private moment soon. Perhaps unknowingly, Holly could be stepping into a sticky situation.

Chapter 4

Phoebe had very aptly held down the fiber castle most of Friday, and Maggie gave her Saturday off, even though it was their busiest day. Ever since she and Charles had started living together, she had been less inclined to be at the shop on Sundays. They were only open from noon to four and Phoebe was fine covering the hours so that Maggie could spend the day with Charles.

On this particular Sunday, they lingered over breakfast and the newspapers and later worked in the garden, raking out the beds. Maggie knew she'd have to clean up the garden around her shop, too, very soon. But that would have to wait for another day.

In the late afternoon she cooked one of Charles's favorite dinners, classic spaghetti and meatballs. She'd meant to surprise him, but when he found her in the kitchen, prodding some of the mixture into dog-bone shapes, he had a few questions.

"What is that you're cooking, Maggie?"

"I'm making you meatballs. This is just a little experiment. We're having dogs at the knitting group meeting this week, and I wanted to make them a special treat."

"You're going to teach dogs how to knit now, too? Not

that I doubt you could do it, if anybody could. But why would they even need to know that?"

She knew he wasn't serious. She hoped not anyway. "Rose Piper needs to bring her therapy dogs with her to the shop. At least one of them. So I told Lucy and Suzanne they could bring their dogs, too. It didn't seem right to leave them out." She looked up at him. "So I decided to have a dog theme."

"I see." He picked up a slice of carrot from the cutting board and crunched down. "I didn't even know you like dogs."

Maggie wasn't sure how to answer. "I like them well enough. I don't know that much about them. Julie liked cats, so she never asked for a dog growing up. I'm starting to see why some people are so devoted. A dog will do anything to please you. Cats are pretty much the opposite."

"I had a great dog when I was a kid. A big old mutt," Charles said wistfully. "His name was Champ."

"Really? You never mentioned him before."

Charles shrugged, remembering his childhood friend. "That dog saved my life. We were out in the marshes, me and a bunch of neighborhood kids. I wandered off and got stuck in quicksand. I flailed around, screaming and sinking deeper and deeper. Really stuck."

"That must have been terrifying."

"Never been more scared in my life, not even under gunfire. Champ ran for help and brought my friends back to find me. They got me out just in time."

"Sounds like a boy's adventure novel."

He smiled. "An old-fashioned one. I've had a lot of adventures you don't know about yet, my dear. You'd be surprised."

"No I wouldn't. But I'll still enjoy hearing about them," she said sincerely.

Lucy's suggestion—her nagging, more precisely—echoed

in Maggie's head. Maybe Charles would like a dog. She could ask him right now. But for some reason, she decided to change the subject entirely.

She stood back from the counter. "I give up. I think I need a bone-shaped cookie cutter. I bet Lucy has one. I'm going to call her."

Charles stared down at the baking sheet and then at Maggie. "Do you think the dogs will really notice?"

Maggie smiled. "Good point. I might be getting a little carried away."

On Tuesday morning, Maggie was preparing for a class that started at eleven when she noticed Holly's green pickup truck pull up and park in front of the shop.

Holly was alone, without Rose or any four-footed family members, and Maggie watched from the window as she took a large shopping bag from the cab and two pots that held bright green plants from the truck's bay.

Maggie opened the door and greeted her. "What a nice surprise. Let me help you with that."

Holly passed the bag to her. "It's just the pans and dishes everyone brought over last week. And I brought you some pansies. A shipment was delivered this morning."

"How thoughtful. They're one of my favorites. There's something so optimistic about pansies. Even if it's still cold out, they always make me feel as if spring is really here."

Maggie set the shopping bag down just inside the door and took the potted plants, one in each hand. The bold-colored blossoms were just starting to open. She stepped outside and placed them at the bottom of the porch steps. "I guess this is a sign. Time to get into those beds and start digging. Sometimes I wish I hadn't planted such a big garden here. Though I do enjoy it when it's in bloom."

Holly had followed her outside. She looked over the flower beds in front of the shop, bordering the white picket fence, the brick path, and the front of the porch. "I can see that there's enough work here to keep you busy all spring and summer. But if it makes you feel better, we have acres to weed right now."

"I bet you do. But not on your own, I hope." Maggie recalled that Holly hired a staff of workers this time of year. More helpers than just Carl Thornton, Dana had said.

"At the height of the season, there are about six to eight in the crew. Right now, I'm down to zero. Well, as of tomorrow."

Maggie was confused. "What happened to Thornton?"

"I don't know. A better-paying job probably. He didn't give a reason. He just told me this morning he was quitting and needs to collect his pay by the end of the day."

"How strange, and it's not very responsible to leave so abruptly, with no notice . . ."

"What can you do? I thought he was a bit of an odd duck, but I was willing to give him a chance. There are a few men and women who come back every year to work for me. They'll start soon. We'll manage fine."

"I'm sure you will." Maggie wondered if Dana knew Thornton had quit. She'd be happy to hear it.

"Would you like to come in for a minute? There's fresh coffee. Or I can make you some tea."

"I can't stop long, but I would like to see the shop. I don't think I've ever been inside."

Holly followed Maggie inside and looked around with interest. Phoebe was at the back table, helping a customer choose buttons from the many drawers in a wooden cabinet, but the morning had been quiet otherwise.

"This is a lovely place. Very cozy. Have you been in business long?" Holly asked.

"Oh, about eight years now, I guess. I'd always wanted to run a knitting shop someday but thought I'd do it once I retired. I was a teacher at the high school. After my husband, Bill, died, I needed a fresh start. I quit my job, found this place, and gambled a chunk of my retirement savings."

"Looks like the bet paid off."

"I can't complain." Maggie smiled. "There are highs and lows, as you know, running your own business. I love knitting, and I'm pretty good at it. But there's a big difference between a fun hobby and a successful business."

"I never imagined I'd take over the nursery from my parents," Holly admitted. "But that's the way life worked out for me. When I was a teenager, I wanted to be an actress. I had the lead in the school play senior year. I was Emily in *Our Town*. I guess the success went to my head, as silly and naive as that sounds." She smiled, remembering. "I imagined I'd live in New York or California and be a big movie star. No wonder my parents were against it."

Dana had told them that Holly was set to go away to college but changed her plans when Rose was injured. She'd never mentioned acting. Maggie didn't want to pry, but she was curious to hear more.

"It doesn't sound silly, not at all. Did you ever find a way to pursue your interest? There are a lot of amateur theater groups around. It's hardly the same, but it could be fun." A way for Holly to socialize more and have some life of her own, besides taking care of Rose, she thought.

"It was just a childhood daydream. I like running the nursery. I like working outdoors and growing things. I couldn't imagine living in a city. Sometimes I think I'm stuck right where I am, like one of the old oaks next to our house. But it's fine for me."

Maggie wondered at her resignation. Wasn't she too young to feel that way? "You're more of a graceful willow or a cherry blossom, if you're a tree at all. I think so anyway."

Holly laughed and seemed to appreciate the compliment. "I guess I'd pick a willow," she replied. "It's been fun talking to you, Maggie, but I have to run over to the bank. The money goes out faster than it comes in lately. I wish I knew how to grow some dollar bills alongside the daffodils."

"No worries. We're still on for Thursday night, right?"

"Absolutely. Rose has been grooming the dogs for their night on the town."

Maggie smiled at the thought. "That reminds me, I have something for her. Some yarn she might like." Maggie quickly located the skeins under the counter, where she'd put them aside. "I thought this weight was perfect for the collars she's been making. It knits into stripes automatically. It has a little stretch, too."

Holly took the skeins and looked back at Maggie. "That's very thoughtful. Please, let me pay you something?"

"It's my pleasure. You've already paid me in pansies. Rose is keeping up with her knitting, right?"

"She's really taken to it. It might be too soon to say, but I think it's helped her already."

"When I have a stressful day, even five minutes of stitching can calm me down. I'm not surprised to hear Rose got some benefit after five days."

"I think she has. You can ask her yourself when we come on Thursday." Holly headed to the door. "I'm looking forward to it."

"I am, as well," Maggie replied. She wished Holly a good day and said good-bye.

After dinner that evening, Maggie sat knitting, wondering what she'd teach the group on Thursday night. She still hadn't fixed on a special stitch or project. Dog outerwear came to mind, but it was still too advanced for Rose and wouldn't interest everyone.

Charles was watching a show about the archaeologists who uncovered the tombs of the ancient Pharaohs. He'd always been keen on Egyptian history and was taking a class in the subject at a college nearby.

"I'd love to go to Egypt and see the pyramids. Wouldn't you?"

Maggie couldn't quite picture herself on the back of a camel, wobbling over the dunes, but tried to sound open minded.

"That would be exciting. Though they say most of the ancient treasures ended up in the British Museum. I'd love to go back to London sometime."

Before Charles could counter with his preferred itinerary, a promo for the local news flashed on the television screen. Maggie saw a video of a building ablaze. Fire trucks and other emergency vehicles rushed into the chaotic scene.

In a long-distance shot, the sign for Piper Nursery appeared as the broadcaster said, "A greenhouse on the outskirts of town went up in flames tonight. Two victims found at the scene were rushed to Harbor Hospital and are listed in serious condition. Details at eleven . . ."

Maggie dropped her knitting, her mouth hanging open in shock. "Did you see that? It was Piper Nursery. Can you wind it back so I can watch it again?"

Charles peered through his reading glasses and fumbled with the remote. He managed to rewind the clip, and they watched until Maggie yelled, "Stop . . . right there. See? That's their sign. It's Holly and Rose's place. Oh my goodness . . . I wonder if Dana knows."

She grabbed her phone and dialed Dana, who picked up on the first ring.

Maggie's words came out in a rush. "I just saw the news. Maybe you already know. There was a fire at the nursery . . ."

"We just heard. A friend of Jack's on the police force called when the report came in. We went straight to the hospital. We're there now, with them."

"Oh my goodness . . . How are they? Were they badly hurt?" Maggie hated to think the worst but couldn't help asking.

"Firemen found them outside the building, thank goodness. There are only very minor burns. Holly is in intensive care. She's had serious smoke inhalation and some other injuries. She's on a breathing device and sedated, so we haven't been able to speak to her. Rose is getting treatment, too. She's not nearly as bad as Holly. But she's in shock. She can't tell us yet what happened, either."

Maggie guessed that Rose was experiencing some of the stress issues that plagued her. Good thing Dana was there to explain her medical condition to the doctors and oversee Rose's treatment.

"Oh, Dana . . . I'm so sorry. How did the fire start? Do they have any idea?"

"No one knows yet. It could have been faulty wiring or a problem with the heating system. The fire department will investigate as soon as they're able."

Maggie's heart went out to both young women. What a horrific experience. But she felt especially bad for Holly, who was already dealing with so much. She hoped Holly would recover quickly, and also hoped her business could withstand this loss.

"What can I do? I can come right now and keep you company," Maggie offered.

"Oh, thank you, Maggie, but Jack is here. We'll be fine."

"If you need anything at all, please let us know. And please keep me posted on how they're doing," Maggie added.

It sounded as if Holly, at least, would be in the hospital awhile, and there would be other opportunities to help as time went on.

"I'm sure I'll be back here tomorrow, but maybe I can stop by the shop at some point. I'll let you know," Dana said good night and ended the call.

Maggie sat in stunned silence a moment, then glanced at Charles. "Holly and Rose are both in the hospital. Sounds as if Holly is in bad shape, with smoke inhalation. Dana said there are some other injuries, too. She's being treated and sedated. Rose was hurt, but not as badly."

"That's awful. Those poor girls." Charles frowned. "What were they doing in a greenhouse at this time of night?"

"Good question . . . Maybe they saw the fire start and thought they could put it out by themselves?"

"Maybe. People panic. They don't realize what they're dealing with. Must have been bad wiring or something mechanical."

"That's what Dana said. Thank goodness they weren't caught in the flames. I hope Holly's insurance will cover the damage."

"A lot depends on the cause of the fire. These insurance companies are very good at avoiding paying out on a claim. Bad wiring or bad sprinklers. Arson isn't covered, either," Charles noted.

"How could it be arson? Are you saying Holly may have set the fire herself?"

"I'm not accusing anyone. But some business owners do set fire to their property. Or pay someone to do it. It's a common tactic when a business is in trouble . . . and the owner usually gets caught."

Holly was feeling financial pressure. Dana had mentioned that a few times, and Holly had even alluded to it on Tuesday at the shop, Maggie recalled. But she definitely seemed optimistic about the new season.

Would Holly really set her own greenhouse on fire? Maggie didn't know her well but doubted Holly was the type to sink so low, no matter how far her business had fallen behind.

"From what I know of Holly Piper, I sincerely doubt it's even a question," Maggie said.

"I hope that's true," Charles replied in his infuriating "always leaving room for the possibility" way. "The fire marshal will conduct a full investigation, and the insurance company will send their own inspectors, too. They'll sniff it all out. It doesn't take them long."

Maggie didn't reply. She felt sure that the findings would be something wrong with the building. The house was comfortable but in need of repair. The greenhouse was probably in the same worn condition.

There were more calls and text messages exchanged with her friends before Maggie finally headed to bed. "Dana said she might stop by tomorrow and give me an update," she told everyone.

They decided to meet at the shop once Maggie knew when Dana would arrive. It was what she called their "rapid response" strategy.

It was hard to carry on business as usual the next day, but Maggie knew she was such a creature of habit and her body had an automatic setting, even if her mind was worlds away.

Phoebe came down early from her apartment, almost as soon as Maggie turned the key in the front door. Highly unusual, but she looked as if she had not slept well or spent much time on her outfit, and her first words were about Holly and Rose.

"Good. You're here early. Any news from Dana?"

"Not yet. I don't want to bother her. She was going back to the hospital this morning. She promised to be in touch." Maggie put her purse and knitting bag on the counter and took off her sweater, a thick cabled coat sweater that she had knit for herself a few years back and that draped down to her knees. It was plenty warm, but it was definitely a sign of spring when she was able to wear it.

"We can call the hospital and see how they are," Phoebe suggested.

"I guess we should. I'd like know how they are, too. Do you want to call? I need to make coffee. I didn't have time for a cup at home."

After all the text messages last night and getting to bed late, Maggie hadn't been able to sleep. The flashing images of the fire had kept replaying in her head.

Phoebe pulled out her cell phone and followed Maggie to the back of the shop. As Maggie put the coffee together in the storeroom, she heard Phoebe using her official voice to deal with the hospital switchboard.

But before Maggie emerged to hear the update, a text came through on her own phone. It was Dana. **On my way to the hospital now. I can stop in for a minute or two. Are you at the shop yet?**

Maggie quickly wrote back. **I'm here. I'll let the others know you're coming. Everyone wants to see you.**

She walked out with two mugs of coffee, one for herself and one for Phoebe, who looked a bit brighter.

"They couldn't tell me much, but a nurse said Holly is in stable condition and Rose is in good condition. Maybe she'll come out of the hospital today."

"I hope so," Maggie replied. "Dana might have more details. She's on her way."

Maggie's alert brought Lucy and Suzanne to the shop within minutes. By the time Dana arrived, the group was already seated on the antique sofa and armchairs near the bay window, sipping coffee and nibbling bits from a box of donut holes Suzanne had brought.

"I picked them up for the office, but this is definitely an emergency."

"A carb emergency," Phoebe agreed, choosing a large hunk covered with sugar and cinnamon.

"First, how are Holly and Rose?" Maggie asked Dana. "Phoebe called the hospital. All they'd say is that Holly is in stable condition and Rose is in good condition."

"Holly is better than last night, but she's still in the ICU, with a breathing device, and she's still unconscious. She has other injuries. Not just from the fire."

Maggie was surprised. "What do you mean?"

Maggie could see it was hard for Dana to talk about it. "She was struck on the head with a heavy object. The fire department is fairly certain that the fire was intentionally set. It appears someone knocked her out and set the blaze. I guess they hoped that she would . . . that she wouldn't wake up in time to escape."

No one spoke. Maggie felt a deep sense of dread.

"That's awful," Lucy said finally.

"What about Rose? Was she attacked, too?" Phoebe asked.

"No, thank goodness. Firemen found her unconscious not too far from Holly, but it doesn't look like she was in the burning building. We don't know yet for sure."

Everyone waited for Dana to say more. She looked tired, with dark shadows beneath her eyes and no make-up to cover her exhaustion and stress. Dressed in jeans, with a hand-knit poncho tossed on top, she didn't look her usual well-put-together self. No wonder about that.

"The more the fire department and the police find out, the stranger the story gets," she added. "The fire department can tell from the pattern of the flames and the fire's epicenter that it was started with a flammable substance. They're running tests but are almost certain it was gasoline."

"Holly keeps gas in a shed to run power tools. Remember when she told Thornton where to find it?" Maggie said.

Dana nodded. "Yes, and the police will try to figure out if that store of fuel started the blaze or if someone arrived with their own supply."

Suzanne was very upset. Maggie could tell by the way she alternately sipped her coffee and nibbled a donut hole. "What awful news. It's bad enough to have a fire on your property, but to think someone purposely put a match to the place? That's terrifying. That person is still out there, wishing Holly and Rose harm. They could come back to finish the job."

Maggie had come to the same conclusions but wouldn't have put it so bluntly in front of Dana. Not right now anyway. But Dana had likely thought of that problem already, too.

"Who in the world would do such a thing to Holly and Rose? And why?" Lucy leaned forward in her chair, upset and angry.

"I was up most of the night wondering that myself," Dana replied. "Who would want to hurt Holly? Not just hurt her but kill her. Thank goodness she got out in time."

"Rose must have saved her," Phoebe said. "She must have seen the fire and heard her sister call for help, so she ran out and rescued her."

"Possibly," Dana agreed. "The dogs were out loose on the grounds. Rose's special trio. Rose may have let them out to chase down a stranger on the property. But one of the firemen thought maybe Rose's big dog Wolf pulled Holly from the fire."

Lucy looked at Maggie. "I hope you heard that."

"Duly noted. Though I'd like to know how the fireman figured that out. Aside from the theory that it makes a very nice human interest story for the news. Has Rose been able to answer any questions yet?"

She didn't mean to upset Dana further, but she could see that the question had made Dana uneasy. "Unfortunately, Rose had a stress episode and blacked out. The EMT techs revived her, but she has no idea how she got outside or even when she saw the fire."

"Maybe her memory will come back once she's had some rest." Maggie had taken her knitting out, but the conversation was too upsetting for her to focus. A rare moment, indeed.

"Maybe." Dana took another sip of tea. "She was in shock last night, and we didn't want to pressure her with questions. Neither did the police. But it's possible she'll never fully recall what happened. It's a common symptom of post-traumatic stress. She has no recall of several events in her past—the night of the car accident, when she was injured, for instance."

Dana had mentioned that before, Maggie recalled. It had to be a way that the mind protected a person from reliving terrifying experiences, and a blessing in most cases, Maggie thought. Clearly, a mixed blessing in this situation.

"What about Holly? Can she communicate yet?" Suzanne asked.

Dana shook her head. "I spoke to her doctor after he did rounds early this morning. Holly won't be able to breathe on her own for a few days, he predicts, and he feels it's best if she remains sedated."

Suzanne began to reach for another donut hole but stopped herself. "Let's hope the police can figure this out, even if Holly can't supply any leads. They have their ways of digging up dirt. Excuse the pun, please," Suzanne said.

"You are excused, all things considered," Phoebe said.

Maggie had to agree. Suzanne had paid her dues in that department. Last fall, when Suzanne's office rival had been poisoned, Suzanne had been at the top of the suspect list. The police had unearthed clue after incriminating clue, most of them circumstantial and purposely planted by the real culprit in order to frame her.

Maggie and her friends had solved most of the puzzle, though in the final moments, Suzanne had cleverly outwitted and captured the killer all on her own.

"It could have been a business rival . . . or maybe Holly owes someone money?" Lucy glanced around at the group as she offered the theories.

"I don't think the nursery was successful enough for any such jealous competitors. But she did feel stressed about finances," Dana replied.

"What about that scary guy she hired? He looked capable of setting stuff on fire," Phoebe said. "Did the police talk to him yet?"

"Holly stopped here yesterday and told me Carl Thornton, the helper, had quit just that morning. He was going to work out the day, collect his pay, and wasn't coming back." Maggie glanced at Dana. "Did you know that?"

Dana shook her head; she looked surprised. "I didn't speak to Holly yesterday. I was going to tell the police about him anyway. He should definitely be questioned. Even if he wasn't involved, maybe he heard or saw something important while he was working there."

"Saw a can of gasoline and some matches," Phoebe murmured.

Maggie turned to her. "We can't jump to conclusions, just because of his appearance. Holly had no complaint about him. She was pleased with his work."

Maggie recalled the way he'd saved Holly from the falling branch. That act alone must have made Holly trust him.

"Did you speak to the police yet?" Lucy asked Dana.

"There were a few at the fire, uniformed officers called

to the scene. But the fire department just determined this morning that it was arson. I haven't heard from any detectives yet."

Dana had barely finished speaking when her cell phone buzzed. She picked it up and read the message. "Spoke too soon. It's Detective Reyes. She wants to know if I'll be at the hospital this morning. She wants to speak to me." She looked up at her friends. "I wonder if she'll remember us?"

"How could she forget?" Maggie said without a doubt.

They'd helped Detective Reyes solve several cases over the past few years—when a film crew came to town and actors were being fatally cut from the script right and left, and when a groom mysteriously disappeared days after a lavish society wedding. She was also the lead investigator when a psychic – with questionable intergrity—was found dead right next to her crystal ball.

"I think Detective Reyes looks on us kindly, though she always rolls her eyes at our helpful hints," Phoebe noted.

"Our helpful hints bumped her up in the ranks, I'd say. She definitely owes us one," Suzanne replied.

"Detective Reyes never needed our help. She's smart, capable, and fair minded," Dana countered. "I'm glad she's on the case." Dana's voice trembled, and she reached for a tissue. Maggie thought she might cry, and who could blame her if she did?

The group sat in silent sympathy.

Lucy, who sat closest to Dana, reached over and rubbed Dana's shoulder. "I know this seems awful right now, but try not to worry. Detective Reyes is very sharp, and she won't give up until she solves this."

"And she won't let anything more happen to the Pipers until this heinous arsonist is found," Suzanne added.

Maggie felt the same, though the situation did seem puzzling. So little to go on and no clues from Holly or Rose.

Dana wiped her eyes. "Thanks for the pep talk. I'd better get to the hospital. It's going to be a long day. I need to hold up better than this."

"Will Jack be there?" Maggie asked.

Dana shook her head as she gathered her belongings. "He had to appear in court today. He tried to pass off the case, but no one was available to step in for him."

"I'll go with you. I'd like to," Maggie said. She knew Dana would resist her offer, so she decided she'd be persistent. "And please don't act all mature and brave and argue with me."

"Maggie is great riding shotgun," Phoebe quickly added, "and I can use more experience managing the shop. For when I open my own."

"Good point. You'd be squelching Phoebe's career plans," Maggie said.

Dana managed a shaky smile. "I'd never do that."

"What about Rose's dogs? Is anyone taking care of them?" Lucy sounded concerned.

Dana looked relieved to hear Lucy ask the question. "Jack looked in on them early this morning. But we can certainly use some help until Rose gets home."

"I'll go right now." Lucy jumped up from the couch, eager to do her part, and Dana told her where to find a hidden key to the Pipers' house.

"I hope Rose's special dogs don't give you any trouble. They'll probably be loose in the house, on guard duty," Dana said.

"Hey, they call me the Dog Charmer, haven't you heard? And I'll bring good treats. That always works."

"Good idea. Bring plenty," Maggie suggested.

"I can go in the afternoon," Suzanne offered. "I'm showing some property out there. Someone text if you need backup and let me know what to do."

A few moments later, they headed in separate directions. It warmed Maggie's heart to see her friends jump into action this way, but she wasn't surprised. When the going got rough, each of them could count on the rest. That was the simple but strong stitch that held them together. That was what their friendship was all about, along with knitting, of course.

She gave Phoebe some unnecessary last-minute instructions and made sure her own knitting was tucked in her handbag, then followed Dana to her car. She felt an unexpected pang about leaving the shop, but Holly and Rose needed all the friends they had right now.

Who could have done such a thing—set the fire and left Holly and Rose to die? She hoped Detective Reyes had some insight about this awful act. She hated to admit it, even silently, but she was truly baffled.

Chapter 5

When they reached the hospital, Dana thought it would be best to visit Rose first. "She should be awake by now. She might be frightened and confused about what happened."

Anyone would be, under the circumstances, Maggie thought, and poor Rose even more so.

As they approached Rose's room, a nurse walked up to Dana. "Dr. Haeger, Rose is still asleep. It's probably best if you don't wake her yet. She became agitated in the early morning, and Dr. Fletcher prescribed a heavy sedative."

Dana's expression was quizzical. "Agitated? Did she have a panic attack?"

Maggie recalled that Rose was prone to such episodes and sometimes even blacked out from stress. She must have been frightened to wake up and find herself alone in the hospital.

"No, not exactly. But she was very upset. Practically incoherent. We tried to calm her, but she became physical. She knocked over furniture and struck one of the aides. We almost had to restrain her."

"Restrain her?" Dana sounded horrified by the word. "Why didn't anyone call me? I told Dr. Fletcher about Rose's condition."

"We didn't need to do that, finally. But I'm not surprised she hasn't woken up yet. I think it will take at least an hour for her to come around."

"We're going to the ICU to look in on Rose's sister. I want you to call me immediately if Rose starts to wake before I return." Dana slipped a business card out of her purse and handed it to the nurse. "Here's my number again. In case it somehow got misplaced last night."

Maggie could tell that Dana was very upset that no one had told her about Rose's episode.

The nurse put the card in her pocket. "I'll keep an eye on her. Don't worry."

The nurse left to visit the room across the hall. Dana and Maggie peeked into Rose's room. Rose was sleeping soundly, a white sheet and blanket pulled up to her chin, her long hair fanned out on the pillow. Except for a few scratches on her face, she looked very peaceful, Maggie thought. Practically angelic. It was difficult to believe she'd caused such an uproar.

As they walked back to the elevator, Dana said, "Poor Rose. It's my fault. I should have stayed over here last night, slept in her room, on a chair. But she seemed to understand what was going on, and the nurses were taking good care of her. Jack and I were here until two. But she must have woken up in the dark and forgotten where she was and what had happened. She hasn't had a hysterical episode like that in a long time."

"It was upsetting to hear about it," Maggie replied. "But maybe she's well enough to come home today."

"I'm really going to push for that," Dana said.

They got off the elevator on the sixth floor and followed signs to the ICU for respiratory patients. Dana had already told Maggie that they would find Holly connected to tubes and machines and unaware that they were there.

Maggie stood at the foot of the bed, while Dana walked

closer to Holly. She reached over and softly stroked Holly's hand.

Maggie was prepared, but the sight was still disturbing, and she was glad to be there, to lend her friend support. Dana was always so calm and levelheaded, their go-to voice of reason. But this time, she was the one who had been blindsided and who was helplessly looking on as those dearest to her were suffering.

"I know I should just be thankful that she survived. But it's so hard to see her like this."

"Of course it is," Maggie replied quietly. "But she's young and strong. The body has miraculous healing powers."

"Yes. It does." Dana sat in the chair at the bedside and watched Holly breathe through the plastic mask that covered most of her face.

"I wish she could open her eyes and see that we're here," Dana whispered. "But the doctor said they can't wake her up yet. She'll struggle against the mask, and they can't risk any strain on her heart right now."

"I understand," Maggie said. "I know it's hard for you to see her this way, but it's helping her heal."

Dana answered with a sigh.

A few moments later, a nurse came in the room. She checked the readings on the machines. "She's doing well," she told Dana. "Her heartbeat is steady."

"Thank you. That's good to hear." Dana forced a small smile.

"We're going to make her more comfortable. If you wait outside a few moments, you can come back in soon."

Dana stood up and smoothed Holly's forehead with her hand, then kissed her cheek. "We'll be back soon, sweetheart. The nurse said you're doing great. You're going to get better very quickly. We love you so much," she whispered.

They walked into the hallway, and Dana wiped her eyes

with a tissue. "I know it seems silly to talk to her, but many studies suggest patients can hear what's being said around them when they're sedated or even under anesthesia. It's important to let her know we're here and she's being well cared for."

"I'm sure she can feel your love, even if she can't hear you," Maggie replied.

"I think that's true, too," Dana said.

Dana seemed lost in her thoughts. Maggie wished there was something more she could say or do for her. A short distance down the hallway, the elevator doors slid open, and Maggie recognized Detective Reyes among the passengers getting out. Maggie touched Dana's arm to get her attention. "Detective Reyes is here. I guess she tracked you down."

Dana followed Maggie's gaze but before she could reply the detective was close enough to greet them. "Dr. Haeger, I'm glad I caught up with you. Do you have a few minutes to talk?"

"As much time as you need," Dana replied. "I have some questions for you, too."

"I can wait somewhere while you two talk." Maggie was glad she'd remembered to bring her knitting. "I'll go downstairs and get a cup of tea."

"I'm sure you can come with us." Dana turned away from the detective and gave Maggie a meaningful look. "Maggie knows Holly and Rose, too. She can help."

A bit of an exaggeration, considering she'd met the young women only last week, Maggie countered silently.

The detective looked doubtful, too, but also amused. Her smooth dark brows were drawn into a quizzical frown over bright eyes.

"If you like, Dr. Haeger. I should know by now how your group sticks together. There's a family room at the end of the hall. We'll be more comfortable there."

Detective Reyes led the way. She was not very tall but moved with grace and a dancer's posture. Maggie wondered if she still coached her daughter's soccer team. She looked a bit older and more mature than when Maggie had last seen her. Her hair was pulled back in a smooth twist at the nape of her neck. Her dark blazer and pants provided an effective camouflage for her femininity.

A small black handbag swung from her shoulder. Maggie wondered if she carried a gun inside it. Or was a firearm on a holster somewhere? Her shoulder or leg? Maggie couldn't see any sign of one, but that didn't mean it wasn't there.

The small room at the end of the hall was filled with functional furniture arranged around a square black coffee table. A framed poster of a ubiquitous sunrise over mountains hung on a pale green wall. It was intended to be uplifting, Maggie assumed. At least there was no corny motto inscribed on it, like *Live, laugh, love* or *Dance like no one's watching.* That was Maggie's least favorite.

She thought most people should always dance as if they knew others were watching. She had never seen dancing any other way turn out well. It was just common sense, wasn't it?

The detective chose an armchair, while Maggie and Dana sat side by side on the hard couch.

"I know you're upset, Dr. Haeger. We're doing our best to figure out what happened to the Pipers, but it will take time to put the pieces together. Especially since Holly is unable to speak to us yet."

"I understand. I heard this morning that you know it was arson, so that's a step," Dana acknowledged. "Is there anything else you've found out?"

"We combed the property and the house for evidence

last night and again this morning," Detective Reyes explained. "Police arrived to assist the fire department, but we weren't treating the event as suspicious. Or treating the property as a crime scene the first few hours."

That didn't sound good to Maggie. Dana was concerned, too.

"What does that mean exactly, Detective? What are you trying to say?" Dana asked.

"I'm afraid that a lot of physical evidence may have been lost or destroyed," the detective admitted.

"You don't have any clues?" Maggie knew she was lucky to be sitting in on the interview and should have kept her mouth closed. But she couldn't help her reaction.

"We have several leads, Mrs. Messina. It might take longer than we'd like, but we will get to the bottom of it. There are some puzzling aspects. For one thing, there are bruises on Holly's chest and other signs on her body that are consistent with CPR. But the EMTs didn't perform CPR. They did notice that her mouth had been wiped clean before they applied an oxygen mask. It appears someone gave her mouth-to-mouth resuscitation prior to their arrival, which probably saved her life."

"Maybe Rose did," Maggie offered. "Rose must have found Holly and tried to get her breathing again."

"I don't think Rose knows CPR," Dana said. "But I guess it's possible she's seen it done on TV or wherever and gave it her best shot."

The detective looked doubtful. "From Rose's physical condition and the stains on her clothing, it's unlikely she was in the fire long enough to pull Holly out."

Dana didn't answer for a moment. "I guess that point is debatable."

Maggie thought Rose must have had heard Holly call for help and saved her sister from the fire, then fainted from the smoke or shock or both. That seemed the most likely scenario. But Detective Reyes didn't seem to think so.

"Do you know if Holly was taking any medication? A blood test from last night showed a high level of Zenotrop in Holly's blood. It's a common drug."

"Yes, I'm familiar with it. It's prescribed as a sleep aid mostly. And for panic disorders. Holly hated drugs. She'd barely take an aspirin."

"I've heard a little about Rose's condition. Does she take any prescription drugs?"

"A number of them," Dana replied honestly. "You should contact her doctor, Timothy Riley, at the Riley-Curtis Wellness Center. He'll give you the most up-to-date list, but I don't think Zenotrop is on it right now."

"Was it ever?" the detective asked curiously.

Dana took a moment to think about her answer. "I'm not sure. Is that important? A lot of people could have access to that drug. You just said so yourself."

"I'm just gathering information, Dr. Haeger. We need to find out as much as we can about the Pipers. We don't know what's significant yet and what's not. I have to piece together as much as I can about their daily routine, business connections, friends, and romantic relationships. Anyone who might have wished them harm, especially someone who may have ill will toward Holly. Can you help me with that?"

"Holly doesn't have an enemy in the world. Not that I'm aware of. She has been very focused on the business and on taking care of Rose. I'd have to say her social life has been very limited. She hasn't had much time for friendships, male or female."

"She isn't involved with anyone romantically? Or even in the past?"

"Not for years, that I know of."

"And you would have known? Holly shares the more intimate details of her life with you?"

"Yes, I think she would have told me. Holly shares her feelings about most things with me. I can't see how she'd be able to date someone and keep it a secret."

Maggie recalled the conversation she'd overheard on Friday, while she'd sat outside Dr. Curtis's office, and realized that she'd forgotten to tell Dana about it. There had been no chance right after they'd left the center with Rose in the car, and after that, it had slipped her mind entirely.

But she didn't think that now was a good time to offer the information, either. She'd tell Dana about it privately and see if she wanted to put it forward to Detective Reyes.

"The only man Holly spent time with recently was a helper she hired last week. Carl Thornton," Dana added. "I had a bad impression of him from the start, but Holly insisted he was qualified to work in the nursery. I was glad to hear that he didn't last very long, but . . . now I wonder. He quit Tuesday morning, the same day as the fire. Strange coincidence, don't you think?"

Detective Reyes was making notes on a small pad. She paused and looked up at Dana, her dark eyes bright with interest. "It could be. Tell me more about him. What do you know?"

With Maggie's help, Dana told the detective how Thornton had appeared Thursday night during the storm, and told Holly he'd knocked down part of the fence.

"Holly insisted she'd sent him a message and told him not to come back. But he did, anyway, at the crack of dawn and then talked himself into a job," Dana told her. "And worked only for a few days."

Detective Reyes made another note. "We'll follow up on Thornton right away. Maybe we can track him down with a phone number."

"He put his number in Holly's phone last Thursday night. You should find it there," Dana replied. "And I think she said he was renting a room in Rowley. She must have put his address in her phone or saved it somewhere in her business records."

"Maybe. But I'd say Piper Nursery is the type of business that mostly employs temporary help. An employer such as that . . . Well, records tend to be thin."

"There must be a lot of ways these days to locate someone who doesn't want to be found," Dana said. "Electronic trails, security cameras and all that?"

Maggie could tell Dana felt frustrated at the possibility that Carl Thornton may have disappeared. Maggie felt the same. She knew it was not wise to jump to conclusions, but he did seem the likely suspect so far.

"We will do our best to track him down, believe me," Detective Reyes promised.

"I remember something, Detective," Maggie said suddenly. "Holly dropped by my shop Tuesday morning. She gave me some pansies. She said that she'd just gotten a large shipment of plants. She was starting to fill her inventory. She also mentioned she had some business to do at the bank. Something about wishing money would come in faster than it went out. I thought she meant she was making a large withdrawal to pay suppliers as she stocked up her business. Maybe she had a lot of cash on hand, and someone knew about that."

"It's possible, Mrs. Messina. Though we don't see robbery as a motive right now. I was in the house this morning. It doesn't appear that anything has been disturbed."

"Holly had some good jewelry that had belonged to her mother. I'll look next time I go to the house," Dana offered.

"Of course. If you notice anything missing, even if it doesn't seem of value, let me know immediately."

"Are there any more questions, Detective?" Dana asked. "We should get back to Rose's room. She might be awake by now."

"Of course. I won't keep you. I heard she had a difficult night. A nurse said Rose was hysterical. She threw things and struck one the aides. Does she often have outbursts like that?"

Maggie saw Dana's cheeks flush. "Rose was in shock. She was frightened and confused. She never behaves like that at home. Well . . . very rarely. Not for a very long time," Dana insisted. "You can ask Dr. Riley, if you don't believe me."

"Aside from her anxiety, she's seems healthy. Maybe they'll discharge her today."

"I hope so. I'm going to work on that," Dana replied.

"We need to speak to Rose as soon as possible. I understand that her mental capacity is impaired, and there are considerations," the detective added. "I'd like you to be present for her interview."

"Absolutely . . . Maybe Dr. Riley should be with us, too. She trusts him. They have a great bond. But even if I take her home today, I doubt she'll be ready for a police interview right away."

"I understand. But the sooner she can tell us what she remembers, the faster we'll find out who attacked her sister and set the fire."

"Rose adores Holly. She'll do everything she can to help you. The problem is, Rose may not remember. It's part of her condition. Extreme stress and fear, like her experience last night, can trigger a fugue state. She's not really aware of her surroundings or even of time passing. Sometimes, she'll black out completely. Either way, she has no memory afterward of what's happened to her."

Detective Reyes sat back and closed her pad, then held

it in her lap. Her lips were drawn in a tight line. She had not expected this wrinkle, that was for sure.

"I didn't know about that aspect of her condition. We still need to speak with her. Even a fragment of a memory could prove very valuable to the investigation right now."

It was not what Detective Reyes said that seemed most important. It was what she didn't say, Maggie thought. With the crime scene unknowingly trampled last night by the fire department and police officers, and with the only eyewitnesses unable to remember the event or unable even to speak, the investigation was grasping for clues.

Dana seemed to understand that, too, and looked distressed.

"I'm sure Rose will try her best to answer your questions. I just doubt she can remember anything that will be helpful."

"We'll be the judge of that. I'll be in touch about the interview. We'd like to do it as soon as she's able." Detective Reyes offered her card, and Dana thanked her. "I know this is a very hard time for you, Dr. Haeger. I appreciate your help. I do hope Holly makes a full and speedy recovery."

Once the police officer was gone, Dana turned to Maggie. "It hasn't even been twenty-four hours. I'm sure there's a lot more to uncover. There's no obvious track to investigate, and she's feeling stumped right now."

"I agree. Maybe it was Carl Thornton, after all. I bet they catch up with him by the end of the day." Maggie wasn't quite as sure he would be found as she sounded, but she wanted to offer Dana some hope that an answer would be found quickly to these dark questions

They had walked down the hall and got into an empty elevator. Dana pressed the number for Rose's floor.

"We forgot to tell Detective Reyes about the branch that fell and nearly hit Holly," Maggie said. "It's probably not important. But she said anything might be helpful."

"I didn't forget," Dana admitted quietly. "I was about to tell her, then realized it showed Thornton in a positive light. Frankly, I didn't want to give Detective Reyes any reason to take him off the top of her suspect list."

"I see your point," Maggie replied. "A very short list right now, too," she added. She was quiet a moment as the elevator glided down another floor. Then she said, "But I'm just thinking now, What if what we saw that day was totally the opposite of what it seemed to be?"

Dana turned with a puzzled look. "Opposite? What do you mean?"

"What if Thornton had *purposely* weakened that branch while he was up on the ladder, and had *wanted* it to fall on Holly? But once you and I appeared unexpectedly, he didn't go through with the plan. And instead made it look as if he was eager to protect her."

Dana looked shocked by the idea and took a sharp breath.

"Maggie . . . that's a terrifying thought. But truly insightful."

Maggie took her words as a compliment. "Just a possibility. Things are not always what they seem."

"A good possibility that makes sense to me. The way he was the first to hear the branch fall and acted so quickly was uncanny," Dana pointed out. "I couldn't reconcile the man who put himself in danger to save Holly with someone who would drug her and leave her to die in a fire. Now it makes sense. He wasn't saving her from the branch, only revising his plan and sparing her a little while."

"Why he would want to hurt Holly is another question altogether," Maggie replied. "But you should tell Detective Reyes. When she finds Thornton, she can ask him herself."

The elevator door slid open, and a bell rang, punctuating their conversation. Like a sign from the universe that they were on the right track, Maggie thought.

When they reached Rose's room, they heard voices within. Maggie expected to find a nurse or a doctor, but when they stepped inside, they found Dr. Riley standing by Rose's bed.

Rose was awake, sitting up against the pillows. She looked pale, with dark rings below her eye and a bleak, frightened expression. Maggie's heart went out to her.

"Aunt Dana . . . the nurse said you were here, but you left. I was worried you went home."

"Of course not, sweetheart." Dana was instantly at Rose's side. She leaned over and hugged her. "I'm glad to see you awake again. How do you feel?"

"Not so bad. I have a smoky smell in my nose and my throat. It's awful . . . What happened to me? Dr. Riley said there was a fire last night in our greenhouse?"

"That's all I've told her so far." His deep voice was calm but somber. He met Dana's glance, his expression deeply concerned.

"What about my dogs? Are the dogs all right?" Rose turned back to Dana, looking very anxious. Dana put her arm around Rose's shoulder to soothe her.

"The dogs are fine. Lucy just went to visit them."

Rose looked a little calmer. Her eyes darted back to Dana. "I want to go home. I feel fine. They should let me out of here. You know how I hate hospitals." Maggie could only imagine why that might be. Dana had never mentioned it, but perhaps Rose had been hospitalized for her condition. Of course, just being in this environment would upset her.

Dr. Riley reached over and squeezed her hand. "You've been through a frightening experience, Rose. It's all right to feel scared and unsettled. Anybody would be. We know you can't remember what happened, but once you feel better we can work on recovering those memories. If you want to," he added.

Rose nodded, her chin trembling. Maggie thought she might start to cry. "Where's Holly? Isn't she coming to see me?"

Maggie was stunned at the question. Then not so stunned. It was likely that none of the medical staff Rose had seen so far were permitted to give her information on her sister.

Dana sat on the edge of Rose's bed and took her hand. "I know you don't remember what happened last night, honey. You and Holly were both hurt in the fire. She's in the hospital, too, on a different floor. She needs more help than you. But she's going to be all right," Dana promised.

Rose sat up and stared at Dr. Riley, then back at Dana. "Holly's hurt? I need to see her."

She threw back the sheet and began to climb out of the bed. She must have been attached to an alarm or something, Maggie realized when a beeping sound started. Dana took hold of her arm to slow her down, and Dr. Riley rushed around to help, too.

"Calm down, Rose. We're going to help you," he said. "Try to sit still for a moment and take a few deep breaths."

Rose stared up at him with a defiant look. If anything, she wanted to move even faster. But corralled by Dana and Dr. Riley, she had little choice but to follow his instructions.

"We'll take you to Holly. I promise," Dana said. "But I want to explain first. She needs a machine to help her breathe, and the doctors have put her to sleep so she can rest and heal. She's attached to a lot of tubes and wires. She won't know you're there or be able to talk to you."

Rose nodded, her eyes glassy with tears. She seemed to be making an effort to stay calm but looked even more determined to see her sister.

"I understand. If you won't take me there, I'll figure it

out myself." She turned to Dr. Riley. "And I don't want any more pills that put me to sleep."

"We understand," he said calmly. There was a bathrobe at the bottom of the bed, hospital issue, and he held it out to her. Dana had found a pair of hospital slipper socks.

"I'll tell a nurse where you're going, and I'll get Rose's discharge rolling," Dr. Riley said. "I don't see any reason why she needs to stay here. I'll meet you in a few minutes at Holly's room."

Rose's doctor obviously had the clout to get things moving in the right direction. Maggie and Dana walked Rose down the hall, and after a silent elevator ride, they led Rose to Holly's room.

Dana stood close to Rose, gently holding her arm. Rose looked frightened but did not hesitate.

The room was dimly lit and very quiet, except for the hum and occasional beep of medical equipment. On a glowing screen, electronic patterns of Holly's heart rate and breathing appeared and disappeared, as if written by some unseen hand.

A woman stood on the far side of Holly's bed, shrouded in the shadows. Maggie thought it was Holly's nurse, then realized it was Dr. Curtis. She stood with her back toward the door as she examined a bag of fluid hanging from an IV pole and connected to Holly's arm through a plastic line.

Dr. Curtis turned. She looked surprised to see them.

"Poor girls." Her gaze full of sympathy, she walked toward Rose, who stood frozen near the doorway. "How are you feeling, Rose? The fire must have been terrifying."

"She doesn't remember what happened," Dana said.

"Oh . . . I see. Not a thing?" Dr. Curtis asked.

"Not yet. But when she feels well enough, she'll work on it with Tim," Dana said. "He sounded optimistic about recovering some memories."

Maggie had wondered if there were methods for regaining lost memories of traumatic events. If there were, these doctors would be experts, though it seemed there had not been much success so far in that direction. Hadn't Dana said that Rose could not remember any details of the car accident that had left her with the injury? But maybe there would be more success uncovering a recent event.

Dana spoke quietly as she led Rose toward the bed. "I know Holly doesn't look well. But she's going to be all right. She needs to sleep until she gets her strength back."

Rose nodded but didn't answer. She stepped closer to the bed and rested her hand on Holly's. "Can I sit with her awhile?"

"Of course you can," Dana said.

"How long will she be like this?" Rose's voice trembled, but she was holding herself together. So far anyway.

"The doctors aren't sure. At least a few days, I think." Dana touched Rose's shoulder. "We should know more when I speak to Dr. Gupta today. He's the specialist who's helping Holly."

Dr. Riley appeared. He took a few steps into the room and stopped. "Emily . . . when did you get back?"

"Early this morning. I heard about the fire on the news and came right over."

Maggie remembered that she had been on a fund-raising trip to Boston and was due to return tonight.

"That was kind of you. Thanks," Dana said.

Dr. Riley didn't say anything, Maggie noticed. He met Emily's gaze and looked over at Holly again.

A nurse came into the room. She checked the medical machinery and made notes on a pad. Then she turned to Dana and spoke in a soft voice. "I'm sorry, we don't allow this many visitors at once in this ICU. You can come back to see her later, for ten minutes or so each time. Close family only."

Dr. Curtis picked up her handbag from a chair. "We'd better get back to the center, anyway, right, Tim?"

"You go ahead. I'll catch up in a little while."

A flash of annoyance crossed the doctor's pretty face but just as quickly vanished. She turned to Rose with a kind smile and touched her cheek. "Don't worry. Holly will be all right, and we're all here to take care of you while she gets better."

Dr. Curtis left, and Maggie glanced at Dana. Would Rose raise a fuss when she had to leave her sister?

Dana rested her hand on Rose's shoulder to catch her attention. "We need to go now, honey. Holly needs to rest. That's the main thing that will help her get better."

Rose didn't answer, her gaze fixed on Holly. When she finally spoke, her tone was bleak. "All right." She got up slowly and kissed Holly on the forehead. Then she shuffled toward the door, her gaze fixed on the floor.

Dana and Maggie followed Rose, but Dr. Riley remained at Holly's bedside. As she stepped out the door, Maggie glanced his way just long enough to see him stroke Holly's cheek with his fingertips. She heard him whisper something to Holly, but she couldn't make out the words.

They headed back to Rose's room on a lower floor, moving through the bustling hospital corridors without speaking. Dr. Riley soon appeared, and Maggie waited with Rose while he and Dana headed off to arrange for Rose's discharge.

Visiting Holly had worn Rose out. She lay down on her bed and curled on her side. Maggie sat next to her bed and took out her knitting, prepared for the long wait of cutting through hospital red tape. Maggie thought she was asleep, but then she suddenly noticed small tears squeezing out from the corners of her eyes.

Maggie wasn't sure how much time had passed before

Dana returned. She did make good progress with Charles's basket-stitch sweater.

Dana sat on the edge of Rose's bed and gently called her name. "Wake up, Rose. Time to go home and see the dogs."

Rose sat up and rubbed her eyes. She didn't smile, but Maggie could see the relief in her expression. Dana had managed to find enough clothes in a workout bag stashed in her car to get Rose decently dressed.

"We can come back tonight to see Holly, if you want to," Dana promised Rose as they left the hospital.

Maggie wondered if Rose would be so eager to return, even to see her sister. Hospital visits were disturbing to many people who didn't even suffer from Rose's stress condition. And she didn't envy Dana, who would have to make the drive again, but Dana's offer seemed sincere. It was clear she would go the limit and then some to make Rose feel safe and secure.

"I'm going to stay with you while Holly is here," Dana added. "Uncle Jack will come at night, too. I'd bring you back to my house, but it would be hard to watch the dogs, and I think you'll feel more comfortable in your own space."

Maggie agreed that was the best solution to watching over Rose right now. Familiarity and routine were important considerations for her.

Rose nodded, accepting the arrangements, though she seemed deep in thought. She stared out the backseat window as they pulled out of the hospital parking lot, her gaze fixed on the building.

Trying to pick out Holly's window? Maggie wondered.

Finally, she turned and faced forward, wringing her fingers together and pulling on the ties of the sweatshirt Dana had given her to wear.

What was she thinking and feeling? Was she worrying about Holly? And feeling scared and vulnerable, despite Dana's comforting presence and promises?

"I can drop you off in town," Dana offered.

"I'll go back with you," Maggie replied. "I'll find a way to get home later," she added. "You'll have some company until Jack gets out there tonight."

Dana glanced at her. Maggie didn't doubt that Dana could handle Rose with love, compassion, and expert knowledge at this difficult time. But it had been a hard morning for Dana, too, having so little sleep last night and seeing Holly in such a state. Maggie thought she ought to stick around to help, if she could.

"Thanks, Maggie. Jack might not get out until late tonight. He's so busy in the office right now and has a business trip coming this weekend. I would welcome your company."

Dana glanced at her and smiled. She didn't say more, and neither did Maggie. The afternoon light was quickly fading behind the thick woods on the road to the Pipers' house. It would be dark before long, and Maggie wouldn't feel right leaving Dana and Rose alone in such a desolate place.

When they arrived at the nursery, the first thing Maggie saw was the charred shell of the greenhouse, circled by yellow crime-scene tape. An area of about fifty feet in diameter was circled, as well.

Rose leaned forward and stared wide eyed through the windshield. "The whole thing burned down? It must have taken hours."

Dana sighed. Maggie could see her searching for the right words. Would she tell Rose that someone had deliberately set the fire? Maggie wondered if that would be good for Rose to know right now.

"It took a while to put it out, but the firemen got it under control quickly. Thank goodness no one was hurt and it didn't reach the house."

That was a blessing, Maggie agreed. The scene looked apocalyptic, but it certainly could have been worse.

The house was dark and empty looking in the gathering dusk. Behind the closed door, the dogs barked wildly, but this time, Maggie found the sound welcoming. Rose certainly did; she lifted her head and smiled, eager for Dana to open the door.

Dana walked in first and flipped the switch next to the door. The foyer was flooded with light.

Rose's rescues filled the foyer and quickly surrounded them, barking and vying for attention. The coat-tree had been knocked down and trampled, and a vase of red roses on a side table had been tipped over, with water spilled on the tabletop and floor.

Rose shouted to shut the door as the three women had no choice but to wade deeper into the canine flash mob. "Quick! Before they get out!"

Maggie did as instructed and had to use her foot to gently block a small schnauzer from escaping. With her back against the wall, she surveyed the scene, confused about what had happened.

Dana pointed to the parlor. "The gate fell down. Look . . ."

Maggie saw that the baby gate that usually blocked the entrance to the dog parlor had fallen to the floor. The hinges that had secured the gate to the molding were now dangling. Either the dogs had broken down the gate or maybe the police investigators had dislodged it by mistake?

It hardly mattered now. The result was much like videos Maggie had seen of the running of the bulls in Spain.

But Rose was already herding the pack back into the parlor, shouting commands and tossing biscuits she had retrieved from the other room.

Just as quickly as they'd flooded the foyer, the dogs ran to follow her and claim their treats. Dana and Maggie ran over to the parlor and propped the gate up. Maggie noticed it had to be stretched and didn't quite reach. She saw one section blocking the bottom of the staircase, and she wondered how it had gotten there.

And from behind the closed kitchen door, Maggie now heard more barking, along with whining and scratching at the woodwork.

Rose ran to the kitchen door and found it locked. "Someone locked my dogs up. Wolf, Oreo, and Queenie."

She was very angry and pulled on the doorknob, shaking it with all her might. She turned to Dana, tears in her eyes.

"We'll get them out, honey. Give me a minute . . ."

Rose didn't wait for Dana to finish. She ran out the front door, and they watched her dash past the dining room window.

"She's going to the back door," Dana said. "I wonder who locked up the dogs? And how the other bunch got loose. I doubt it was Lucy's doing."

"Maybe the police, when they searched the house? The dogs may have been hard to control or overly protective."

Dana was about to answer; then her gaze cut to the staircase. "Someone's coming. Someone is in here."

Maggie heard footsteps, too. Someone was slowly walking down the staircase.

"Who's there?" Dana shouted.

No one answered. They backed up toward the front door, and Maggie scanned the foyer, looking for a possible weapon to defend herself, but didn't spot a thing. Where were her knitting needles when she really needed them?

A figure emerged from the shadows, and Dana pulled out her phone and began to dial 911.

"Stop right there . . . I'm calling the police. Who are you?"

Chapter 6

The visitor laughed, a mocking sound. "Aunt Dana . . . after all these years, that's the greeting I get?"

Dana looked shocked, but Maggie could tell she recognized the stranger. "Toby? What are you doing here?"

He came down to the bottom of the staircase, then stepped over the gate with a swing of his long legs.

"Can't I visit my little sisters? From what I hear, they could use my help."

"Holly never mentioned you were coming."

"She didn't? That's funny. I left a message a few days ago. I was in Portland on business. I told her I'd come by to say hello. Maybe she forgot to tell you." His gaze challenged her. Dana didn't answer right away.

"We didn't see a car. You startled us," Dana said.

"I left it around back. I knew I had to get the key from the shed."

Maggie recalled that Ava Piper had a son from her first marriage and that he'd left the area when George Piper died, about ten years ago. Clearly, his appearance was an anomaly and not the casual visit he'd implied.

He took a step toward Maggie and extended his hand. "Toby Nash, the prodigal son. Stepson to George, to be precise."

"Nice to meet you. I'm Dana's friend Maggie."

His smooth smile and unnaturally white teeth reminded Maggie of a crocodile. He held her hand a little too long and gave her fingers an inappropriate squeeze. She sensed that the self-deprecating charm worked for him, usually.

He was not bad looking, but he was a man who had hit his prime early on, she'd guess, and was now working off depleted capital. His straight brown hair, carefully combed, was thin on top, obviously dyed His blue eyes were bright and his tanned face deeply lined; the cut of his jaw, soft and sagging. His wrinkled gray suit and dark red tie were designer discount quality, and it looked as if he'd slept in the outfit.

"Terrible about this fire. What a nightmare for those girls. I was driving when I heard the story on the radio. I nearly lost control of the car when I realized it was poor Holly and Rose. Who the heck would do such a thing? Do the police have any clues?"

"Not yet. They have a lead or two."

"What sort of business are you in, Mr. Nash?" Maggie asked.

"I'm in sales. Call me Toby. Everybody does." He looked around, checking out the dogs, who were secure again behind the gate in the parlor and were watching him warily. One or two growled low in their throat. "Where are those other dogs? The wild ones? They don't seem to like me."

"Is that why you locked them in the kitchen?" Dana asked.

He shrugged. "They wanted to tear my throat out. Especially that big white one. I was lucky to outrun them. I guess the girls need watchdogs, but that one is plain vicious."

Maggie had never been the least bit afraid of Rose's big dog, and she wondered what Toby had done to set Wolf off.

"You're lucky they let you inside," Dana said.

"Just barely . . . Hey, you forget, I'm family, too. What was I supposed to do? Wait out in the car? I called the hospital. They said Holly was still in ICU, so I figured it was best to wait here and visit her tomorrow."

Maggie had a strong feeling Dana would have preferred to have found Toby waiting in a car, if she had to find him here at all. But, of course, she didn't say that.

"Holly is under sedation. She's not able to breathe on her own yet. The doctors want to give her more tests, but her condition isn't stable enough."

"Poor kid. I sure hope she rallies." His gaze was downcast; he shook his head. "In the meantime, at least I'm here to hold down the fort. Keep my eye on Rose and the business."

Maggie doubted his plans sat well with Dana, but she didn't show any reaction. "Rose is very fragile right now, Toby. She's had a huge shock, and she is upset about Holly. She doesn't remember anything that happened last night, either."

"Really? I bet the police weren't happy to hear that."

"No, they weren't. She might remember something, in time. But please try not to talk about it. Please don't say or do anything that might cause her more distress. And—"

"I know how to handle Rose," he said, cutting in. "I know all about her condition."

"She may not remember you," Dana concluded in a blunt tone.

"Of course she will. I'm her big brother. I taught her how to ride a bike and climb a tree. She looked up to me. Seems to me you're the one with the faulty memory, Aunt Dana." The endearing title sounded sarcastic on his tongue.

"She hasn't seen in you in a long time. That's all I'm trying to say. Ten years maybe? It may take her a while to feel comfortable around you. Please be patient."

He drew in a sharp breath. "I bet she does remember me. I'm her brother, for goodness' sake. I'm here to help her."

Maggie suddenly saw Toby as a little boy with an affectionate attachment to a younger sister and also as a child who felt the anguish of never quite fitting in with his family. She did feel some sympathy for him in that way.

But even though she hated to rush to judgment, she didn't like the grown-up Toby very much. Shouldn't he be worrying more about Rose than his own wounded ego? According to Dana, he'd chosen to cut all ties with his half sisters. Yet here he was, proclaiming his noble intentions.

Dana left to find Rose at the back of the house, and Maggie sent Charles a text, asking him to pick her up. She hoped he wouldn't come all that soon. She knew she was being silly, but she felt uncomfortable leaving Dana with long-lost Toby.

He strolled toward the parlor, hands in his pockets, nervously jangling his change. His approach caused the dogs to growl again, and he scowled at them.

"Shut up, you stupid mutts." He glanced over at Maggie. "This house used to be a showcase. My mother kept it like a picture in a magazine, but my sisters have turned it into a stinking dog kennel. My mother must be turning over in her grave."

There were a lot of dogs, but Maggie disagreed with his assessment of Holly and Rose's housekeeping. Repurposing the front parlor for the needs of the rescue project would not be found in any decorating books. That was true. But overall, it was a very tidy and clean home, even in the dogs' lair.

She didn't bother to argue the point with him, just watched as he gazed into the large room after venturing as close to the gate as he dared.

"George used to keep his whiskey in there. In crystal decanters, like a real gentleman," he said, recalling his step-father. "I could use a drink right now, but I'd rather walk out of here on two legs." He glanced at the unhappy dogs and back at Maggie.

"Probably not worth it," she agreed.

"I bet Holly got rid of all that fancy stuff anyway. She never appreciated it. There's still some nice furniture. Real antiques," he noted, continuing his inventory. "My mother had good taste for a woman who came from nothing. And George Piper had the money."

An interesting way to sum up the relationship of your parents, Maggie thought. Maggie wondered if he'd ever called George Piper "Dad" while he was growing up. He didn't seem attached to the affectionate title now.

Dana returned with Rose, her hand on the young woman's shoulder. Rose's special dogs were not at her heels, as they usually were. Rose and Dana must have thought it best to leave them in the kitchen.

Just as well, Maggie reflected.

Toby's face strained with a wide smile. He walked over to Rose and leaned down, then talked into her face, as if she was hard of hearing or had difficulty understanding what people said. "Hey, Rosie-posie . . . It's me, your big brother, Toby. You remember me, right?" He glanced at Dana, eager to prove his point.

Rose looked confused but finally nodded. "I guess so. We haven't seen you in a long time, Toby. Where have you been?"

He laughed. "Good question, kiddo. You always got right to the point. Your brother has been around the track a few times, let's just say. But I'm home now. How about a hug?"

He opened his arms, and Rose stared at him. She glanced back at Dana for some cue. Dana crossed her arms over her chest. Finally, Rose stepped forward, gave her half-brother a brief, loose embrace, and quickly stepped back to a safe space.

Toby looked a little frustrated by the cool greeting but forced his face into a smile again. "That fire was just awful, wasn't it? Poor Holly. But you don't have to worry. I'm here to take care of you now. Everything is going to be just fine. What do you think of that?"

Rose's expression closed, like certain flowers that fold their petals to the cool night air. She moved even closer to Dana.

"Aunt Dana and Uncle Jack are staying here until Holly comes home. Why would you need to stay, too? We hardly know each other anymore." Her tone was both puzzled and matter of fact.

He laughed quietly and shook his head. Maggie still had a feeling that he was angry. "That's my Rosie. Never pulls a punch. I know that I haven't been around much, honey. But when there's trouble, family sticks together. *Real* family." He glanced at Dana. "That's why I'm here. To protect you. If I ever catch the guy who set that fire and hurt our Holly, he'll be one sorry dude. Believe me." He made a fist and punched his hand.

Rose jumped at the gesture and the sound of flesh striking flesh. She glanced at Dana and then looked down at the floor.

Dana lightly rubbed her shoulder. "He won't come back, honey. The police will make sure of that."

Behind Rose's back, Dana glared at Toby. He'd promised not to upset Rose, but it hadn't taken very long for him to forget, Maggie noticed.

"Hey, let's not even talk about it. If no one objects, I'll make some dinner. I'm pretty good at making a tasty meal from whatever I find in the fridge." He finally caught Rose's eye. "Just keep those dogs away from me. Leash them up or something, all right?"

Maggie had not seen one of the dogs on a leash so far. She was sure Rose didn't like the idea.

"Why? Are you allergic?" Rose asked.

"Let's put it this way. If the dogs don't bother me, I won't bother them. Understand?" His tone was harsher this time. Rose read it clearly.

"I'll put them outside. They can use some air." Rose turned toward the kitchen, and Toby followed.

Maggie was left with Dana in the foyer. She kept her voice low, wary of being overheard, though the door to the kitchen was closed and she could already hear the clatter of pots and pans. "You told us that Ava had a son from her first marriage. It sounded to me like he'd more or less disappeared."

"He did. It's hard to remember how many years it's been since he visited Plum Harbor. Probably about ten. I hate to sound harsh, but I find it very odd that he's suddenly surfaced."

"Crawled out of the woodwork," Maggie would have said, but she didn't want to be too hard on the guy. She'd barely met him. "It sounds like he plans to stay awhile."

"Doesn't it? Ostensibly, to take care of Rose, who neither needs him nor wants him here. He wouldn't know the first thing about taking care of her, either," Dana replied, the annoyance in her tone rising with every word.

"She doesn't seem to like him much," Maggie agreed. "But I guess you have no choice. He is family, and it's his house, too."

"I'd never tell him he was unwelcome here. For one thing, it's not my place. But the house and everything in it was left to Holly and Rose, along with the business. George Piper left Toby a very generous cash gift, which he quickly burned through. Come to think of it, the only time Toby has ever come back was a few years after George died, to press Holly for a loan, which he never repaid."

"Oh . . . I see." The Piper family history—misdeeds and grievances—was becoming clear. "Toby feels cheated? Short-changed?"

"I'm sure he does. I felt sorry for him, in a way. Ava was always running interference between her son and her husband. George tried to help him. He really did. Paid for all sorts of schools and gave him loans for business schemes. It always ended with debt and even lawsuits. No one was surprised when George didn't leave him a share of the business. Except for Toby."

"What are his rights in regard to Rose? I mean, if anything happens to Holly . . . heaven forbid," Maggie said.

Dana's expression clouded with worry. "I'm really not sure. He is related by blood . . . and I'm not. Holly and I talked about her wishes for Rose if she was ever unable to take care of her sister, but we never drew up a formal agreement. I have to ask Jack. He handles all Holly's legal matters. If Toby makes any claim, Jack will know what to do." She glanced at her phone and sighed. "He's probably running even later than we thought. Stuck in a meeting. But I'll ask him when he gets here tonight."

"Good plan. But I'm sure Holly will be home soon."

"Yes, she will." Dana looked too upset to say more than that. "Thanks for spending the day with me. I'm not sure I would have gotten through half of it without you."

"Of course you would have. But I was happy to help," Maggie said sincerely. She heard a buzz from her own phone and glanced at a text from Charles. "And it looks like I'll be staying for dinner. Charles has a meeting at the historical society, and he won't be here until at least nine o'clock."

Dana looked cheered by the news. "I'll let the chef know there's an extra guest. If he's so able in the kitchen, it shouldn't throw him at all."

She rolled her eyes, a gesture very unlike her. But Maggie could see that Toby Nash definitely tested her limits.

True to his word, Toby was clever with working with what he could find in the kitchen and soon announced that dinner was served. He had found a large container of chili in the freezer that Holly had set aside, and had defrosted it in the microwave. The rice he'd made from scratch was seriously undercooked. Maggie pushed it to one side of her dish but ate with a grateful smile.

"It wasn't a bad start. I bumped it up with plenty of spices," he explained, taking ownership of the dish. "Makes all the difference."

"I noticed that." Maggie took a few sips of cold water. The chili had a slow burn effect, the spices were seeping into her tongue and creeping down her throat. She'd be searching for the antacids tonight.

Rose pushed her dish aside. "I'm not as hungry as I thought. I'll just have an apple. In my room."

Toby's eyes narrowed. "I thought we were going to have a nice family dinner and catch up."

Dana gave him a warning look. "That's all right, honey. You must be tired. Don't forget to take your medication."

Rose left the table, grabbed an apple from a bowl on the counter, then slipped into the mudroom, where her three comfort dogs were leashed. She walked them on leads through the kitchen and then toward the front of the house.

When the kitchen door closed behind her, Toby said, "So, Rose has taken over the best room in the house for stray dogs. That would change real fast if I lived here. Does she sleep in there, too?"

Dana dabbed her mouth with her napkin and took a sip of water. Maggie could tell she was taking her time to keep her temper under control.

"Most of the time, though all her clothes and belong-ings are still up in her bedroom," Dana replied. "Jack and I will be in Holly's room. The bed in the guest room is made up, if you'd like to stay there."

"What happened to my old room in the attic?"

"I think Holly uses that spot for storage now."

"Figures. It didn't take long to forget I ever existed, did it?"

"Only ten years," Maggie wanted to reply. But of course, she didn't.

"I'll stay in the guest room, as long as those dogs don't bother me. Maybe Rose should leave them in the backyard at night. I saw a pen back there."

Maggie knew Rose would never leave her dogs outside all night. It would be unthinkable to her.

"I'll tell Rose to keep the dogs with her. They're very well trained."

"You could have fooled me." Toby helped himself to another plate of chili. He had found a beer somewhere. Or perhaps had brought it with him? He drank from the opened bottle, then smothered a belch with his hand. "Ex-cuse me," he mumbled.

Toby cleaned his dish with gusto, clearly enjoying the meal he'd served. Dana did not eat meat and had carefully picked out some beans and set them on her dish. The rest of her plate was filled with green salad, which she'd quickly tossed together before they had sat down.

Dana's phone rang, and she pulled it from a pocket. "Sorry . . . I have to take this."

She rose from the table and wandered into the mud-room. Maggie couldn't tell who she was speaking to. She looked distressed, and Maggie hoped it wasn't bad news about Holly.

A few moments later Dana joined them again at the table. "That was Detective Reyes. She heard that Rose is home, and wants to speak to her."

A bit of food stuck in Maggie's throat, and she swallowed it quickly. "Tonight?"

"She did want to come by tonight, but I put her off. She's going to meet up with us tomorrow at the center. She'll be there in the morning to interview Dr. Riley and Dr. Curtis."

"What do they have to do with this?" Toby asked.

Dana shrugged. "I don't know. She said they needed to speak to everyone Holly and Rose deal with day to day. I guess she's covering all the bases."

Toby was forking up the last few bites on his plate. "I thought you said Rose doesn't remember anything."

"The detective needs to see for herself, I guess. Maybe she'll ask Rose a question that will trigger a memory. Or maybe something Rose says will help the investigation. Right now, it's pretty much at a dead end."

"Except for Carl Thornton," Maggie added. "Have they caught up with him yet?"

"She didn't mention him. I guess she would have told me if they'd found him."

"Who's Carl Thornton?" Toby pushed back from the table and picked up his beer.

"An old man who worked here a few days. A drifter, I guess you'd call him." Dana picked up her plate and carried it to the sink. She'd hardly eaten a bite. Was it nerves or Toby's cooking? A combination, Maggie guessed. "He was a rough-looking character, but Holly said he worked hard. He quit Tuesday morning, very abruptly, and Holly was attacked that night."

Toby threw up his hands. "What are the police waiting for? That's got to be the guy. Track him down. Lock him up. Game over. He must have come back to rob the place, and Holly tried to stop him."

"That's what we think," Dana agreed. "But the police

aren't big on the robbery part. The house was not disturbed, and nothing appears to be missing."

At least, not yet, Maggie thought. She recalled now that Dana had mentioned there was some jewelry in the house and she assumed Dana would look for it later. But how would Carl Thornton, or any random intruder for that matter, know where to find hidden jewelry in such a big, rambling house? The robbery motive seemed unlikely to Maggie. But obviously not so to Toby.

"She must have caught him before he could grab anything. He got scared and ran off . . ." Toby declared, " and then he tried to burn down the greenhouse to cover up the crime. So Holly wouldn't be around to accuse him. I bet that bum didn't even give Holly his real name." He shook his head, looking disgusted. "I know you two are going to give me grief for saying this, but women are too soft and trusting to run a business like this. You can't believe every seedy old guy with a hard-luck story. If you do, this is what you get."

Maggie bristled at the slight to her gender. "I run a business. A successful one, too. I wouldn't call myself naive. Or call Holly naive, either, for that matter."

"No offense." He raised his hands in a mock sign of surrender. "Most women, I mean." When that didn't seem to satisfy her, he added, "Okay, *some* women."

"And some men," Dana noted.

"All I'm trying to say is, What's the mystery? It doesn't matter if Rose remembers a darn thing. They'll catch up to this lowlife in a day or two. It won't take long."

"I hope so," Dana replied.

Maggie wanted to believe that was true, too. Though her intuition balked at the simple solution. *You do have a tendency to complicate things. To turn a knit one, purl two into a zigzagging argyle*, she reminded herself. *Some-*

*times the obvious answer is the right one. Who else could
have done this but Thornton?*

"Thanks for making dinner." Dana rinsed a dish and set
it in the dishwasher. "Don't worry about the kitchen. I'll
clean up tomorrow."

Maggie stood up and cleared her place. "Thank you for
making such a nice meal for us," she said politely, though
he hadn't actually made it. Just heated it up. "Let's see
what Rose is up to," she said to Dana. "I thought we
could do some knitting while I wait for Charles."

"Good idea. I have my project in the car." Dana seemed
pleased for the excuse to leave the kitchen.

Toby had finished his beer and left the empty bottle on
the counter, along with two other empties. He must have
downed those beers while cooking dinner, Maggie thought.
He pulled open the fridge and took out another. "Guess
I'll head upstairs. There's used to be a good TV in the guest
room. I'll probably have to wrestle some dog for the remote," he muttered.

Maggie was glad she had her back turned. It was easier
to hide her laughter.

Maggie was much more comfortable in the dog parlor
than she had expected, once Rose pulled a sheet off the
couch and cleared a space for her. Most of the dogs were
dozing. Some were curled up together on another couch,
and a few had claimed their own armchairs or had
stretched out on the patterned area rug. There were even a
few in dog beds, she noticed. It was relaxing to see them
sleeping or chewing on rawhide toys.

Two of the favorites rested at her feet, the largest and
smallest, Wolf and Queenie. Oreo, the black-and-white
border collie, was curled next to Rose on a love seat, with
her soft head in Rose's lap. An arrangement that didn't
seem to impede Rose's knitting in the least.

Rose was making dog collars with the finger-knitting

technique, a project that suited her, Maggie thought. The rows were only two stitches in width, and it didn't take long to stitch up the length. She had already finished one for Wolf and was working on a second, for Oreo.

"Nice work, Rose. Lovely, even stitches. Well done," Maggie said, examining the finished project. "I have buckles in my shop, to complete the ends. I'll bring some next time and show you how to attach them."

"That would be great. Maybe you can teach me how to make dog sweaters, too. Some of the little ones get cold."

"I'd be happy to." Maggie was pleased that Rose had taken to knitting so quickly. It did seem to calm her, just as Dana had hoped.

Never mind Rose. You feel calmer, too, and so does Dana, she thought, glancing over at her friend, who had claimed an armchair.

Dana was working on a shawl, knit in very soft yarn with a lovely purple hue. Maggie guessed it was gift. She knew her sedate friend rarely wore such bold colors. Dana glanced at Rose over her reading glasses.

"Detective Reyes called. She'd like to talk to you tomorrow. She's going to meet us at the center. We'll go there after we visit Holly."

Rose put her knitting down and stroked Oreo's head. The dog sighed, her eyes half closed. "Will she ask me too many questions?"

Dana sat back and gave Rose her full attention. "I'll be with you the whole time. I'll make sure it's not too many."

Rose nodded. Maggie could sense her gathering her courage. "I want to help Holly. I just don't think I can." She seemed sad and disappointed with herself, as if she had already failed.

Dana leaned over and squeezed her hand. "Sweetheart . . . it's all right. Just do your best. Everyone understands that it's hard for you to remember what happened."

Rose sighed, sounding frustrated. "All right. Maybe I will remember something." She picked up her knitting again and, after a few stitches, said, "That dinner was awful. I need a peanut butter sandwich."

Dana laughed. "Good idea. My stomach is grumbling, too."

"I'll pass on the sandwich, but I'd love a cup of tea," Maggie said.

By the time Charles arrived, Maggie had packed her knitting and slipped her jacket on. She'd wanted to show him the puppies, but it seemed silly now. It was late. They had to get home, and she needed to get ready for a workday tomorrow.

She said good night to Dana, then gave Rose a hug at the door. Even though she'd known the young woman only a short time, she felt close to her. Rose's expression was so sweet, and her eyes were so clear and trusting, Maggie had no choice but to offer some hopeful words.

"I know this is a difficult time, Rose, but everything will be all right. You'll see."

As Rose returned her hug, Maggie had to wonder. Was it fair or even honest to offer such a blanket reassurance? But it seemed the kind thing to do. As Rousseau said, "What wisdom can you find that is greater than kindness?" Maggie believed it, too.

She walked out with Charles to the car and stared up at the clear night sky and a sliver of silver moon. Away from the village, the stars and the moon glowed with a brilliant light, she noticed, but they didn't offer any answers.

Dana stood in the doorway and watched Charles's SUV disappear down the drive and turn onto the main road. She shut the door and rubbed her arms for warmth. Or was it from a feeling of dread that seemed to creep into the house, along with the chilly night air?

But she had to put forward a calm, optimistic face for Rose. The fire, as well as Holly's injury, had shaken everyone to the core, and now Toby had appeared out of the blue, disrupting things even more.

Dana peeked into the parlor. The TV was on, tuned to a nature show, as usual. Dana wasn't sure who liked the channel more, Rose or the dogs. Many of them did seem to be watching the flickering images on the screen.

Rose sat in her favorite spot, in the middle of a long sofa, bookended by snoozing hounds. She had put her knitting aside and seemed to be dozing off, as well. Dana walked past quietly and took a few steps up the stairs, to the first landing.

All the lights were off on the second floor, except for a thin beam that glowed under the guest-room door. She heard the TV on in there, as well, the raucous cheers and buzzers of a basketball game. And beyond that, someone snoring.

The sound of Toby fast asleep gave her courage a boost. She crept down the stairs again and turned at the bottom, heading for Holly's office.

Detective Reyes had asked her to report if any valuables were missing, and she knew George Piper had installed a safe in the house a long time ago. Dana was fairly certain it was in the office, which had been George Piper's before Holly took over the business.

It was certainly possibly that someone, like Carl Thornton, or maybe someone else who had worked there at some point, knew about the safe, and that the whole situation was a robbery gone haywire.

With Toby in the house, there was even more reason to keep an eye on the valuables. She hated even to think of it, but she had to face the facts. She had known Toby since he was a boy, and wouldn't trust him as far as she could throw a pot of that nasty chili he'd cooked tonight.

It would not surprise her one bit if he started snooping around the house, looking for jewelry or even the good silverware, and found some way to rationalize that some, or even all it, should end up in his pockets.

The hinges creaked as she pushed the door open, and she winced. *Toby won't hear. Not until the beer wears off. But I need to be fast.*

She switched on a small brass banker's lamp that sat on the desk, and glanced around the room. The big old desk stretched from wall to wall and was covered with piles of papers, folders, and envelopes. Either Holly was a very messy businesswoman or she was simply overwhelmed.

Dana quickly looked through the pages, trying to determine if any would yield a clue. It all seemed very ordinary, orders and receipts for supplies and plants, and utility bills.

If only Holly had kept a diary. But she had never been the type, even when she was at an age when most girls passed through that stage, Dana reflected.

She looked around, wondering where to search next. There was a bay window behind the desk, an old armchair in front of it, and floor-to-ceiling bookcases on the other three walls.

There was little space for photographs or art work on the walls, but Dana did see a family portrait. She looked closer and guessed it was taken during Holly's graduation from high school. Everyone looked so young and happy, so optimistic. Little did they realize what was to unfold for the family by the end of that summer

Right below the photo, a framed print of lilies hung. It was a botanical drawing in pen and ink and watercolor wash. Dana lifted it, wondering if it hid the safe. It looked as if it had been there for ages, and but all she found underneath was a stained square of paint.

She checked the back of the print, not even sure what

she was looking for. It was blank. No note or mark of any kind. She set the print back on the wall hook and gazed at it a moment. George Piper loved that particular flower she recalled, and cultivated all types—tiger lilies, Asiatic lilies, classic white trumpets, so prevalent at Easter, weddings, and funerals. The nursery had been known for its lilies in his lifetime.

A wall calendar hung in a space beside the door, the day of each month neatly crossed off, one by one. Dana lifted it and was not surprised that the safe was not under there, either.

She noticed some squares marked with notes about Rose's appointments and scheduled deliveries. She wondered why the police had left the calendar. Had they missed it somehow? She decided to take it with her later and look it over more carefully before she went to bed.

It was more important to find the safe, if she could. Was it in this room at all?

The bookcases were little more than shelving hung against the walls. She pushed aside books on each row and searched behind them. Most of the books were thick, dusty guides to plants and trees, or insects and plant diseases. There were books on garden design and landscaping, as well. An entire shelf was devoted to masonry.

A shelf on the very bottom held only romance novels. Dana found that surprising. Ava's legacy? Or was Holly a closet fan? She seemed so sensible about men, but sometimes Dana wondered if she was secretly holding out for a knight in shining armor. A true romance novel hero who would sweep her off her feet and make her life divine.

The poor girl was entitled to her fantasies. If only Holly would recover quickly and meet and marry a wonderful man someday. Maybe reading romances would help her recognize Mr. Right when he finally came along.

The dust suddenly got to her. She stepped back, overcome by a sneezing fit, and quickly covered her mouth and nose with her hands so she wouldn't wake the entire house, then stumbled backward, trying hard to suppress the sound.

Her boot caught on the edge of the area rug and flipped up the corner. She found a box of tissues, then knelt down to smooth the rug back in place. She looked around, her spirits sinking. If the safe was in this room, she couldn't find it.

She'd felt so sure about it. Where to look next? Perhaps the master bedroom? It was too close to the guest room to investigate tonight, that was sure.

She straightened the rug, preparing to go, but felt something jiggle. A loose floorboard? Why would that be? She quickly leaned over and pulled back the rug. A section of a board, a little over a foot long, was neatly cut on either end. She found a letter opener on the desk and easily levered up the board's edge.

Sure enough, it was loose and came up easily. She felt almost giddy at the sight of a small black metal safe tucked beneath the floorboards, the silver knob for a combination lock stuck in the middle. She twisted the lock, wondering if it could possibly be open for some odd reason. It was locked tight.

She pondered possible combinations and started to try one, Holly's birthday. No luck, She tried Rose's next. The door wouldn't budge. She recalled Ava's birthday and tried those numbers, without success.

She couldn't remember George's birthday, and couldn't think of any other significant numbers in his life off the top of her head. This was probably a good puzzle for her friends. Lucy, in particular, was good at cracking codes. Still, she wished that she could open the safe tonight and see what was inside.

She sighed and stood up. The rug flopped back into

place. Where would she find the combination? George or Holly must have it written somewhere.

The police might be able to break the lock, but she wanted to get in first. Holly's desk seemed a logical place to look first. *Try to be positive*, she coached herself. *You might find it easily.*

She sat behind the desk and began to search, starting at the top. A white china box held only stamps and paper clips. A pencil cup yielded nothing unexpected, too.

She pulled open drawers next, then sifted through rubber bands, paper clips, stationery, business cards, and file folders. The last drawer was full of bank statements. She pulled out a few for the current year and put them aside. After hours of listening to clients, Dana had concluded that most people's problems stemmed from either love or money.

Holly's finances could certainly yield some clues. Dana stuck her arm in the drawer and felt around the back. Could the combination be written on a card and taped somewhere? Maybe on the bottom of a drawer or even the chair? She pulled the entire drawer out, and a folder full of pages spilled out on the floor.

"Aunt Dana . . . catching up on some bookkeeping? You ought to leave that to me. It *is* a family business."

Toby stood in the doorway, half hidden in the shadows.

Dana sat back and got her bearings. She did feel as if he'd caught her up to something nefarious. But she had every right to be in here. She was trying to help Holly.

"Detective Reyes asked me to look for a calendar or a datebook. It could help the investigation."

"Really? Maybe I can help." He stepped into the room and pointed at the calendar that hung beside the door "Is this what you're looking for?"

He reached out and yanked it off the wall. Then tossed it on the desk.

Dana had to steel herself. She wouldn't be intimidated by him. "I'm not the enemy, Toby. I'm trying to help Holly and help the police find out who attacked her."

"You were always very helpful. A big support to the girls after Mom died. No one would deny that. But I'm here now. Things are going change. I'm just warning you."

Dana stood up. He was a schoolyard bully, and she wouldn't be intimidated. "Warning me? You disappeared for ten years, with no concern at all for your half sisters, and suddenly, you're warning me off? Lord of the manor, staking your claim?" Her hands were shaking, but she pressed them flat on the desk. "I don't know what you're up to, but I do know Holly and Rose are protected legally. Jack and I have seen to that."

Toby came closer. He tossed his head back and stared down at her, his eyes cold with anger. "Jack, that legal genius who drew up my stepfather's will. Who cut me out of everything I was promised. Holly and Rose, the little sweethearts, got it all. Jack saw to that."

"Those were your stepfather's wishes, not Jack's. George left you a gift, a generous sum, I recall."

"Generous? It was peanuts compared to what this place is worth now, and you know it."

Dana stood up straight and took a step back, away from him. "You challenged the will. It held up. I'm not sure what you think you can go after at this point," she said bluntly.

"Aunt Dana, what a thing to say. I admit, I've been remiss," he said with mock sincerity. "But I'm here now, to help my little sisters. I worry about Rose. Holly is her legal guardian, but she's not able to carry out her role right now, is she? Hope for the best, but prepare for the worst, I always say."

"Meaning what exactly?" Dana was afraid to hear the answer.

"I've hired a lawyer. He's filing a petition for Rose's guardianship. I am her closest relative. You seem to forget."

Dana's blood ran cold. His words left her speechless. A court would never name Toby as Rose's guardian while Holly was sick . . . would it?

"Hire all the lawyers you want. You won't even get a hearing. Count on it."

Dana held his gaze, determined not to show her fear. Then scolded herself for losing her temper. Threatening a person like Toby was the worst approach. You didn't need to be a psychologist to know that.

But he only shrugged and replied in a mild, innocent tone, "I have to try my best. I do worry about poor Rose. If you and Jack have done such a great job watching over my sisters, why were they nearly killed last night? Any judge worth their salt will want to know the answer to that."

He turned and left the small room. Dana heard his soft laughter as he climbed back up the stairs. The sound gave her chills.

Chapter 7

Maggie had tossed and turned most of the night, worrying about Rose and Holly. And Dana. As if there wasn't enough on Dana's plate, now she had to deal with the predatory half brother, Toby.

Maggie was standing on the porch, unlocking the shop door, when, as if mere thoughts had conjured her up, she heard Dana call to her from the street.

"Maggie? I'm glad you're here. I was just going to phone you." Her voice sounded relieved and a bit breathless, and when Maggie turned, Dana was already walking up the path.

Rose stood at the gate, with Oreo on a thin blue lead attached to the dog's halter. Rose looked up and waved, and Maggie waved back.

"What's up? Is everything okay?"

"We were on the way to the hospital to see Holly. But Detective Reyes called. She can't meet up this afternoon to talk to Rose. She asked if we could stop at the station but . . ." Dana paused and glanced back at Rose

Maggie didn't need to hear more. "That's not a good place to bring Rose," she said flatly. "Not at all."

Maggie had been interviewed at the police station once and still felt anxious thinking about it. She considered herself very solid in stressful situations. Usually unshakable. But under police scrutiny she had been shaken, to her very core. It would be doubly stressful for Rose.

"You'd think Detective Reyes would be more sensitive. You've told her about Rose's condition."

"I guess she doesn't understand the whole picture. She's very busy and needs to keep the investigation moving." Maggie thought Dana was being very generous, though her points were probably true. "Could we possibly meet her here? Just until you open. I'm sure it won't take very long. It's such a comfortable spot. Almost as nice as sitting in someone's house."

"Of course I don't mind. That's a very good solution." Dana's office wasn't far, but the shop was definitely cozier. "I don't open for at least an hour. I can hold back my fans a little longer, if need be. Does Detective Reyes agree?"

Dana already had her cell phone out. "I'll explain it to her. It's only to her benefit if Rose feels calm and comfortable. The police station would scare her, and she's liable to not say a thing."

"That's true, and it should convince the detective."

Maggie stepped inside, while Dana remained on the porch to talk to Detective Reyes. A few moments later, she came inside with Rose. Rose stood at the door for a second, seeming hesitant to enter.

"Come in, please. Oreo is welcome, too," Maggie said, sensing Rose was about to ask.

"She'll stay right next to me. I'll hang on to her lead." Looking relieved, Rose sat in an armchair, and the dog settled at her feet.

While Maggie wondered how to pull Dana aside, Rose looked around. "What a nice shop. There's something interesting to see in every corner."

Dana smiled at Maggie, looking pleased that her plan was working out.

"Thank you, Rose. I'd love to show you some projects and yarns if you have time later. Which reminds me, I need to find those buckles for the dog collars."

Rose shrugged. "When you get to it. I sewed a big button on and pushed it through the stitches. See?" She showed Maggie Oreo's collar, which had been finger stitched with the self-striping blue yarn Maggie had given Holly on Tuesday morning.

"That was a clever idea. But a real buckle will hold better. A button might slip open."

No harm done if the collar did slip open, Maggie realized. Rose used halters on her dogs, not leads that were attached to a loop on a collar. The halters stayed in place even if the dog collar slipped off or popped open. The truth was, her dogs were so well trained, there was little danger of one ever running away or getting lost. As far as Maggie could see, they all wanted to stay as close as possible to their mistress.

Dana sat down next to Rose. "Detective Reyes will be here in a few minutes."

Rose took a deep breath, then reached down and stroked Oreo's head. "I'm ready . . . I think."

Dana took her hand. "I'm right here the whole time. And so is Oreo. You'll be fine. I promise."

Maggie saw a gray Camry park across the street from the shop. After a moment, Detective Reyes climbed out.

"Here she is now," Maggie said.

She walked to the door and opened it as Detective Reyes came up the porch steps.

"Good morning, everyone," Detective Reyes greeted them as she stepped into the shop. Once inside, she slipped off her black weatherproof jacket and sat on a chair opposite Rose.

"Thanks for meeting us here," Dana said.

"Not a problem. As long as we have some privacy." She looked straight at Maggie.

"I have work to do in the storeroom. I'll close the door, too," Maggie said.

Lucy was the only one liable to stop by at this hour, and a quick text would take care of that, Maggie thought. She headed to the back of the shop, and Detective Reyes seemed satisfied. As Maggie glanced around, she saw the detective take her pad and pen from her purse and balance them on her lap.

Maggie slipped into the storeroom and shut the door with a little more force than necessary, to instill confidence that the interview was private, though she was actually aching to hear what was being said. She put her ear to the door but could hear nothing but murmuring voices.

She sighed and began her daily ritual. First, making a fresh pot of coffee. As the coffee dripped, she sent Lucy a short text explaining why the shop was off limits right now. She felt sure that Lucy would stop and circle the block with her dogs a few times, until she could get in to hear the latest news.

When the coffee was done, she considered bringing out a tray for the others, in the hopes of catching a few snippets of conversation, then decided the detective would get annoyed by the obvious ploy. It was best to keep her word and not embarrass Dana.

She filled her mug and set up the yarn swift, clamping the device to the counter. Might as well use the time productively. She did need yarn wound for a class this afternoon.

As she worked, watching the swift merrily spin, the door slowly creaked open. She wasn't surprised. The shop was a crooked old house with uneven floors, windows, and doorways throughout. Part of its quirky charm, she'd always thought.

Now she had a moral dilemma. Shut the door or leave it open? She paused her winding and could hear the conversation clearly. She stepped closer. It was far too tempting. She couldn't help it, despite her best intentions.

And she did want to help Dana and the Pipers. Couldn't she help them much more if she knew what was being said right now?

"Take your time, Rose. There's no rush. Try to tell me everything you can remember from Tuesday. Let's start in the morning. What did you do when you got up?" Detective Reyes coaxed her.

"I took care of the dogs, like I always do. They need to go out early, and then I give them fresh water and breakfast. Then I get dressed and have my own breakfast. After that, I exercise them in the yard and train the new rescues. Sometimes people come by to see if they want to adopt one. But nobody was coming that day."

"What was the weather like? I'm not sure I remember," Detective Reyes said. Maggie had a strong feeling she did remember, but this was some sort of interview tactic.

"It was sunny and felt warmer. More like spring. A delivery truck came in the morning, with pansies and daffodils. Carl helped Holly unload the flats. Holly doesn't sell a lot of annuals, but she says the spring flowers bring customers in. Everyone likes them."

That was true, Maggie thought. The bright, cheerful blooms seemed to mark the official end of winter, even when it was still chilly at night and in the early morning. Pansies rarely complained.

"So Carl Thornton was there in the morning, working with Holly. What time did he get there? Do you know?"

"I'm not sure. Before I came out. He just always seemed to be around once Holly hired him. I thought he lived in the woods or something," Rose said.

"Why would you think that?" the detective asked curiously.

"I saw him there once at night, when I was walking Wolf and Oreo. They started barking, and he ran away."

"Are you sure it was Mr. Thornton, Rose?"

"He's not the type of person you'd mistake for someone else, and he had that red bandanna on. It was him. I'm sure."

"Can you remember what night that was, Rose? Was it Tuesday?" Detective Reyes's voice was calm and even, though Maggie sensed the answers were important to her.

Rose didn't answer for a few moments. "No . . . I don't think so. I think it was Monday night. When I came back inside, I was going to tell Holly. But she was talking to Dr. Riley."

"On the phone?" Dana asked.

"No . . . He was at our house. They went into her office and closed the door."

Maggie found that information interesting. Maybe he'd come to talk to Holly about Rose's condition, and they hadn't wanted Rose to hear? Or maybe the conversation had been personal, about a matter that didn't involve Rose, only the two of them.

Once again, she recalled the argument between the two doctors that she'd overheard on Friday, while she sat in the hallway, waiting for Dana. She realized that she still had not told Dana about it.

"They were in there a long time," Rose recalled. "I heard them arguing about something. I took my medication and went to bed."

Medication that made her sleep soundly, Maggie assumed.

"Did you hear what the argument was about?"

Maggie didn't hear Rose answer. She must have shaken her head.

"Could you guess?" the detective said next.

"I couldn't hear what they were saying. I asked Holly in the morning, but she said they were just talking and got a little emotional. It wasn't anything important, and she promised it wasn't about me, either."

Which sounded to Maggie like more of Holly shielding her sister. She doubted Holly would have told Rose the whole story, even if it had been important.

"Did you ever hear or see Carl Thornton argue with Holly?"

"No, never. Carl didn't talk much. He worked all day and did whatever Holly said."

"Do you ever argue with Holly?" Detective Reyes asked in a quiet but pointed tone.

Rose seemed surprised and even a bit defensive. "We get along fine. Most of the time," she said. "Sometimes, I don't want to go to appointments, or I forget to take some pills," Rose admitted. "Once in a while, I'll make a mess in the kitchen, and she'll get upset." She paused. Detective Reyes did not fill in the silence. "Or maybe the dogs get on her nerves. I know it's not always easy for her, taking care of me."

Maggie could not see Rose but imagined her drawing comfort from Oreo. The dog was probably sitting beside her on the sofa, perhaps even with her head in Rose's lap.

"We never stay mad for long. I can always make her laugh and snap her out of it," she added. Maggie heard the small smile in her voice.

"Does she get upset often about the dogs?" Detective Reyes asked. "Does she ever complain about the mess or, say, the cost of taking care of them? Maybe she told you it was too much bother or she couldn't afford to take dogs in like that anymore, and you and Holly had an argument?"

Maggie heard Dana cut in with an objection worthy of

any attorney. "Detective, those aren't exactly questions. I think you're trying to put words in Rose's mouth now."

Before Detective Reyes could answer, Rose said, "Of course not. I love Holly . . . and she loves me. Why would I fight with her? She does everything for me."

Rose sounded near tears. Maggie felt a pang in her heart.

"I think that's enough questions for now, Detective," Dana said. "Rose is getting tired, and we need to leave for the hospital."

Maggie checked her watch. They had been talking about ten minutes or so, but it felt much longer.

Maggie knew that these sorts of interviews could last for hours in a police station setting. But this wasn't that sort of interview, she reminded herself. Rose was not a suspect, just a witness, without memories of the actual event. Though she had supplied some useful information so far. Maggie was encouraged by that.

"I do need to touch on a few more points, Dr. Haeger. It's probably better for everyone if we can just get this done, don't you think?"

Dana didn't answer. Instead, Maggie heard her ask Rose, "What do you think, Rose? Are more questions okay with you?"

Maggie heard Rose sigh. "I want to help Holly."

"Good. You are helping, Rose," Detective Reyes replied. "So back to Dr. Riley. Did he visit your house often?"

"Not usually," Rose answered slowly. "He did stop by a few times last weekend. He would talk to me awhile, ask me how I felt and all that. But he really came to see Holly. I know he likes her. He sent her flowers."

"The bouquet in the foyer?" Dana asked.

Maggie had noticed the flowers, too. Not that it would be unusual to find fresh flowers in the home of someone who owned a nursery. But manicured long-stemmed roses didn't seem like a choice she'd make for herself.

"Holly wouldn't tell me who they were from. But I know she didn't buy them. She hates red roses."

"When did the flowers come? Do you remember?"

"Let's see . . . on Tuesday morning, I guess. Holly was outside with Carl, unloading a delivery of new plants. A car drove up, and a guy gave Holly the box of roses. I was behind the house, with the dogs."

Maggie was trying to keep a timeline in her head: Dr. Riley visited the house this past weekend, pursuing Holly. They argued on Monday night, and on Tuesday morning flowers arrived. Probably from him, but that would be easy enough to check out with local florists. And Rose saw Carl Thornton in the woods on Monday night, as well.

Did this information give Detective Reyes anything more to work with? Maggie hoped so.

"Tell me about Tuesday night again, Rose. Was anyone at your house besides you and Holly? Did anyone come to visit or even to deliver anything?"

"It was just us two. And the dogs. Holly went into the village in the morning, and she brought back pizza for dinner. It's hard to get deliveries where we live. We ate around six thirty. Holly told me Carl quit and wasn't coming back."

"What did you think about that?"

"I didn't care, except that he helped Holly a lot. He scared me at first, but then he didn't seem so bad. He was kind to the dogs, and they trusted him."

Maggie found that tidbit interesting. She'd heard of crooks who were very adept at winning over watchdogs and tossed the fur guardians hunks of steak or sticks of butter and then proceeded to easily rob a house. Did Thornton have that knack, charming even Rose's dedicated pack?

"What did you do after dinner?" Detective Reyes asked in a conversational tone.

"Holly went into her office to do bookkeeping and pay bills. It always puts her in a bad mood, so I stayed in my room with the dogs and watched TV. And worked on my knitting," Rose replied. "I let the dogs out again around ten o'clock and took my medication. Then I went to sleep on the couch in the parlor with them."

"Was Holly still awake at ten, do you recall?"

"She was still in her office, and I said good night to her from the door. She was busy. She hardly looked up. It looked like she was still paying bills."

"Was she making out checks? Reading invoices?" the detective asked. "On the phone with anyone?"

"She was counting money, and she doesn't like to be interrupted when she's doing that. There was a big pile of money on her desk." Rose's voice was very matter of fact.

Detective Reyes replied quickly, "Does she usually pay money that way? With cash?"

"Sometimes," Rose said.

"Did you ask who the money was for?"

"Why would I do that? Holly runs the business. I only help with weeding and watering. Things like that. She reminded me to take my pills, and I went to bed." Rose paused. Her voice was growing thin and a bit shaky, Maggie thought. "I fell asleep quickly. I don't remember anything after that."

The room went silent.

Then Dana said, "I think Rose is very tired, Detective. Honestly. Can we stop now?"

Will she ask me too many questions? Maggie recalled Rose ask Dana. This was certainly a lot of questions, probably way too many for her.

"I'm sorry, Rose. I don't want to wear you out. Just one or two more, and we'll be done."

Maggie doubted that. There were always more questions, once the police got started.

"All right. I'm okay, I guess." Rose's voice trembled.

Maggie dared a glance into the room. She saw Oreo's head on Rose's knee, the dog's way of lending Rose support and calm, warm energy.

"Did you know there was a container of gasoline at the nursery?"

"Of course I do. Holly kept it in the potting shed for the power tools. Did the person who set the fire use it?"

"Possibly. We know it was set with gasoline, and some further tests will show if that was the same blend. There are fingerprints on the container. We're trying to find a match for them."

"Detective . . . are these details really necessary?" Dana's tone was strong.

The detective didn't answer her. She kept talking to Rose. "I know you don't remember what happened Tuesday night, Rose. But we know that you got out of bed and went outside. We also know there was gasoline on your hands and feet and splattered on your pajamas. We need to figure out how it got there. Do you remember anything at all about that?"

Maggie's breath caught in her throat. She turned to see Rose's and Dana's reaction.

"I don't know how it got there . . . I don't remember . . . I never used the gasoline. Holly didn't let me." Rose was upset, her voice thin and anxious.

Maggie heard Rose's breathing become fast and labored. She stepped out of the storeroom, unable to stay hidden any longer. Oreo had her head pressed to Rose's lap and softly licked Rose's hands. Dana put her arm around Rose's shoulder.

"This interview is over, Detective. I hope the information Rose gave you helps." Dana's tone was fiercely protective, and Maggie wondered if the detective would back off.

Detective Reyes took a deep breath, her mouth pressed in a tight line. Maggie knew she could be tough, but there seemed no chance now of Rose answering any more questions. Her head was bowed, and she trembled as Dana softly rubbed her back.

"I'm sorry to upset you, Rose. I have to ask these questions in order to understand what happened Tuesday night. We need all the information we can gather in order to find out who hurt your sister," Detective Reyes explained in a patient tone. She looked at Dana. "Can we speak outside a moment?"

No one had noticed her in the back of the room. Maggie saw her opportunity and stepped forward quickly. "I can sit with Rose while you talk."

Detective Reyes glanced over at her. Maggie had the feeling the detective knew very well that she'd been listening, but couldn't do anything about it now.

"Is that all right with you, Rose? I won't be long," Dana said.

The young woman nodded, her gaze troubled and unfocused as she stroked her dog. Oreo was sitting up and gently licked Rose's face.

Dana stood up and followed the detective to the door. As Maggie took a seat beside Rose, she saw the two women standing across the street, near Detective Reyes's car. Detective Reyes was doing most of the talking, and Dana was listening, her arms crossed over her chest in a defensive pose.

"Detective Reyes thinks I hurt Holly . . . doesn't she?" Rose asked quietly.

The last few questions had veered in that direction, like an out-of-control car skidding off the road. But Maggie was reluctant to be the one to validate Rose's conclusion.

"I know her questions upset you, but Detective Reyes has to consider a lot of possibilities. Some that are very unlikely or even unthinkable."

"I'd never hurt Holly in a million years . . . or do anything like that. Pour gasoline all over the place and set a fire."

She was agitated again, trembling and short of breath. Maggie hoped Dana would return quickly.

"I know, Rose. We all know that. It will get sorted out. Take some deep breaths, dear, and try to relax."

Rose nodded and closed her eyes. Was she going to black out? Maggie hoped not. Rose squeezed her hand and followed her instructions, drawing in several slow breaths, which started to calm her. Oreo's comforting attention helped, as well, Maggie noticed.

Rose and Maggie sat side by side, holding hands, for a few quiet moments. Oreo had somehow draped herself across both laps, and Maggie had ended up with the softly wagging tail end. The dog's fur tickled her nose, but she didn't mind nearly as much she thought she would.

"How are you doing?" Maggie asked quietly after a few minutes had passed.

"Better, I think." Rose opened her eyes and met Maggie's gaze. "But what if I really did those horrible things . . . and I just don't remember?"

Her wide blue eyes filled with tears and panic again. Maggie wasn't sure what to say or do. She leaned over and took Rose in her arms.

Logically, Maggie knew there was some chance that Rose's very worst fear—everyone's worst fear—was true. But Maggie pushed aside her doubts. It wasn't true. She just knew it, deep in her heart. Rose Piper did not harm her sister or set that fire. Some diabolical individual, who was still out there, did all of it and may have even intended to make Rose the easy target for the blame.

"I'm sure you didn't do it, Rose. I promise, I'll do everything I can to help find out who really did."

Before Rose could answer, Oreo jumped up and stood with her front paws on the back of the sofa. She stared out the window and barked wildly.

Lucy had arrived and was tying her dogs to the porch rail. Or trying to. They had caught sight and scent of the canine visitor inside and were barking like crazy now, too.

Maggie pressed her hands to her ears. "Oh my . . . sounds like a barking contest."

"I'll bring Oreo outside. They'll calm down once they're properly introduced."

Rose was just the person to accomplish that, too, Maggie thought. "Would you, Rose? That would be a big help."

Dana and the detective had not finished their conversation. The sight made Maggie uneasy. She doubted Rose could overhear them up on the shop's porch, especially with the dogs going wild, and the conversation had to be done soon.

As Rose slipped out, Lucy walked in. "I saw Detective Reyes outside with Dana. I assume the coast is clear?"

"Almost," Maggie replied. "It's been a long morning, and it's only"—she glanced at her watch—"eight forty-five? Can that possibly be?"

Plenty of time to clear the mini dog pack from the porch before customers arrived.

Outside, not only had the three dogs quieted down, but they also sat in a circle around Rose, staring up at her alertly. *A small but remarkable feat*, Maggie thought. She really did speak their language.

Lucy had walked back to the storeroom and returned with a mug of coffee. She sat on the sofa and took a sip. "How did the interview go?"

"Fine, at first. I think Rose was very helpful to Detective

Reyes. She answered a lot of questions about Tuesday and the days prior—about things that were going on at the nursery. But it took a troubling turn toward the end."

Lucy sat up and set the mug down. "How so?"

"The police have determined that Rose had gasoline on her hands and feet and on her clothing. And they've pulled fingerprints from the gas container. They haven't matched the prints yet, but Detective Reyes seems to think it's a valid lead."

"Such as . . . Rose set the fire?"

Maggie nodded solemnly.

"That's outrageous!"

"That's what I think, too. Let's face it, anyone with Rose's condition is vulnerable to accusations. Even the most outrageous. If she can't remember the events of the evening and present her own version of what happened that night—what she heard, what she saw—the police can put the pieces together in any number of ways. And she can be accused of most anything."

Dana walked in. They both turned to look at her.

"What did Detective Reyes need to tell you in private?" Maggie had a feeling it wasn't anything good.

"She wants Rose to make a formal statement at the police station. And give fingerprints."

"That's ridiculous. It wouldn't prove a thing," Maggie insisted. "There are a million reasons why her fingerprints would be all over the place, including on the gas container."

Maggie did recall Rose saying that Holly didn't allow her to handle the power tools or the gas. But still, it wasn't evidence that would hold up in court.

"There's another reason." Dana drew a sharp breath. "A shovel was found in the woods, with Holly's blood and strands of hair. There are prints on the handle, as well, and probably they've tried to collect some DNA. That takes a long time to process," Dana explained. "But it's still a consideration. Reyes claims they just need to rule Rose out. But this whole line of questioning worries me."

Maggie felt her stomach drop. She knew it was a corny cliché, but the phrase *Sure, that's what they all say* quickly sprang to mind. This was serious.

Lucy looked worried, too. "What did you say?"

"I told Detective Reyes that she'll hear from Rose's lawyer by the end of the day. And I just called Jack and got him working on it."

"Good move. That's exactly what you need to do now," Lucy said.

"Rose is hardly the only possible suspect. There's still Thornton. Or someone we don't even know about yet. Holly and I are close, but I can see now that there are things going on in her life I have no idea about. Which is only natural." Dana flipped her beige shawl around her shoulders. She seemed upset, and Maggie's heart went out to her.

"Did you ask Detective Reyes if they've made any progress tracking down Thornton?"

"So far, it's all dead ends," Dana said. "The cell phone was a cheap throwaway kind. The address in Rowley exists, but the landlord had no record of anyone like him renting a room there."

"That's too bad. But they still might find him," Lucy said.

"If they keep looking." Dana hooked her handbag over her shoulder and sighed. "They might stop looking if they get focused on making a case against Rose."

Maggie knew that was true, but didn't want to encourage a negative outlook. "Jack will find Rose a good lawyer, who will pressure the police to keep looking."

"Maybe Helen Forbes will take Rose as a client," Lucy suggested. "She saved Suzanne's bacon when things looked grim."

"She did," Maggie agreed. "But please don't ever phrase it that way in front of Suzanne. You know how sensitive she is about her . . . bacon."

Dana responded with a small smile. "I was thinking the same thing. I mean about Helen. She's smart and tough and thrives on complications."

"No lack of them here." Maggie smoothed some dog hairs from the sofa cushion. She didn't have time to get out the hand vacuum and hoped that none of her customers today were allergic.

"Backing up the police with a good attorney is one thing," Lucy said. "But it doesn't solve the problem of their focus on Rose. Are they looking at anyone besides this mysterious Thornton character?"

Dana sighed. "Dr. Riley's name came up. He was visiting Holly for some reason over the weekend. Rose overheard an argument but couldn't hear what they were talking about."

"And a big bouquet of roses was delivered the next day," Maggie added.

"A lovers' quarrel," Lucy said. "I didn't know they were involved."

"I didn't think so, either. Now I'm not so sure," Dana said. "Maybe he likes Holly, but she isn't interested in him?"

Lucy reflected. "Rejection is an aphrodisiac for some men. They thrive on a good chase."

"It is a pattern with some people. When the object of their affection is just out of reach, he or she seems more desirable," Dana agreed. "And beyond that, I've always thought that he and Emily Curtis were together. An on-again, off-again affair, I'd heard. They do keep their private life private. Maybe that's over, and he was pursuing Holly."

Maggie felt a bit embarrassed, as if she'd kept something important from Dana. But the conversation she'd overheard hadn't seemed that important with everything else going on. It seemed to have relevance now.

"I probably should have mentioned this sooner, Dana. I overheard Dr. Curtis and Dr. Riley arguing last Friday, when you took me to the center. I was going to tell you, but I put it off, and it just felt too much like gossiping, I guess," Maggie admitted. "And Rose was in the car."

She quickly had the full attention of both her friends.

"Sounds interesting. Go on," Lucy coaxed.

"I was waiting for Dana to come out of her office, and the door to Dr. Curtis's office was open. Dr. Riley and Dr. Curtis were having a spat. She knew he had an appointment with Holly that afternoon, and she was upset. And jealous. I got the distinct impression that he and Dr. Curtis are not just business and scientific partners but also a romantic pair. At least she seems to think so."

Dana's expression was thoughtful. "They might be together. If so, they keep it very quiet. Maybe for professional reasons. But maybe Holly knew, and that's why she didn't want to get involved with him."

Lucy had taken out her knitting but left it on the table. "Perhaps it's one sided for Dr. Curtis. Maybe she's yearning after a guy who keeps dancing out of reach."

"I did get that feeling," Maggie agreed. "Then again, it's impossible to judge an entire relationship from one brief conversation. I may have misinterpreted. Either way, it sounds like Detective Reyes does plan on interviewing Dr. Riley. You might mention it to her?"

"I will. But I don't think she'll look at either of them as persons of interest. Does anyone really think that someone like Dr. Riley could react to romantic rejection by trying to kill Holly? Or that Dr. Curtis could be so crazed with jealousy she'd do such a thing? I can't imagine that either of them is responsible, any more than I think Rose is."

Maggie followed Dana's gaze through the big window in the front of the shop. Rose stood on the small square of lawn, with full control over the three dogs as she put them through their paces with sit, lie, and stay commands. The perfect distraction for her after the police interview.

"It does sound out of character for any of them," Maggie agreed. "But who would be angry enough to go to such extremes?"

"Toby is angry." Dana turned and met Maggie's glance. "I didn't want to talk about him in front of Rose. I don't want her to be afraid of him. But I gave Detective Reyes an earful."

"Whoa . . . Who's Toby?" Lucy asked. "I can't keep the scorecard if I don't know the players."

"He's Rose and Holly's half brother. Ava's son from her first marriage," Dana explained. "He's already had . . . issues and feels very much the victim in the family. His stepfather, George, lost patience and didn't leave him any share of the business. So he has his grievances."

"Oh, I see. I'd put him on the top of my list if I were Detective Reyes. He should definitely distract her from focusing on Rose, don't you think?" Lucy's tone was hopeful.

"I've barely met the man," Maggie said, "but he was definitely sugarcoating his bitter feelings and seemed completely insincere about coming home to help his sisters."

"When he showed up yesterday, I was surprised, but I was willing to give him the benefit of the doubt," Dana said. "Now I'm totally suspicious. I'd like to know where he was Tuesday night, when the fire started, and if there's any gasoline on his shoes or clothing."

"I was thinking the same thing. I felt uneasy leaving you

alone with him last night," Maggie said. "I hope Jack wasn't too late getting out to the house."

"Late enough. Toby and I had a very ugly confrontation. He found me in Holly's office. I was looking for the home safe or anything to help figure out what happened to her. He lost no time reminding me I'm not a blood relation and claims that he's filing a legal petition to become Rose's guardian. At least temporarily, while Holly is unable to fulfill her responsibilities."

Maggie felt her heart clutch. "That would be awful. He doesn't even know Rose. He treats her in such a condescending way and he clearly disdains the dogs. Can he really persuade a judge to do this?"

Lucy was alarmed, too. "Holly has been sick only two days. Wouldn't it take a while for a legal decision like that to be worked out? She might be awake and aware before he could even get in front of a judge."

"Normally, that's true. But because of Rose's disability, things can move very quickly. I feel stupid now for not working out some official arrangement with Holly in case anything like this happened. At least I'm her official health proxy, or Toby would be taking over Holly's medical decisions right now, too."

"What does he hope to gain by this maneuver? Can you figure that out?" Maggie asked.

"Oh, it's very clear to me. He's still bitter about George Piper's will. He wants the business and the property, or whatever part he can get his hands on. Who knows what damage he can do, even in a short span of time?" Dana took a deep breath. Maggie could see she was very upset but was trying to lay the facts out clearly. "If, heaven forbid, the unthinkable were to happen and Holly didn't survive her injuries, everything goes to Rose. Since she's deemed mentally incompetent, her legal guardian would control her inheritance."

"That is a dark scenario," Maggie said quietly.

"And plenty of motive to attack Holly and leave her in a fire to die," Lucy pointed out.

"More than enough, I'd say. Even if he's arrived by co-incidence and is just trying to take advantage of the situation, checking out Toby's story should deflect attention from Rose for a little while," Maggie pointed out.

"We hope so. And we aren't taking any chances with his threat," Dana assured them. "Jack thinks he can nip Toby's legal move in the bud. He's filing a counter petition, asking that I be named Rose's temporary guardian while Holly is incapacitated. Even if we need to appear in court, it will certainly slow down Toby's plan, and Holly might rally by then."

"Oh my . . . this is so much all at once for you," Maggie said.

She leaned over and gave Dana a hug. Lucy did the same, and Dana finally smiled, though her eyes grew glossy and she looked about to cry.

"It must be so awkward staying in the house with him now," Lucy said. "Even if Jack is there with you."

"He can't stand the dogs and announced this morning he was moving into the apartment over the garage. It's furnished, and sometimes Holly rents it out, but it's empty now. He'll take what he needs from the house, I guess. I think his biggest concern is hooking up a TV."

"Maybe he'll disappear again, once his petition is thrown out of court," Lucy said.

"With any luck," Dana agreed. "At least with him out of the house, I can poke around some more. I found some bank statements and I did find the safe, hidden in the floor of Holly's office. Unfortunately, I can't find the combination. Yet. I know I should tell Detective Reyes, but I don't want to until I get it open. There might be something important inside."

Something that might contribute to the theory that Rose was guilty? Maggie wondered. Was that what she was afraid of?

"Toby interrupted me before I could do a good search of the desk," Dana said.

"It's a big place. The combination could be hidden anywhere. If it's even written down." Maggie hated to sound negative by pointing that out, but it was true. Maybe Dana was better off taking her chances and letting the police open the safe.

"Don't remind me. I'm trying not to psyche myself out," Dana said. "If I go room by room, I'm sure it will turn up. It might even be in the one of the outbuildings. Maybe the garage or potting shed? Not the greenhouse, I hope." She sounded worried about that possibility.

"We should help you. We'll come there tonight." Lucy turned to Maggie. "We can't sit here, happily knitting away, while poor Dana is trying to figure out who tried to kill Holly . . . and the super-creepy half brother is lurking around."

"I did think we should call off tonight's meeting," Maggie admitted. "But gathering at the Pipers' to knit and help Dana dig up pieces to this puzzle is the perfect compromise."

"Would you really do that? That would be a great help." Dana's face finally lit up with a smile. "We'll act like it's knitting night as usual, in case Toby gets suspicious."

"I'll take care of dinner," Maggie offered. "It's my turn to do the main dish."

"Something we can eat quickly. There's a lot of ground to cover and not much time." Lucy sounded serious and psyched, already in her investigation mode. "I've been meaning to search Carl Thornton on the internet. I'll do that today, and I'll do some research on Toby Nash. From what you've said about him, I doubt his background check comes up lily white. Which would help fend off his play for Rose's guardianship."

"Thank you, Lucy," Dana said sincerely. "Someone in Jack's office might work on that angle, too. Let's hope the combination turns up. I have a feeling we'll find more than cash and jewelry in that safe. Holly has probably stashed some precious secrets there, too."

Maggie thought it was wise of Dana to admit the truth. It did seem now that Holly had hidden parts of her life from Dana. Dana prided herself on her close relationship with her goddaughter, but as a psychologist, she surely knew that everyone held at least a few secrets close to their heart, and even hidden relationships.

Had one of Holly's secrets nearly killed her? That was starting to look very possible.

Chapter 8

"Well, gang, as Yogi Berra said, 'It's like déjà vu all over again.'" Suzanne pulled up in front of the Pipers' house, parked the SUV, and shut off the engine. She pulled down the visor mirror to fluff her hairdo and freshen her lipstick, though there was no one joining them tonight to admire her appearance.

"Yogi was right, too." Maggie climbed out of the backseat, where she had sat beside Phoebe. She grabbed two pans of food from the hatch—there was much less to carry tonight since she'd been determined to keep the meal simple—and headed up the path with her friends toward the Pipers' house.

Exactly one week later, and here they were again. It did feel like déjà vu. A chilly wind tossed the branches above the rooftop, and the dogs inside barked and howled. The small lamp above the portico cast a yellow glow, and the front door slowly opened.

Except that Holly wasn't standing in the doorway this time to welcome them. It was Dana and Rose. And though it appeared that they were visiting for another knitting session, their real objective was to search the house and the property for any clues the police may have missed. For any bits of evidence that proved Rose did not carry out such a cruel, heartless act.

Despite their serious purpose, or maybe because of it, the mood was upbeat and cheery.

"I heated the oven for you," Dana said as Maggie and the others followed her into the kitchen.

Rose was at the table, setting it for six. The everyday china tonight, Maggie noticed, though she certainly didn't mind.

She opened the oven door and slipped in the two trays she was carrying, then pulled off the foil covers.

"Is that pizza?" Maggie could tell from Rose's tone that pizza was one of her favorite meals.

"Flatbread." Maggie closed the oven and smiled at her. "Which is just a trendy word for the same thing."

"You're in luck, Rose. Maggie's homemade flatbread is a culinary treat. You'll never look at ordinary pizza the same," Lucy warned.

While the flatbread heated, Dana tossed a green salad with some dressing she'd mixed earlier.

"Ta-dah!" Suzanne pulled two bottles of sparkling water from her knitting bag, as if arriving at a picnic with bottles of champagne. "I know it's a no wine night, but a few bubbles couldn't hurt."

"Not at all. They might even help," Maggie replied.

They had decided to forgo their usual bottle of wine with dinner. They needed to keep their wits sharp for the search, and it was a long drive back to the village. But sparkling water did make the meal more festive and might even spur some creative thinking. There were plenty of puzzles and baffling questions to answer.

Suzanne poured the sparkling water as if it was a fine vintage and Dana served the salad. The oven timer buzzed and Maggie peeked at her flatbreads, to check that they were ready.

"Here it is, hot from the oven." Maggie cut through the crust with a sharp pizza wheel and set down the trays in the center of the table. Conversation stopped as she passed out slices, and everyone happily munched on their dinner. "Best to eat this while it's hot. Oregano anyone? I brought my shaker from home."

"You mean the one you carry in your purse," Phoebe said between bites. "You're the biggest oregano fan I've ever met. You can put it on practically anything."

"I can," Maggie agreed. "Could be my genetic makeup. I've heard it's very good for you. Lowers the blood pressure."

"As long as it has tomato sauce and mozzarella, I'm good," Rose promised.

"I'm with you, kid. But I love to see what else Maggie has tossed on top. Roasted artichokes, mushrooms, asparagus . . . chicken," Suzanne noted, surveying one of the breads. "Not to mention this one, with the blue cheese. You do come up with some very creative combinations."

"This is scrumptious, Maggie. I need to get the recipe," Lucy said.

"Not much to it. Some store-bought pizza dough and any tasty odds and ends you can find in the fridge."

"Some refrigerators have a much better selection of odds and ends than others," Phoebe pointed out. "If you looked in mine, you'll see a few shriveled carrots, some hummus, yogurt, and a bag of chocolate Kisses."

"Chocolate flatbread. Maybe a few nuts or mini marshmallows on top? That has possibilities," Suzanne mused.

Dana nearly laughed. "What a combination. I was thinking more like roasted brussels sprouts."

"Sounds about right." Suzanne dabbed her mouth with a napkin.

"Speaking of combinations, I've been thinking," Lucy

cut in. "Didn't you say the safe has been in the house for a long time?"

"That's right. Holly's father installed it." Dana helped herself to more mixed greens and passed the bowl down the table.

Lucy took another slice of flatbread, choosing the blue cheese and mushroom. "Maybe we should try to figure out where George, not Holly, would have hidden the combination."

Dana seemed to like that idea. "Good point. Toby said he found the spare house key in the potting shed, right where their mother always hid it for them. It seems that Holly didn't change that family tradition. She may have just stuck with the tried and true for the combination, too."

"So, where would George stash it? What was he like? How did his mind work?" Lucy asked. "Did he have any prized possessions around the house, where he may have stuck it for safekeeping? In a trophy cup maybe? Or a favorite book?"

"His favorite book was the Bible," Rose said. "My dad was very religious."

Maggie glanced at Rose. "I'm sure Aunt Dana has already asked if you remember where the combination was written, Rose."

"She did. I can't remember." Rose shook her head. "But I do remember him. He loved growing flowers and trees. He loved lilies the most, and he loved our family. He always said he'd do anything for me and Holly. He was quiet and kind and went to church a lot. The only thing he didn't like was when someone went in his office. We weren't allowed there."

"That makes perfect sense if that's where the safe is. The combination must be in there somewhere, too," Suzanne said. "Sorry to say it, but even if Rose doesn't remember, Toby might know where both are hidden. He may have already gotten to it."

"You're right. I didn't even think of that. He's been alone here for hours today, ransacking the place, for all I know. We'd better check." Dana jumped up from her seat. Lucy, Maggie, and Phoebe followed.

Suzanne rose, too, and began clearing the plates. "I'll stick around here and be the lookout for Toby."

"Me too," Rose offered. "I can always distract him with dogs. He hates them, and the feeling is mutual."

"Good plan." Maggie was the last out the kitchen door.

It was good of Suzanne to stand guard, but Maggie wondered why Rose didn't want to come. Perhaps she was still abiding by her father's rules and was too well trained to go in his office? Or now that it belonged to Holly, it upset her to be in such a personal space?

Dana was moving quickly. Maggie, Lucy, and Phoebe raced to catch up to her. They walked past the staircase, then down a short, dark hallway.

Dana pulled open a heavy wooden door. Once inside, she switched on a lamp. and the others followed "This room is small and packed with furniture. I hope we all fit."

"I won't take offense at that comment, even though I may have put on a few pounds since I got married. And so has Matt," Lucy admitted.

"Chubby hubby syndrome?" Phoebe teased.

"Nonsense. It means you feel comfortable with each other," Maggie said.

"Lazy is more like it," Lucy laughed. "We don't seem to mind."

Dana quickly looked around the room and then pulled open a few of the desk drawers. "He's definitely been in here. The papers have been moved. The folder with credit cards bills and the bank statements are gone. At least I have the most recent ones. I was hoping we could look them over tonight, too."

"So, he's lived up to your worst expectations. I'm not surprised," Maggie said. "We'll have to sort that out later. What about the safe? Do you think he found it?"

Dana turned to them with a grave expression. "I probably can't tell, unless he was dumb enough to leave it open." She pushed aside an armchair. "Help me roll back the rug. It's under here."

Lucy helped with the rug as Maggie and Phoebe backed up toward the doorway. Dana knelt down and pried up a piece of floorboard.

"There it is," she said, leaning back.

Maggie saw a small black metal safe. The silver knob of the combination lock stared up like a cyclops's eye, daring them to battle for its secrets.

Dana grabbed the handle and jiggled it. "It's still locked, but that doesn't mean anything. He could have been in there."

"It's very solid looking, isn't it?" Lucy said.

"No one is opening that baby without the combination or something explosive," Phoebe replied. "We can look on the internet for a recipe to blow it open. I hear fertilizer is a key ingredient. There must be a lot of that around here."

Maggie knew she was joking, but even the suggestion was alarming. "No need to panic. Let's take a deep breath and think this through."

"Lucy had a good idea. Let's try to guess where George would have hidden the combination. There must be some note reminding him around here."

"Did you search the books?" Lucy asked. Before Dana could reply, Lucy began pulling out the books on the shelves nearest to her. "It might be, written inside the cover, or noted on a page. Something like that."

"Good idea. Let's check all the books." Maggie started on another section, and so did Phoebe.

"He did love his family. Look at the photos. I guess Holly never took them away," Lucy remarked. "Here's one of Holly and Rose on Christmas morning, opening their presents. It's very sweet."

Dana glanced at the photo, her expression softening with a smile. "That was years before the accident. They were just little girls."

And no one could foresee the many challenges the future would bring, Maggie added silently. She hoped with all her heart this latest chapter of their story did not take an even darker turn.

"Wait . . . look, a Bible. Rose said that was George's favorite book." Lucy pulled a thick volume bound in dark red leather off the shelf.

She set it on the desk and then quickly searched inside the front and back cover. "It's inscribed. I'll read it. 'Presented to George William and Ava Marie Piper on the event of their wedding, September seven, nineteen eighty-two.' " Lucy looked up. "Let's try that date or some variations. Nine, seven, nineteen, eight-two."

"Aren't combinations three numbers?" Maggie didn't know much about locks, but she did remember that.

Dana started spinning the dial. "I'll try nine, seven, eight and two, as the first numbers. Let's see."

They waited quietly, watching her twist the silver dial. With no luck. She tried every combination of the date and finally gave up.

"I tried birthdays last night. That didn't work. either," she said.

"Maybe it's in the Bible. A margin note or something," Lucy said. She wasn't giving up on her idea, Maggie could see. She hoped they weren't wasting valuable time.

"It's the Bible, Lucy. It will take a week to search the pages," Phoebe said.

Lucy didn't answer, flipping through the flaky-thin pages like a deck of cards. "I don't see anything, not a mark. Looks like he wasn't the type to write in books."

"I never do. I don't think it's right. No less a Bible," Maggie said.

Lucy wasn't listening. She sighed and finally placed the Bible back on a shelf. "I guess we can keep looking through the books."

"That's still a possibility. I just have a feeling that if the combination is in the room, it will be in a more obvious spot. Where he could access it quickly if he'd forgotten the numbers." Maggie pulled out a copy of a guide to flowering trees and shook it. The dust made her nose twitch.

Dana stood up and sighed. She rubbed her fingers, which had to be sore from all the lock twisting. Maggie wondered if professional safecrackers did special exercises.

Dana tilted her head back and talked to the ceiling. "George? Can you at least give us a clue? We're trying to help Rose and Holly. We know you loved them."

Phoebe ducked her head. "I hope he doesn't answer," she said under her breath.

"Look at this print." Lucy pointed to a finely etched botanical drawing. It looked antique to Maggie.

"George loved lilies. That was his specialty. I noticed that drawing last night," Dana said. "I thought the safe might be behind it, stuck in the wall."

"Maybe there's something written on the back?" Phoebe suggested.

"I checked. No luck there," Dana replied.

"Never mind the back. There's verse underneath, written out by hand." Lucy took the print from the wall and drew it closer to the light. " 'Consider the lilies of the field, how they grow; they toil not, neither do they spin. And yet I say unto you, That even Solomon in all his glory was not arrayed like one of these.' Matthew, chapter six, verses twenty-eight through twenty-nine." Lucy said the numbers slowly and looked at Dana.

Dana sighed and knelt down next to the safe again. "Six . . . twenty-eight . . . twenty-nine," she said aloud.

They hovered over her, holding their breath, as she spun the dial. Maggie heard something click. Dana turned the handle, but the safe didn't open.

Everybody groaned.

"I'm doing something wrong. I'm terrible with locks." Dana stood up. "Someone else should try."

"Don't look at me." Lucy shook her head. "I was always late for gym class. I could never open my locker in time to get my uniform." She looked at Maggie. "I think Maggie should try it. All that stitching? Your fingertips must be very sensitive and nimble."

"You're kidding, right?" Maggie's gaze moved to the rest of the group. From their expressions, Maggie could tell they were in unanimous agreement with Lucy. She had been elected to try spin the dial again.

"Okay, if you insist. I'll give it my best shot. Tell me the numbers again, slowly."

Maggie knelt down and slipped on her reading glasses, and Lucy read the numbers. "Six to the right, twenty-eight to the left, twenty-nine to the right."

Maggie turned the knob as carefully as she could, secretly doubting the attempt would be successful. But, as if by magic, she heard something metallic in the belly of the black box grind into place. She turned the handle, and the door creaked open. Then she quickly stood up and stepped aside so Dana could check the safe's contents.

Lucy patted her shoulder. "I knew you could do it. Now we need to add safecracking to your long list of talents."

"Beginner's luck," Maggie replied, feeling secret pride at her victory.

Dana pulled out a flat wooden box inlaid with an intricate design. "Here's the jewelry. I'm actually afraid to look inside. What if Toby got here first and it's empty?"

Lucy took the box from her and lifted the lid. "There's a lot of good stuff in here—rings, necklaces, bracelets. Would he have left so much if he was ripping the place off?"

Dana looked relieved. "Probably not. Unless he took just one or two good pieces, so no one would notice right away. Put it on the desk. I'll check later."

"What else is in the safe? Anything interesting?" Phoebe peered over Maggie's shoulder.

"Not too much. There are some letters." She took out a stack of envelopes secured with a rubber band and set them aside on the floor, then held up a book covered with pale green cloth. "And this record-keeping book."

Maggie took the book and flipped it open. She quickly scanned the pages. "It looks like a gardener's journal. That makes sense. But why did Holly keep it in there?"

"Good question. But let's figure that out in the kitchen. I'm afraid Toby might come back any minute."

Maggie wasn't sure how long they'd been in the office but Dana had a good point. Best to put the room back in order and sort out what they'd found in the kitchen.

Dana slammed the safe door closed, swirled the lock, and slipped the wooden floorboard back into place. With Lucy's help, the rug flopped back into place, and Maggie helped move the armchair.

Not a moment too soon, they suddenly realized. They heard the dogs burst into a fit of barking.

Phoebe had already left the room but suddenly appeared in the doorway again, her eyes wide with alarm. "Hurry up in there. He's coming. I hear him in the kitchen. He must have come in through the back door."

Dana turned off the lamp, and they softly crept up the hallway into the foyer.

"Now what?" Lucy whispered. "We can't just march in there like a chorus line. He'll wonder what we've been up to."

Maggie grabbed her tote bag from the bench near the coat-tree. "We went to get our knitting. Of course."

Dana grabbed her bag, too. "The mere sight of a flock of yakking women and knitting needles should chase him off for the rest of the night."

"The combination is automatic man repellant," Phoebe agreed as she dug her knapsack out from under the pile of coats.

They headed toward the kitchen door, with Maggie in the lead.

Dana stopped. "Wait . . . I have to hide this stuff. I almost forgot." The jewelry case and the pile of letters were tucked under one arm, and she shoved both in her bag. But she still held the journal in her other hand.

"I'll take that. Your bag is already bulging." Maggie slipped the book into her knitting bag and pulled some yarn over it. "Heads up, shoulders square. It's showtime."

They proceeded to the kitchen, and Maggie pushed open the door. She had already met the irascible Toby and braced herself for an ugly confrontation.

But, much to her relief, it seemed that Suzanne had the situation well under control. She stood at the stove, in full charm mode, all dimples and batting eyelashes, as she heated some leftover flatbread slices and listened in rapt attention to Toby, who sat at the table, sipping a beer.

His back was toward the door, and he didn't seem to notice the women slip into the room.

"Wow. You've had it rough, haven't you?" Suzanne said, oozing sympathy. "I know how it is. We all have our war stories. Give me your card. I'll ask around for you."

Toby pulled out his wallet and fumbled for a business card. He turned to glance at the women, and a few cards dropped to the floor. Maggie noticed they all had different logos and information.

Interesting, she thought.

He turned back to Suzanne and dropped a card on the kitchen counter near the stove. "I'm needed around here, the way things are going. But it's always good to have options."

"My motto exactly." Suzanne pulled a pan from the oven, then met the curious glances of her friends. "Hey, gang. Ready to knit?" Her tone was falsely bright, but she'd obviously picked up on their cover.

"Hello, Toby," Dana said. "This is my knitting group. We're having a little get-together. I thought it would be a nice distraction for Rose."

Toby turned to face Dana. His dark gaze narrowed. "I won't be in your way. Just waiting for my pizza to heat up."

"It's flatbread," Maggie quietly corrected, though no one heard her.

Toby must have been scrounging in the fridge for something to eat, Maggie reasoned, and had come up with just a beer. Feeding him the leftovers was preferable to Toby staying in the house to cook himself a meal.

Suzanne slipped the slices on a plate and handed it to him with a flourish. "Enjoy . . . And here's your beer. Hey, take two." He was already holding an open bottle in one hand, and she stuck another in his pocket.

Then she turned to her friends and rubbed her hands together. "Let the stitching begin."

Maggie and the others had already taken seats at the

table and pulled out needles, yarns, and projects, waiting for Toby to get the hint.

"Party on, ladies. Don't get too wild now."

"We'll try not to disturb you," Suzanne replied sweetly.

The back door slammed shut, and they all breathed a sigh of relief.

"Where's Rose?" Maggie asked.

"She took a few of the dogs out for an evening stroll. She should be back soon," Suzanne said.

"I'm glad she missed Toby. He makes her very anxious." Dana had pulled the jewelry case from her knitting bag, along with the letters and bank statements. "All right. Let's get to work. I'll look through the jewelry. I should be able to tell if anything important is missing. Lucy and Suzanne can read the bank statements. You're both good with that sort of thing."

Maggie pulled the clothbound book they'd found in the safe from her knitting bag. "Phoebe and I will study the gardener's journal." Maggie opened the book and glanced at the pages. "It looks like the usual sort of notations about temperature and rainfall, the acid level of the soil, and so on. But there must be some reason she kept it under lock and key."

"What about Holly's letters? Should I start reading them?" Phoebe asked.

"What letters?"

They turned to see Rose. She walked into the kitchen, followed by her three faithful hounds, Wolf, Oreo, and Queenie. She must have come back inside through the front door, Maggie realized.

"We managed to open the safe and found a few things in there. Nothing of huge value, except for the jewelry your mom left to you and Holly," Dana explained. "And there were these letters," she added, picking up the packet.

She glanced at the postmark and the return address on the envelope on top. She looked disturbed by what she'd read. "They're addressed to Holly, but not at this house. In care of a post office box in town," she reported, with a note of surprise. "And now I see who they're from. Jeremy Carlson. While he was in prison."

Rose stepped closer, to see the letters for herself. "Holly wasn't allowed to be in touch with him after the accident. My father would have had a fit if he'd known they were writing to each other."

"Who's Jeremy Carlson?" Lucy asked.

"Holly's boyfriend. Used to be in high school, I mean," Rose replied.

"He was behind the wheel the night Rose was injured," Dana added. Her concerned glance at Rose told Maggie she was worried the conversation might be upsetting, and she didn't want to say more.

Rose was the one who answered unspoken questions. "He and Holly weren't hurt badly, just me. But someone out on the road died. A motorcycle rider. Jeremy went to jail."

"He never went to trial. He plead guilty to manslaughter and driving under the influence. He was sentenced to twenty years, I think."

"Oh my . . . That is a tragic story." Maggie looked around the table. Their productive, "Let's do it" mood had suddenly turned somber.

"My parents didn't like him, but he was always nice to me," Rose said. "He was sweet to Holly. He always made her laugh. She hardly ever does now."

Fifteen years had passed since that tragic night, Dana had once told them. A night that changed the lives of both young women forever. And robbed poor Holly of laughter, Maggie thought.

Dana rested her hand on the letters. "These must be

very personal. Holly might not even want me to read them. I guess it's best if I'm the only one treading on her privacy."

"Yes, I think that's best, too," Lucy said. "You're the only one who will be able to understand the significance of what she has written there, too."

Maggie agreed with that.

Dana tucked the letters back in her knitting bag and started on the jewelry again. She opened the box and took out a satin roll that was tied in the middle. "Why don't you look in here, Maggie. I'll check the rest of the box."

"Will do." Maggie took the jewelry, then noticed Rose was still standing by the table. She slid over to make space. "Why don't you sit with me, Rose. We can help Dana."

Maggie wondered about that, considering the state of Rose's memory. But maybe she could remember the past clearly. It was just the night of the car accident and other deeply traumatic moments that overloaded the circuitry in her nervous system.

Rose seemed pleased by the assignment and pulled up a chair. She lifted a strand of pearls and ran it along her palm. "My mother loved this necklace. I remember helping her with the clasp sometimes. She looked so pretty all dressed up."

Rose's memory made Maggie sad. She glanced at Rose and saw a soft smile of fond recollection, and somehow, that made her sadder.

"Do you ever wear it now?" Maggie asked.

"I can if I want to. Holly and I share the jewelry," she explained. "But we never go anyplace fancy enough to wear it."

Her admission made Maggie smile. "I feel the same about my good jewelry. It's sitting in a safety-deposit vault in the bank."

Dana had been spreading out the rings and necklaces on

a blue velvet cloth she'd found within the jewelry box and suddenly looked up.

"You just reminded me of something, Maggie. You said that on Tuesday morning, Holly told you she was going to the bank, and Rose remembered that night she was counting out a large pile of cash."

"That's what she told me. I sensed she was stressed about the errand."

"It was a thick pile of bills. She put it in a manila envelope," Rose added.

"You told the detective about that," Dana said. "Even if she expected to pay for a delivery on Wednesday, why didn't she put it in the safe overnight?"

"Do you think Toby weaseled his way in there and took it?" Suzanne asked in a harsh whisper, her dark eyes wide.

"Why are you whispering? He can't hear you all the way in the garage." Rose didn't seem to be mocking Suzanne in any way. She just sounded curious. Which made it all the more amusing.

"Suzanne enjoys a little drama," Maggie explained. She glanced at Dana. "What do you think? You said before it didn't look as if he'd gotten into the safe, but maybe this changes things."

Dana didn't answer for a moment. She seemed lost in her thoughts. She looked up suddenly and caught Maggie's gaze.

"I don't think he found the money. He could never keep a secret. I think it would show in some way if he'd ransacked the house and had a big payday."

"He would have treated himself to a night out, a steak dinner at least. Instead of scrounging around here for left-over pizza," Suzanne said.

"It's flatbread . . . Oh, whatever," Maggie sighed. "But that's a good point. And raises an excellent question.

Where's the money she withdrew from the bank? How much was it?"

Lucy had opened the bank statements and shook her head. "These statements won't show that transaction if it just happened on Tuesday. Maybe we can find a checkbook register or something like that."

"There's a drawer full of receipts in the desk," Dana said. "Maybe I can find it in there."

"A woman after my own heart. Receipts are so important," Suzanne insisted. "You never know when one will come in handy."

Suzanne was a champion receipt saver, as everyone knew. A receipt for a cup of coffee and some streusel bites had even provided her with an airtight alibi when the police were on her tail.

"Look for a withdrawal slip. Maybe she saved those separately somewhere," Suzanne advised.

"I'll read these old statements carefully. I'll make a list of any big cash withdrawals. Maybe there are others," Lucy said. "Don't you think the police are doing the same thing, but much faster? Finances are one of the first places Detective Reyes will look in a situation like this."

"I'm sure that's true. But the detective didn't mention any red flags to me. Not yet anyway," Dana said.

Maggie smoothed her hand over the cover of the gardener's journal. "I'll read this tonight and bring it to the shop so you can look at it, too," she told Phoebe.

"I think we should work on our assignments and reconvene tomorrow morning." Suzanne glanced at her watch. "It's getting late. We need to head back to the village soon."

"Good plan. Let's meet up at the shop first thing tomorrow." Maggie handed Dana the jewelry she'd been examining and Dana put it all back in the jewelry box Then stuck the box in her knitting tote, though it didn't fit very well, Maggie noticed. "Rose and I will stop in early on our way to check on Holly."

"How is Holly? Is she making any progress?" Suzanne asked.

"I spoke with the specialist again today. He's hopeful, but her condition is very much status quo. We must wait for her lungs to heal before they can remove the breathing tube and reduce the sedatives. It's hard to see her like that, but I keep reminding myself it's for her own good and at least she survived the fire."

"It could have been worse. A lot worse," Lucy agreed.

"It's been only forty-eight hours," Suzanne reminded them. "Give the woman a chance."

Rose stared down at the table and rubbed her hands together, which was a technique for self-soothing, Maggie had once heard.

She reached over and touched Rose's shoulder. "I'm sure Holly will recover in a few days. She's young and strong and getting wonderful care."

"I agree," Dana said in a decided tone. Whether for Rose's benefit or her own, Maggie was not sure. "The best thing we can do now is hold positive thoughts. And a prayer or two wouldn't hurt, either."

"Not one bit," Maggie agreed.

The dogs in the parlor began to bark, and everyone at the table was instantly alert. "Someone's coming," Rose said. "It must be Toby. I'd better settle the dogs down."

Maggie could see she was frightened of her half brother. That was not good for her at all.

Rose ran to the dog parlor, and Suzanne jumped up from her chair. "Hustle, you guys! Pull out some knitting. Get busy . . . Hide that jewelry box, Dana. I can spot it a mile away."

Dana struggled to hide the box better. She covered the

top with a few skeins of purple yarn from her project, then slipped the bag under the table.

Maggie tried to exchange her knitting and needles for the journal, but the corner of the book got caught on something, and it wouldn't slip down in her bag. As heavy footsteps approached, she yanked it again and sat on it.

As the door swung open, the group was a picture of sedate female companions, each of them wielding knitting needles, with pleasant smiles fixed on their faces.

"Hello, everyone. I didn't know you were having a meeting here tonight."

Maggie released a breath she hadn't even realized she'd been holding. She turned and smiled at Dana's husband, Jack, who had just come in from a long day at work.

Jack was in his mid-fifties, with thick silver hair and warm brown eyes. Maggie knew he was a sharp attorney, but he also very kind and had a way of lightening even the heaviest conversation with a spark of humor. He'd been on the local police force many years before moving to a career as a lawyer. He knew the system well, and his many connections around town kept him informed. Though so far, if he'd offered Dana any inside news about the investigation into the fire and Holly's attack, she had not shared it with her friends.

Which, in Maggie's mind, amounted to the fact that Jack had not heard anything yet.

Dana rose to greet him and kissed him on the cheek. "Just finishing up. Did you have anything to eat tonight?"

"I grabbed something at the office. Don't let me interrupt. I want to visit with Rose a little. Helen Forbes has agreed to represent her. She just sent me a text."

Dana looked happy and relieved, and Maggie felt sure the rest of her friends shared the reaction. "Good news. Thanks so much for reaching out to her, honey."

"Not a problem. I know she'll do a good job. I spoke to Detective Reyes, and this track of the investigation, honing in on Rose, worries me," he admitted. "I'm hoping some new lead pops up and turns them in a different direction."

"The right direction," Maggie added.

"It's so unfair. It makes me so upset," Dana admitted. "Rose had nothing to do with Holly's attack or the fire. We're lucky she wasn't hurt, too. All this so-called evidence, it's totally circumstantial."

"You know what they say, my friends. 'The truth will out.'" Suzanne glanced around the table and patted her knitting bag.

Maggie understood her meaning. Maybe they'd found some new leads in the safe, in the bank statements and the letters. Even the gardener's journal might turn up a clue.

By tomorrow morning they could have some important news to bring to Detective Reyes. Some breakthroughs that no one could have foreseen or imagined.

Chapter 9

Maggie arrived at the shop just before eight on Friday morning. There was a distinct touch of spring in the air, and she loosened her muffler and opened her jacket as she headed up the path. The beds cried out for a spring cleanup. The persistent, green leaves of tulips and daffodils poked through hard, dark soil and clumps of dead leaves.

T. S. Eliot had famously written, "April is the cruelest month." But Maggie did not agree. March seemed far more unkind with its rough winds and bouts of harsh, cold rain. Though not exactly cruel, either.

Unless you were a bulb or a seed, she mused, annoyed at being forced to wake up and grow. One that preferred to stay dormant, buried in the cold, dark earth. She knew that feeling, too, reminded of the contents of the safe and the secrets they may have dug up. Perhaps some that would be better left buried?

Once inside the shop, she hung up her sweater coat and put the coffee up. Then took the gardener's journal from her knitting bag and set it on the worktable.

She'd stayed up very late the night before, sitting in her favorite armchair and studying the notations. She had read the book through at least two times and had even marked a few spots with yellow Post-it Notes.

Charles had gotten up from a sound sleep to fetch her, then had guided her stumbling steps to their bed. A comforting gesture, Maggie had to admit. She'd felt very cared for.

The innocent-looking tome had made for interesting reading, and Maggie had formed a few theories about the cryptic entries.

But once they were together a short time later, Suzanne was the first to speak. "Lucy and I already compared notes," she began. "Holly had some weird spending habits lately."

Lucy jumped in to clarify, leaning forward in her chair. "You gave us statements from the past three years. In the older records, there's the same pattern of income and withdrawals for supplies, payroll, and shipments of plants. Things like that, which she mainly paid for by check," Lucy explained. "The cycle starts this time of year and gradually tapers off around October. Over the winter, she barely spends a dime for the business."

"But this past winter, Holly's been withdrawing big lumps of cash every few weeks from the business account," Suzanne continued. "She even drew a credit line against the property. What was she spending it on?" Suzanne looked around at her friends. "We know it wasn't wild weekends in the Caribbean."

"And it's way too much for dog food," Lucy added. "Even for that pack."

"Interesting," Maggie said. "The timing coordinates with the gardener's journal. I also noticed quirks in her record keeping."

Suzanne had brought a box of mini muffins from the bakery. She claimed that oat bran was healthy, but it looked decadent enough to Maggie. Maggie sliced off a bite and ate it very slowly. She needed a little sugar today to jolt her awake, she rationalized.

"What sort of quirks?" Dana asked. She peered at Maggie over a mug of tea.

"It reads very much like a typical gardening record. At first. But look at the entries for last winter." Maggie flipped the pages to those marked with yellow stickers. "She starts talking about a bug attacking the rosebushes, then notes a remedy, a solution of pesticide, and various dates and amounts she's applied. And keeps complaining she can't get rid of it."

"What's so odd about that? Maybe a bug did attack the roses," Lucy said.

"In November and all through the winter? Roses are attacked in the spring or even the summer. She can't seem to get rid of it, no matter what she tries. 'Pest lingers. Applying stronger remedy twice this month.' And she has some numbers jotted down, which would typically mean the ratio of ingredients in the insecticide, but I think they mean amounts of money."

Lucy quickly flipped through the bank statements, which she held in her lap. "What was the date on that?"

"That was January twentieth, about two months ago," Maggie replied.

Lucy had found the appropriate statement and quickly scanned it. "I do see two withdrawals that month, one on January eleven and another two weeks after." She looked up and met Maggie's gaze. "I think we're getting somewhere."

"I think she was being extorted or blackmailed," Suzanne said. "What else could it be?"

Maggie didn't want to say it aloud, but another possibility came to mind. "An addiction? Gambling, drugs?" She glanced at Dana. "I'm sorry. I don't mean to sound harsh. From the little I know of Holly, I sense that's highly unlikely. But we can't rule it out entirely. Or maybe she was trying to help someone with that sort of problem?"

"I understand. It's only logical to consider those possibilities." Maggie could see Dana was upset, and who wouldn't be? It was a difficult conversation.

"As Suzanne said last night, 'The truth will out.' But sometimes it's not a pretty sight," Phoebe said quietly.

Dana looked troubled. "I'm fairly certain that Holly did not have a drug addiction or a gambling problem. But after reading the letters last night, I have to wonder if she was being blackmailed."

"Why would someone blackmail Holly? What would she have to hide?" Suzanne said.

"Maybe you don't want to tell us. Maybe it's too private." Lucy glanced at the others, her gaze silently urging them to slow down and give Dana some space. Anyone could see this was a very difficult reckoning for her.

Maggie felt the same. She could see her dear friend Dana struggling, torn between sharing the truth she'd discovered and violating Holly's privacy. Which seemed to be the unexpected cost of trying to help her godchild.

Dana released a slow breath and looked up at them. "I will tell you. But it can't go beyond this room. Not yet." She reached out and rested her hand on the packet of letters. "I mentioned last night, Holly was writing to her boyfriend Jeremy Carlson, who was in prison for vehicular manslaughter and driving while intoxicated. There were also mitigating circumstances and grounds for an acquittal. The accident investigation by the police showed that the motorcycle driver had passed the car on a curve and had gone over a double yellow line. The motorcycle driver had some drugs in his system, as well. But Jeremy had an inexperienced lawyer, too, appointed by the court, who didn't defend him very well or even try to cut a deal.

It was clear that the DA was out to make an example of him. The maximum sentence for the crime is fifteen or even twenty years, and I think that's what he got."

Maggie was interested to hear the full story of the accident. Until now those details had not been disclosed. But she did wonder where this was leading.

"The thing is," Dana continued, "even though Holly and Jeremy never say it outright, I can tell that Holly was driving the car the night of the accident, but Jeremy took the blame. They met in the woods a few miles from the house. Holly didn't realize it, but Rose had followed her. Of course, they had to bring Rose home. Jeremy had been drinking, so he gave Holly the keys to his car. The road was dark, and it began to rain . . . You know the rest . . ." Her voice trailed off.

"And since Rose didn't remember anything afterward, they were free to make up their own story?" Maggie asked.

"That's right," Dana said quietly. "I don't want to judge Holly. All these years, hiding this secret . . . The burden must have been overwhelming. When you read the letters, it's clear, she and Jeremy truly loved each other. They had plans to run away together before the end of the summer, to live in New York and study acting."

"While her parents thought she was going to start college in Vermont," Lucy said. Maggie recalled Dana had told them about Holly's intention to attend college. But that seemed to be her parents' plan for her future and not her own.

"That's right. Who knows what would have happened if there hadn't been an accident that night," Dana replied. "But I do understand now why Holly has never dated anyone for very long or been in any serious relationships since."

"She never got over Jeremy." Suzanne tossed her hands

in the air and then picked up another mini muffin. "The guy gave up his life to protect her. If that ain't true love, I don't know what is."

"He was thinking of Rose, too," Dana added. "He knew that George and Ava were overwhelmed by Rose's injuries and talked about a facility for special care. But Holly was fighting to keep Rose at home and had to be free to care for her."

"Maybe he asked Holly to meet him that night, so he blamed himself for the whole thing," Lucy said. "Even if he wasn't driving, he felt responsible."

"That seems to be true, and it shows great character, I think," Dana said.

"He must have been in jail for years. Did she write the whole time?" Lucy asked.

"Not at all. Only for the first few months. He cut off all contact and told her to forget him. He wanted her to live a good life."

"Poor Holly. Poor Jeremy . . . poor Rose," Phoebe sighed.

"And poor Dana," Maggie wanted to add. To discover that someone she held so dear had kept this dark secret to herself all these years . . . Maggie was sure that Dana was not angry with Holly. Nothing like that. But clearly shaken and shocked, and maybe even hurt that Holly had never confided in her.

"This is big, Dana. Especially when you factor in the cash withdrawals from her bank account. Maybe Jeremy got out of jail and wasn't feeling that noble anymore. Maybe he'd grown bitter about all he'd done for the Pipers, and wanted some cash compensation?" Suzanne said around a mouthful of muffin.

Lucy gazed at Dana with a sympathetic expression. "I was thinking the same thing. Do you have any idea if he's been released from prison?"

"I have no idea. I have to look into it," Dana replied.

"I can help. I'll do a search. If he's been released, I can also find out where he ended up," Lucy said.

Lucy was very adept at internet research. They often teased her that she must have been a librarian in a former life.

"Would you? I'm not sure where to start, and if I ask Jack about it, he'll ask me a lot of questions. I'm not sure I'm ready to talk to him about this. He's an officer of the court. Learning that Holly was driving the car and gave false testimony after the accident could create all sorts of problems for him, too."

"Oh dear. That's right. We don't have Jack to help us out on this," Maggie murmured.

"If Jeremy Carlson wasn't extorting money from her, I'm stumped," Suzanne said. "I can't imagine that Holly told anyone. She kept the secret in a safe. How did they figure it out?"

Lucy stood up; she seemed restless. Dana's discovery had disturbed everyone. "I know this sounds far-fetched, but what if Jeremy told someone in prison? A buddy or a cellmate? That person could have tracked down Holly after they got out of jail and been exploiting her."

Dana had been drifting in private thoughts but suddenly looked up. "That doesn't sound far-fetched at all. That could be it."

Suzanne brushed some crumbs from the front of her sweater. Lilac cashmere, with a draped collar, Maggie noticed—a very Suzanne style. "All this talk of ex-cons brings one guy to mind. Mr. Thornton. He could have been pressing Holly anonymously and then decided he wanted a bigger payoff. So he shows up on her doorstep, hangs around a few days, and confronts her."

Maggie squinted as she considered the theory. "I do agree that the blackmailer could have been operating anonymously, and Thornton certainly fits my idea of what a former felon might look like. But why would he go to all the trouble to work at the nursery and try to win her confidence?"

"I'll be the first to admit I didn't like the idea of him working at the nursery," Dana admitted. "But Maggie and I were standing right there when he practically saved Holly's life. Or at least saved her from a very bad accident," Dana reminded them.

Between Dana and Maggie, everyone else had heard about the fallen tree limb and Thornton's quick thinking. Though Maggie still wasn't sure how to interpret the act.

"I know. You told me. But what does that mean? Of course he tried to save her. She was his meal ticket." Suzanne was getting carried away with her emotions, as usual. She still had not learned to control her short fuse. "Who knows what he was scheming by putting boots on the ground at the nursery. Isn't it exactly the sort of creepy thing a stalking, blackmailing ex-con would do? Didn't you ever watch a movie on the Lifetime channel?"

"Calm down, Suzanne... No one wants to argue. We're trying to look at this from all angles," Maggie reminded her.

"I lost it. I'm sorry. My bad." Suzanne pursed her lips, looking repentant. "It's just that my intuition insists Thornton figures into this. I can't put my finger on exactly how, but I'd bet a week of lattes he's in the mix." She picked up another muffin, then put it down again. "And this entire conversation is triggering a carb binge. Will someone please take this box out of my face?"

Phoebe leaned over and moved the box of muffins to the far side of the table. "If you change that bet to a week of chai teas, I might take you up on it."

"Consider it done, sweet pea." Suzanne smiled warmly at her younger friend.

"I can understand the problem with telling Jack," Lucy

said to Dana. "But what about Detective Reyes? You're going to tell her about the letters and the bank withdrawals, aren't you?"

"They've probably noticed the withdrawals already," Suzanne pointed out. "They have had access to Holly's financial records since day one."

"That's true. But the letters certainly supply a logical explanation for what happened to the money," Maggie added.

Dana sat back in the armchair and cradled her mug of tea. Maggie guessed it was cold, and she would have normally jumped up to warm some more water. But she was too riveted by the conversation to be a good hostess.

"Calling Detective Reyes was the first thing I thought of. Now I'm not so sure. What if the police go after Holly? Jeremy Carlson can only gain by clearing his name, and his romantic motive for protecting her may have totally evaporated by now. Even if Holly can't be charged after all this time, the word could get out and her reputation would be ruined."

"It is . . . complicated," Maggie agreed. Dana was caught in a moral dilemma, between the proverbial rock and a hard place if ever there was one.

Lucy had opened Maggie's laptop, which was sitting on the counter, and had been tapping at it for a bit. She glanced at Dana over her shoulder. "The statute of limitations for vehicular manslaughter is six years. Holly can't be charged at this point."

Maggie heard Dana sigh out loud. "That's good news. But what about a civil suit? Or if the charge is upped to murder by the prosecutor? Who can predict what they will do? The young man who died, I forget his name. His family might come forward and sue her for wrongful death."

"Spoken like a woman who's been married to a lawyer for over twenty years," Suzanne noted. "I wouldn't have even thought of that."

"Let's see . . ." They waited while Lucy searched for answers to the questions, typing at a lightning-fast pace. "The time limit for a civil suit has run out, as well." She looked up from the computer. "Though the victim's family might find some other angle that would get Holly into court."

"That's very true. You'd be surprised what some attorneys can come up with," Dana replied. "I just don't know what to do. What if she was being blackmailed, but it's not related at all to what happened Tuesday night? It's a Pandora's box, and Holly is left open to all sorts of new problems. Including Toby's challenge to Rose's guardianship. If—and it's a big one—his challenge ever reaches court, the information that Holly was driving that night could come out and be a black mark that causes her to lose Rose," she said quietly. "Not to mention how she's going to feel about my rummaging through the most private pockets of her life and giving away her darkest secrets."

"Toby . . . I almost forgot about him," Maggie admitted. "His agenda certainly puts another wrinkle in things, doesn't it?"

"Without a doubt." Dana's tone was gravely serious.

"How's that going? Did he really start the legal ball rolling to win guardianship of Rose?" Suzanne asked.

"Jack heard through the grapevine that he hired a lawyer somewhere around here, but no documents have been filed yet. He also heard that Detective Reyes questioned Toby and checked on his whereabouts Tuesday night. He wasn't very far away. Definitely not in Portland, like he told us."

Maggie was encouraged. "So he was in the area on Tuesday night?"

"That's right. Now they need to call him back and confront him with the lie. He must know his return looks suspicious, and wanted to avoid attention. But it is a red flag for the police."

"A big one." Phoebe was the only one who had taken out her knitting, but she suddenly looked up. "Maybe he's been blackmailing her anonymously all this time. It's not hard to imagine that he knows she was the driver. He still lived with the family at the time of the accident. But the blackmail payments were not enough, and he got greedy. He could have lured Holly from the house, attacked her, and set the fire."

"And he has a truckload of motives to want her out of the way, so he can get his hands on the business and the property," Suzanne said. "I see your point now, Dana. If it turns out Toby is behind this, Holly's secret will be exposed, and she's liable to suffer the consequences for no reason."

"That's my problem exactly," Dana sighed, truly torn. "No matter what I decide, to tell the police or not, we can't let Rose know. There's no telling how she might react, and it's certainly not my place to disclose this to her. Holly is the only one who can do that."

"People often say that with great power comes great responsibility. I think it's true about knowledge, too," Maggie said. "This kind of knowledge anyway."

"It appears that our little safecracking moment unleashed more than we bargained for," Lucy said. "Now Dana is left juggling a stick of dynamite."

Dana offered a small smile. "Knitting has made me nimble enough to juggle, I hope. I will say that I'm glad I told all of you. I trust you completely, and you've been very patient, hearing me out."

"Except when some people yelled at you," Suzanne added.

Dana offered her a warm smile. "And offered some excellent insights and advice. And you didn't really yell . . . just spoke very strongly."

"That's what I should tell my kids. 'I'm not screaming. I'm just talking to you strongly.' " Suzanne laughed. "I don't think they'll buy it."

"Patient? We've been on the edge of our seats with this story, Dana," Phoebe replied.

"And we want to help in any way we can," Lucy reminded her.

Maggie noticed the time. It was getting close to nine. Customers usually didn't drift in until half past or even at ten, but there were always a few early birds.

Suzanne's phone buzzed with a call, and she sent it to voice mail. "Wish I could hang out longer, but the exciting world of real estate sales beckons."

She gathered her things and headed to the door. "Let me know if there are any developments. You know how I hate to be left out of the loop."

"We'd never dream of it," Lucy promised.

With a quick wave and her trademark sassy grin, Suzanne was out the door.

"I'd better get going, too," Lucy said, peering out the window at her dogs. "Tink and Wally have been suspiciously well behaved out there."

"Maybe Rose trained them so well the other day, they're turning over a new dog leaf?" Phoebe glanced at Dana. "Where is Rose?"

"Jack took her to the center this morning for her appointments and sessions. I need to see one or two clients in town. Then I'm going to pick her up and bring her to see Holly."

Dana's phone rang, and Maggie saw that it was a call from her husband. She picked it up quickly. "Hi, hon. What's up?" Dana listened a moment, and her fair complexion turned pale as paper. When she finally spoke, her voice stammered. "I can't believe it . . . what awful news. Are they sure?"

Everyone froze in the midst of their movements and sat perfectly still, listening to Dana's side of the conversation.

"Who found her?" she continued, her voice low and trembling. "I see. Yes, tell them I'm on my way. I'll leave right now."

Lucy was the first to speak. "What happened, Dana? What's wrong?"

"Please tell me nothing happened to Rose . . . Or Holly?" Phoebe sounded beside herself at the thought.

Dana had already jumped up, but her knitting tote and purse had slid to the floor. "It's Emily Curtis. It's just awful. Her cleaning service came to her apartment and found her . . . She's dead . . ." Her voice trailed off. She looked frozen and confused.

The news was shocking. Maggie pictured the vital, confident young woman she'd met just a week ago. Young and successful, at the top of her game, it had seemed. It was hard to believe she was no longer among the living. Tomorrow was not promised to anyone. That was true enough.

Maggie pulled herself from her bleak thoughts. Dana needed her attention. She stood up and touched Dana's shoulder. "Don't run off like this. You're too upset."

Dana turned to her. "I'm worried about Rose. She loved Emily. Jack says she's taking it very hard."

"Of course you want to be with her quickly. But Dr. Riley is there and lots of others. She'll be all right." Lucy stood up now, too, and picked up Dana's purse and knitting bag.

"What happened? Did Jack tell you?" Phoebe asked.

"No one knows yet for sure. She died alone, so there

will definitely be an investigation and an autopsy." Dana held her shawl but didn't put it on. Maggie could see she wasn't herself, but she was still determined to get to Rose.

"I'll drive you there," Maggie offered.

Without waiting for Dana to answer, Maggie grabbed her poncho and purse off the counter and fished out her car keys. "Dr. Riley may need your help today. This is very sad news for the entire staff and all the patients. I can keep Rose company. I've grown very fond of her, and I think she's come to trust me."

Dana looked about to speak but then stopped, as if she'd decided not to argue. Lucy helped her on with her shawl and carried Dana's bags. "I'll walk you out, and I'll stop at the Pipers' later and look in on the dogs."

As they climbed into Maggie's car, Dana looked a bit calmer and was grateful for her caring friends. She was usually cool as a cucumber, the super-centered friend whom everyone relied on. But Maggie could see that this time Dana needed their help and support as much as anyone.

Maggie drove as fast as she dared, while Dana used the time to call clients and make new appointments. She also called Dr. Riley and left a message that she was on her way.

"Tim must be beside himself," Dana said. "Everyone must be looking to him for support, and he's lost his right-hand, his best friend, and business partner. His significant other in every sense of the word."

"It must be a great blow," Maggie agreed. She recalled the contentious conversation she'd overheard between the two doctors and wondered if Dr. Riley regretted the way he had treated his friend, business partner and, most likely, his lover, as well. She wondered if they'd ever made up, or if Dr. Curtis had passed away with their relationship left on a bad note. That would be hard for him.

She knew it was an odd turn of thought, but she couldn't help thinking that with Dr. Curtis gone, the way was clear for Dr. Riley to continue his pursuit of Holly, if Holly's main objection had been his entanglement with Dr. Curtis. But when she factored in the lost love revealed in the letters, Maggie had a feeling Holly's rejection of Dr. Riley was rooted in something deeper.

Maybe Holly kept her distance from all men to protect the dark secret in her past. Or maybe it was simply that she'd known real love, and every connection after that had seemed a shadow.

The buildings and grounds at the Riley-Curtis Wellness Center looked exactly the same, but Maggie felt something different in the air compared to her first visit. A sense of heaviness and disruption. The parking lot was nearly empty, and she steered her car into a space near the entrance to the main building. They climbed out of the car quickly. As they approached the big doors, she saw a white sign, its message typed in large letters, taped to the glass:

ALL APPOINTMENTS AND TREATMENT SESSIONS
ARE CANCELED TODAY. PLEASE CALL TO RESCHEDULE.

Dana pushed open the heavy door. The waiting area was empty, as well as the front desk.

"Let's go upstairs. I need to find Rose. I texted her from the car, but the reception is bad out here."

Maggie followed Dana down the hallway. Their footsteps seemed to echo in the silence. The office doors were closed, and Maggie wondered if Dana would start knocking in order to find somebody. Or just shout out loud, "Is anybody here?"

Dana peeked in the office she shared with another therapist, but it was empty. "No luck. Maybe we should try the new building," she said.

Before Maggie could reply, a door swung open. It was

Dr. Curtis's office, Maggie remembered. Though she was certain the esteemed neurologist would not walk out.

Dr. Curtis's assistant, Beth, emerged. She quickly shut the door and locked it, then twisted the knob to be sure it was secure. She held a ring of keys in one hand and a sheaf of files cradled to her chest. She seemed unaware that they were watching. Her head was lowered, and a curtain of fair hair hid her expression.

"Beth," Dana called to her. "We just heard the news. I'm so sorry. You must be shattered."

Beth looked up and started to speak but was overtaken by tears. Dana swept to her side and put an arm around her shoulder.

"I can't believe it. I keep thinking someone is going to tell me it's a huge mistake. Some sort of mix-up or a really awful joke." She was sobbing, her head pressed to Dana's shoulder. Maggie could barely discern her words.

"It's a great shock. I can barely take it in," Dana said, sympathizing.

Beth lifted her head, her face streaked with tears. "I spoke to her last night on the phone. She seemed perfectly fine. She called to let me know a big shot she'd met in Boston agreed to fund the center with a huge donation. It was such good news for everyone. A real victory for her. It makes it even harder to understand why she'd do such a thing."

Dana's gaze turned troubled and confused. "What do you mean? Are you saying she didn't die from natural causes?"

"Please don't repeat it. It was just something I overheard. I was with Dr. Riley when the police came here, and I overheard them talking. The police suspect suicide, from what they've seen so far. Or an unintentional overdose, I think they said. I really don't know why."

Dana's arm slipped from Beth's shoulder, and she took a

step back. "I guess we have to wait to hear more from the police. I agree it's not wise to repeat what you overheard. The police really don't know what happened yet."

Maggie thought so, too. The term *unintentional overdose* echoed in her head. It suggested Dr. Curtis had been abusing drugs. Maggie would have never suspected that, though she'd met the woman only briefly. It was true that doctors were in a high-risk field, with easy access to painkillers and other habit-forming medications.

"They should know what happened soon. An autopsy will take a while, but the police will find out a lot from the postmortem," Dana said.

"That's what they told Dr. Riley."

"How is he doing?" Dana asked quietly.

Beth sighed and shrugged. "It's hard to tell. He didn't faint or cry, or anything like that. He just seems stunned. Of course, he's had to put his feelings aside to support everyone. A few patients who had early appointments were here. We managed to keep the rest away. There was such confusion for a while."

Maggie could imagine how such terrible news had rocked this little world. A world that Dr. Curtis had helped to create.

Her death marked a sea change for Dr. Riley, there was no doubt. He was probably having trouble wrapping his mind around the far-ranging consequences.

"Here he comes. You can ask him yourself." Beth tucked the files tighter to her chest, as if cradling a baby. But Dr. Curtis doubtlessly had piles of sensitive, highly confidential records in her office. Information that needed to be protected and kept private.

Maggie turned and saw Dr. Riley and Rose and Oreo walking toward them. Rose broke into a run when she saw Dana. With Oreo beside her, Rose met Dana halfway down the hall, and they shared a tight hug.

"Aunt Dana . . . did you hear? Dr. Emily is dead. I feel so bad. How can that be? I can't believe I'll never see her again."

"I know, Rose. I feel very sad, too. Heartbroken." Dana hugged Rose again and stroked her hair. She glanced over Rose's shoulder at Dr. Riley.

His complexion was ashen, and deep shadows beneath his eyes added years to his looks.

"Dana . . . I'm glad you're here."

"How are you holding up, Tim?" she replied.

"As well as I can. Which is not too well at all. I keep thinking Emily would be so much better at reassuring everyone right now." He drew in a sharp breath, his eyes growing glossy as he struggled to hold back tears. "I can't understand how this happened. Why didn't I see some sign? Of all people, I should have been able to help her . . ." His words trailed off, and he covered his eyes with his hand.

Maggie wasn't sure what to say, as his grief was so raw. He seemed to blame himself for Emily Curtis's death, even though the question of suicide or accidental overdose had not yet been established.

But perhaps a psychologist would reason there was no such thing as an accident? Especially in a case such as this.

"It's okay, Dr. Tim. You can cry if you need to. We're all very sad now." Rose reached out and patted his shoulder.

"Thank you, Rose. I've spoken only briefly to her family. I don't know if they've made any arrangements yet for a funeral, but I think everyone here, the staff and patients who knew her, should get together next week to honor her memory. Once we've all had time for this dreadful news to sink in." He paused and took a deep breath. "In the meantime, the center will remained closed. There is no replacing her, and no chance of filling the gap she's left in our organization. And in our hearts. I need to figure out how to keep things going without her. She would have wanted her work to continue. I'm sure of that."

His sorrowful words touched Maggie's heart. It was so hard to see anyone struggle as they tried to come to grips with such a loss.

"Give yourself time. It's so much to take in," Dana said. She glanced at Rose. "We'll talk more about this later, Rose. I think we should head home now." She turned to Tim Riley." Unless you need me here a little longer?" Dana asked.

"I'll be fine. But before you go, can we speak a moment, privately?"

"Of course," Dana said. "Let's go in my office."

Dr. Riley glanced at Beth. "Could you wait here for me a minute, Beth? I'd like to go over Emily's contact list. I'm still not sure I've reached everyone who needs to know."

Beth nodded. "Of course."

Dana and Dr. Riley walked toward Dana's office, and Rose turned to Maggie. "Oreo needs some air. We'll wait in front of the building."

Maggie wondered if she should follow Rose or wait for Dana.

But she had a feeling that like her dog, Rose needed some air, and some time alone to sort out her feelings. It was hard to be Rose, Maggie thought, with everyone watching your every reaction and mood, especially when a challenging situation like this arose. Maggie thought the young woman deserved a respectful distance to deal with this loss on her own terms.

Left alone with Beth, Maggie wasn't sure what to say. "I'm very sorry about Dr. Curtis. I met her only once, but she was a very impressive woman. You must have known her very well."

Beth nodded, and her chin trembled. "Emily was amazing. She had a tough side, but she needed to be that way at times to keep this place in order. When she treated a patient, she was the kindest, gentlest, most understanding person you could ever imagine. And brilliant at her work."

"That's what Dana told me. She said that Dr. Curtis was an outstanding therapist and researcher."

"I'm sure. But did she add that Emily let *him* take all the credit?" Beth was clearly angry on her idol's behalf.

"Dr. Riley, you mean?" Maggie asked quietly.

"That's right. Our resident genius, Timothy Riley. If she did kill herself, it's all his fault." She sounded angry, which Maggie knew was a common reaction to such dreadful news. "I don't mean he actually did it with his own bare hands," she added quickly. "But he may as well have, the way he treated her. He drove her to it. She deserved so much better. I don't know why she couldn't see it."

Maggie wasn't sure what to say. Had Emily Curtis's despair over Tim Riley's wandering eye driven her to end her life? In the glimpse she'd had of the couple, Maggie had sensed simmering anger, but not desperation.

Dr. Curtis had also seemed to hold important cards that gave her control of their emotional game. He had certainly rushed to appease her, Maggie recalled.

Then again, they now knew Tim Riley had visited the Pipers several times last weekend, while Dr. Curtis had been away, and had probably tried to romance Holly.

Beth had adored her mentor and was still reeling from the blow. People said a lot of things in that state that they realized later were emotional exaggerations or were simply not true. Maggie reminded herself of that fact. But Beth's accusations were spoken with such conviction that her words were convincing. And troublesome.

Dana and Dr. Riley came out of her office. She met Maggie's glance. "Where's Rose?"

"Oreo needed to go outside. I think she wanted a breath of air, too. She's waiting near the parking lot for us."

Dana nodded. She seemed distracted. She turned and said good-bye to Dr. Riley and Beth, who then headed in the opposite direction. Maggie walked with her to the staircase. She sensed Dana had something to say but didn't want to run the risk of anyone overhearing.

They got to the bottom of the staircase. The entrance area, with its many seats and the front desk, was still silent and empty.

Eerily so, Maggie thought.

Dana turned to her. Her expression revealed that she was excited but at the same time anxious. "I have some news. Rose is starting to remember what happened Tuesday night."

Chapter 10

Maggie stopped in her tracks. She saw Rose through the glass, waiting by the Subaru. "Dr. Riley just told you that? What did he say?"

"Nothing definitive. He was holding a session with Rose and a few other patients this morning. He was sitting in for Dr. Curtis, with Beth's help. At that point, everyone thought that Dr. Curtis was just running late. Rose related a bad dream she had last night," Dana continued. "As she described it, she realized that it wasn't a dream. She was remembering what happened the night of the fire."

Maggie's head spun with questions. "Any significant details?"

"Dr. Riley said it was very vague. But he does feel it's a positive sign. He wants to move slowly so she's not overwhelmed and he doesn't shut down the process. He says her memory is working hard to put the pieces together. But pinning her down right now, pressing her with a lot of questions, might shut the door again."

"As you know, I'm not a doctor. But that explanation make sense to me. Does Dr. Riley plan to tell Detective Reyes that Rose's memory is coming back? Maybe he expects you to tell her?"

"I asked about that. He said I can tell Reyes if I like, but he doesn't think it's a good time to bring the police in. He said it will help Detective Reyes more if we wait a few days and see if the memories become any clearer." Dana glanced at her. "He said there was a drug he could administer that would speed up the process. But I'm wary of that approach. These are strong medications, and they might interfere with her stability. She's worked so hard to get to this point. And I don't think it's right for me to authorize that step. That's something Holly would need to decide."

Maggie sensed that Dana was troubled. This was another piece of potentially important information for Detective Reyes, but there were complications and consequences in sharing it.

"I see his point," Dana continued. "But I think Detective Reyes should be told what's going on. She's smart enough to understand the consequences of pushing Rose too hard too soon. I think she'd make the right decision."

Maggie thought that was true. "Have you heard any word from Helen Forbes about Rose's interview at the police station?"

"Helen is dragging things out," Dana said. "But I'm sure Detective Reyes will put her foot down soon."

"Especially if she hears there's a chance Rose might remember something."

"There's another wrinkle I'm concerned about." Dana pushed open the glass door and waved to Rose, who was still standing next to Maggie's Subaru with Oreo. "Dr. Riley wasn't sure how the shock of Dr. Curtis's death would affect Rose's memory. He said it could go either way. It might submerge recollections about Tuesday night or help bring them forward."

Maggie found that point very interesting. "We'll have to wait and see."

As they walked to the car, Maggie gazed up at the sky. The sun was high, and she felt its warmth on her skin.

Birds swooped between the branches, and a light breeze ruffled her hair.

It didn't seem right that Emily Curtis had died this morning, on such a perfect spring day. It didn't seem right at all.

Once they were in the car and on their way, Dana said, "I guess we need to head back to town and pick up my car." She turned to Rose. "Do you still want to visit Holly? It's all right if you don't feel up to it, Rose."

"I still want to see her. Now more than ever." Losing Emily had frightened Rose, Maggie realized. She must have been wondering if she would lose Holly, too. "I wish Holly could talk to us," she added quietly. "Do you think it will be much longer before she can breathe without the machine and can see that we're there?"

"I don't know, Rose," Dana said honestly. "I haven't spoken to her doctor yet today. There might be some progress."

Maggie sensed Dana's frustration with Holly's condition, too, and saw how she struggled to keep a calm front for Rose's sake.

They drove along in silence for a while. Maggie didn't know what to say. The concerns of the day seemed far too serious to make idle conversation.

They were passing the turnoff for the nursery when Maggie spotted the convenience store and gas station at the crossroads. "The needle is almost on *E*. I'd better stop, or we won't make it to the village," she told the others.

As she pulled over and turned into the station, Dana nudged Maggie with her elbow. "Look, it's Toby."

Maggie followed Dana's gaze and recognized Toby, standing at a set of pumps just ahead She stopped the car and got out to pump the gas. Dana stayed seated but slid down the window when Toby walked over.

"Headed back to the house?" he asked.

"We're on our way to the hospital to see Holly," Dana said.

"Oh, so you heard the news? I wasn't sure if they called you."

"What news?" Dana's tone was sharp. Maggie looked up, careful not to spray gas all over her shoes.

"Her doctor is taking the oxygen tube out today. She's coming off the sedation. They're going to see if she can breathe on her own."

"That's wonderful." Dana sounded both relieved and overjoyed. "I don't understand. Why didn't Dr. Gupta call me?"

Toby shrugged. "I don't know, Aunt Dana. I did stop in to see her the other day and listed myself as the first contact. Being her brother, I am the only real family relation. Maybe that's what happened."

Dana didn't reply.

The tank was only half full, but Maggie was sure that Dana would want to make a beeline to Harbor Hospital. Without sparing Toby a glance, she jammed the fuel nozzle back in place, closed the tank, and jumped behind the steering wheel.

Rose was so excited at the news, she was practically bouncing up and down in the backseat, next to her dog. "I just made a wish that would happen. Isn't that amazing? It really came true."

"So it did," Maggie agreed, sharing her euphoria. "What a coincidence."

"It's not a coincidence, Maggie. It's a real wish," Rose insisted.

Maggie felt duly chastised. "Yes, I think so. I definitely see the difference, too."

Dana turned and cast a loving smile in Rose's direction. "That was a powerful wish, Rose. You love Holly so much. That must be why it came true." She glanced at Maggie.

"I'm going to call Holly's doctor, but let's get over there before Toby, if at all possible."

"I know a back route. We'll arrive in no time. Hopefully, he'll sit in traffic on the highway."

Maggie pressed her foot to the gas as hard as she dared, and focused on the road signs. There were a few tricky turns along this back route, and she needed to watch carefully so she wouldn't miss them. She smiled to herself, feeling like the getaway driver in a movie about bank robbers. Though it wasn't really getaway driving . . . more of a get-to situation. Either way, she was determined to beat Toby to Holly's bedside. They needed to be there to rally around her, to give her love and encouragement. Who knew what Toby Nash's intentions were?

A short time later, they exited the hospital elevator on Holly's floor and headed to her room. Holly's doctor was just leaving and met them outside the doorway.

"How is she doing?" Dana asked. "Did you take the breathing tube out yet?"

"We just completed the procedure. She is able to breathe on her own and is mostly awake and aware. It will take time for the sedation to wear off completely. We need to watch her closely, to make sure her respiration remains stable." He offered a small smile. "But you can visit for a little while. Just don't let her talk too much. Her throat is still very irritated. She really needs to rest."

"Thank you, Doctor. We won't overdo it." Dana paused before entering the room. "Did you tell her what happened to her, Doctor? About the assault and the fire?"

Dr. Gupta shook his head. "Very little. Only that she had been injured and was being treated for smoke inhalation. I thought it would be best to let a family member tell her the details. Once she's alert enough to understand."

Dana nodded and let Rose lead the way into Holly's room. Sunlight filtered through half-drawn shades. Holly, free of the heavy plastic mask that had covered her face, was raised up in the bed. She lifted one hand and offered them a smile.

There were still tubes and wires trailing from her body in all directions, and machines around her beeping and buzzing. Rose ran to her bedside, then leaned over and did her best to gently hug her older sister.

Rose was crying. *But happy tears*, Maggie thought. She felt a little misty herself, watching their reunion.

"Holly . . . you woke up. We were waiting and waiting. We came every day to see you. I love you so much. I kept wishing and even said some of the prayers Dad taught us."

"Rose . . . sweetheart . . . don't cry." With her free hand, Holly managed to pat Rose's back. Her words were thick and slow. "It's all right now. Please don't worry."

Dana walked to the other side of the bed. She also looked tearful and took Holly's other hand. "It's so good to see you awake, honey. I can't tell you."

"The doctor said I was in a fire, but I wasn't burned."

Dana shook her head. "No, thank heaven. You got out in time, somehow. You were unconscious when the firemen found you. Someone knocked you out and set the greenhouse on fire. It appears your assailant also drugged you, so you wouldn't wake up."

Before Holly could answer, Rose called out from the other side of the bed, "They think I hurt you, Holly. They think I set the fire. You know it wasn't me, right? I could never do that. You know that . . . I'd hurt myself first instead . . ."

Rose's distress was building. She sat down on the chair next to Holly's bed, put her head down and hid her face with her hands. Her body started to tremble. Maggie felt concerned, and she could see that Dana was, too.

But Holly's touch and her calm, though choked words quickly soothed her younger sister. "Of course you didn't,

Rose. I know it wasn't you." Reaching as far as she could, Holly touched Rose's long hair and cheek.

"Do you know who did it?" Dana asked quietly.

Holly didn't answer. Maggie wondered if she had heard Dana's question or perhaps was having trouble speaking.

The other night, they had more or less determined that Holly was being pressed for money by someone who knew her secret and that the blackmailer had attacked her. Was she about to give up that person's identity?

"It was very dark. Someone came up behind me," she replied in a halting, raspy tone.

So, she didn't actually see her attacker. Maggie's heart fell. That statement wouldn't rule out Rose for the police.

"Why did you go out to the greenhouse at that hour? Did you see the fire starting?" Dana asked.

Once again, there was a long silent pause before Holly answered. She took a ragged, wheezing breath.

"Maybe we should get a pad and pencil," Maggie suggested, concerned that Holly was getting tired and was even feeling some discomfort.

Holly raised her hand and seemed to gather her strength. "I had to check the thermostat. For the new plants. Was a cold night," she managed to say.

It had been chilly Tuesday night. The temperature had dropped considerably compared to the day, Maggie recalled. Still, she wondered if Holly had really gone out to meet her blackmailer, as they had theorized, and was reluctant to admit that, even to Dana.

"You're still groggy. The doctor said you shouldn't talk too much," Dana sounded concerned.

Holly nodded. She glanced at Rose, who had sat up and wiped her eyes. Holly softly smiled and touched Rose's hand again; the contact seemed a great comfort for both of them. "Rose . . . are you all right?"

"I'm fine. Aunt Dana and Uncle Jack are staying with me. But Toby came back. He's coming here to see you."

"Toby? What's he doing around here?" Holly struggled to sit up higher, and Dana softly touched her shoulder.

"Don't fret, sweetheart. It's fine. Please . . ."

It was too late. Holly began to gasp and pressed her hand to her chest. Her eyes were wide with alarm; she couldn't speak and seemed to be choking. The lines on the screens around her bed shot up and down in urgent zigzags, and low but insistent bells sounded.

Maggie ran to the door. "I'll get a nurse."

But the alert staff had already noticed Holly's distress at their station, and two nurses and Dr. Gupta rushed into the room.

"We'll take care of her. We need you to wait outside, please," a nurse said.

Maggie followed Dana and Rose into the hallway. The nurse shut the door to Holly's room and pulled the shades.

Rose looked shaken. Maggie guessed she blamed herself.

"It wasn't your fault, Rose," Dana said quickly. "I was just about to mention Toby, too. They'll give her more oxygen and some medication, and she'll need to rest quietly. She needs to heal."

Rose nodded but still looked worried. Maggie bet that she was wishing she had one of her dogs with her right now. Some hospitals did allow therapy dogs to visit patients. Perhaps when Holly was further along with her recovery, Oreo could visit.

I should mention that to Rose later, to cheer her up, Maggie thought.

They found a row of chairs along the hallway, not far from Holly's door, and waited for some news. Maggie had her knitting with her, but she didn't feel inclined to take it out, which was a rare moment, she realized.

Rose was rubbing her hands together nervously, and Dana gently took one in her own.

"Look . . . There he is. He's coming," Rose sounded alarmed.

Maggie turned her head to look down the hall. Toby was walking briskly toward them.

"How did you get here so fast?" He hovered over Dana and stared down at her.

"Holly isn't allowed to see visitors right now," Dana replied.

"Oh . . . she didn't wake up, after all?"

"The breathing apparatus has been removed, and she did speak to us for a short time. But she was struggling to breathe, and her doctor is taking care of her now."

Toby was obviously annoyed. He looked at Dana as if it was her fault.

Ironic, Maggie thought, since the mere mention of his name had sent poor Holly into a coughing spasm.

"If she can't see visitors, what are you still doing here?"

His gaze swept over them again. Rose stared down at the floor. Dana still held her hand, even firmer now.

"I'm waiting to speak to her doctor," Dana said evenly. "I don't know what you told the staff, but I'm still Holly's medical proxy. I can show you the proof. Perhaps you want to challenge that in court, too?"

Toby's gaze narrowed. Maggie wondered what he'd say next. She gave Dana full marks for asserting herself and leaning in, which seemed to be the only thing a bully like Toby could understand.

"I want to talk to the doctor myself. I'm still her brother."

Half brother, Maggie silently corrected.

"There's no law against that, right?" His jaw set at an angry angle.

He took a seat a few spaces down from Maggie. He sat back and crossed his arms over his chest. Maggie heard a crunching sound. She turned her head a bit and peeked at him. She noticed a thick envelope tucked in the deep front pocket of his cold-weather jacket. She wondered what was in it and why he had taken it into the hospital, when he could have left it in his car.

Dana didn't answer. She stared straight ahead and took out her phone. Maggie noticed that she was texting Lucy and asking her to look in on the dogs soon. That was a good idea. They might be here a while longer.

A doctor dressed in green scrubs emerged from Holly's room. His badge said RN–ICU, and Maggie had to scold herself for her gender stereotyping. He was a nurse.

Dana was the first to jump up from her seat. "What happened? Is Holly all right?"

"Ms. Piper is stable, but she needs to rest. She shouldn't speak or have any more visitors until tomorrow."

Toby had also sprung from his seat. "I'm Holly's brother. Can't I just look in on her a second? You let these ladies go in."

The nurse considered the request. "Of course, sir. Come with me." He led Toby to the large windows that framed Holly's room. The shades had been pulled up again so that the staff at the nursing station had a clear view.

Dr. Gupta and other staff stood on either side of the bed, working on the machines and making Holly comfortable. Holly lay with her eyes closed and an oxygen mask over her nose and mouth again.

"We've given her something to help her sleep," the nurse explained. "Nothing like the heavy sedatives she had before. But she needs complete rest. Her body has to get used to breathing on its own again. She remains at risk for cardiac arrest."

Maggie didn't like that the sound of that, but doctors and nurses were obliged to disclose the worst possible scenario, she reminded herself.

Toby looked frustrated, but Maggie doubted it wasn't out of concern for Holly. He'd waited ten years to visit. His own thwarted intentions and schemes, whatever they might be, were likely the real source of his ire.

"Well?" He stared at Dana. "The doctor said we should go. All of us. No one can see her right now."

"I heard him. Maybe we'll see you later at the house." Dana's polite tone masked her true feelings well, Maggie thought. She was sure Dana hoped they would not see Toby for the rest of the night. She'd known her dear friend long enough to recognize that fire in her eyes.

Toby turned and stalked back to the elevator. Maggie heard Rose sigh.

"I hope he doesn't get home before us. What if he hurts the dogs or lets them loose again, just out of spite? I don't understand why he hates them so much."

Dana touched Rose's shoulder. "I sent Lucy a text. She's going over right now. She doesn't live far. She'll definitely get there before him."

Maggie felt relieved to hear that. Toby had looked to be in a terrible temper. No telling how he might express it. But Maggie guessed Toby had a fearsome temper and doubted he knew how to control it.

His undisguised loathing of Rose's furry friends was curious, too. Had he been bitten by a dog in his childhood? That might explain it. Whatever the reason, the feelings seemed to be mutual; the dogs clearly disliked and distrusted him, too.

They peeked at Holly one last time, and Rose blew her a kiss through the window.

"I'll call her nurse later and see how she's doing," Dana said as they headed for the elevator. "This is just a setback. Overall, she's definitely improved. We'll visit first thing tomorrow. She might be able to talk again."

From the tone in her voice, Maggie felt Dana was trying to convince and console herself as well as Rose. Maggie sent up a silent prayer for Holly, that she'd rebound by tomorrow and speak to them again. How much easier it would be for everyone involved.

When they arrived at the Pipers' house, Maggie saw Lucy's white Jeep parked near the back of the house and Toby's dusty black sports car in the driveway. Blocking it, she'd have to say, so her only choice was to turn her car and park on the grass, next to the drive, or she would be blocking him. The lights were on in the apartment above the garage, and she wondered if he had tried to make conversation with Lucy.

"Lucy's still here," Maggie said as they got out of the car. "I think I hear her in the yard, with the dogs."

Dana nodded. "Good. Let's tell her that we're back."

She fell into step beside Maggie as they headed for the path that led behind the house, and Rose ran ahead.

"Toby's back, too, I see," Dana remarked. "I hope he doesn't drop by tonight."

"He probably has his own stock of beer and food up in that apartment by now, don't you think?" Maggie replied.

As they walked by Toby's car, Maggie noticed a large manila envelope on the passenger-side front seat. A distinct crease down the middle suggested it was the same one she'd spotted crammed in his coat pocket. Perhaps it had fallen out or he'd forgotten it there. She paused and leaned over to get a better look.

Dana turned and backtracked a few steps. "What are you looking at in there? Mounds of fast-food wrappers and empty soda cups?"

"That too. Mainly, that envelope on the front seat. See it? I noticed that Toby was carrying one just like it when he came to the hospital." Maggie looked up at her. "It has his name written on it, but no postmark or stamps. There is a return address typed or stamped in the corner. I can't make it out. Can you?"

"I can try. Though it's getting dark out here. Not much light." The package had definitely captured Dana's interest. She put on her reading glasses and leaned closer, then took out her cell phone to use the flashlight. "Watch his windows. Let me know if he looks outside."

"Good point." Maggie stepped into the long shadows close to the house and fixed her gaze on the windows of the garage apartment, yellow squares of light, with shades drawn down low. A shadow crossed the middle window at one point, but luckily, Toby did not peer out.

"What are you doing?" she whispered to Dana.

"I can't make it out. Maybe if I take a picture with my phone, we can enlarge it and see what is says."

"Very clever," Maggie whispered back. She heard the click of the phone as Dana took a few photos and then Dana's quick, light step as she walked toward Maggie.

"I don't know if this will work, but it's worth a try. It looked distinctly legal, and that worries me."

The observation worried Maggie, too. From what she'd seen and heard, Toby seemed capable of anything. He was a desperate man. You could see it in his eyes and even smell it on him. Well, the dogs probably could, Maggie reasoned. Maybe that was why they disliked him so much.

The sight of Lucy and Rose in the mini dog park quickly dispelled her gloomy thoughts. The dogs raced and scampered around, leaping and dodging each other and their mistresses. Laughter floated above the sound of pounding paws and joyful barks. Behind a fringe of trees, the sun slipped into a pile of rose- and lavender-colored clouds, casting one last blast of golden light over the stretch of open fields around the Pipers' house.

Maggie took a deep, calming breath. She could smell the damp, cold river just beyond the woods. An invisible but powerful and important neighbor.

It had been a difficult day. It helped to take a moment to pause and regroup. All the excitement about Holly's recovery had pushed aside the shocking news about poor Emily Curtis. Maggie closed her eyes, offering a silent moment of respect.

"Are you all right?" Dana asked quietly.

Maggie's eyes opened. "Fine. Just thinking. It's a beautiful sunset. It takes you out of yourself for a few moments."

"Yes, it does. If you let it," Dana agreed. "I hope the pink clouds forecast not only good weather but also a better day tomorrow, for everyone."

Rose led her dogs back into the house as an off-leash pack, and Lucy had her two, Tink and Wally, on leads. She jogged over to Maggie and Dana. Her cheeks were rosy from the weather and exercise, and her eyes were bright. "I need to talk Matt into bringing more rescues home. They're so much fun. Dogs really know how to have a good time."

"Don't they?" Dana agreed. "It cheered me up just to watch them. I'm not sure what we're doing for dinner, Lucy. But you're welcome to stay."

"I'd love to. Matt took Dara on a Girl Scout trip to Philadelphia this weekend. They won't be back until Sunday." Dara was Matt's daughter from his first marriage. Lucy adored her, and they spent a lot of time together. Lucy had even taught Dara how to knit this past winter and brought her to the shop. She never minded when Matt and Dara had one-on-one Dad time. She actively encouraged it.

"As for dinner, I know you've all had a long day, so I

brought a surprise—pasta primavera with spring vegetables. I even found some fresh pesto in the freezer. Totally vegetarian," Lucy added, glancing at Dana.

"Bless you, Lucy. I'm so hungry, I'd eat a burger and fries right now."

"I doubt that," Maggie replied. "But at least you don't have to. That was very thoughtful of you, Lucy."

Lucy shrugged. "Or a clever way to wrangle an invitation. And I was in the mood to slack off with work. I have a deadline but ended up surfing the internet today. I found a few articles about the car accident. I want to show them to you."

Maggie caught Lucy's glance as she stepped through the back door and entered the house. But she didn't reply. Rose was in the mudroom, tending to Bella and her puppies. Maggie stood stone still as the yipping little pack romped toward her, then circled her feet and ankles.

"Oh, sorry . . . They got past their gate. Don't let them get away." Rose ran toward her and scooped up puppies with both arms.

Maggie bent down and grabbed the closest one, a little round ball of brown fluff, with a black nose and golden marks on her eyes and muzzle. The little dog was surprisingly strong, and she held on with both hands, then finally hugged it to her chest. She stared down into its bright brown eyes, and it stared back up. Then the pup stretched her head up and licked Maggie's nose.

"My goodness . . ." Maggie pulled her head back with surprise. "You little sprite."

Lucy laughed at her. "I don't know, Mag. I think, you just kissed a dog, and you liked it."

Maggie caught her gaze. She wasn't sure what to say. She had to hug the little dog closer so it wouldn't squirm away. She felt its soft, warm body pressed to her chest like a baby. A fur baby.

The puppy tipped its head up again and licked her chin. "She must be hungry. She'd probably lick anybody right now."

Rose took the pup and set it behind the baby gate. But it didn't run to play with its brothers and sisters. It spun around, then sat and stared up at Maggie. At least Maggie felt as if the puppy was staring at her.

"Dogs know who they like, Maggie. We don't choose them. They choose us," Rose said.

Maggie didn't know what to say to that. "Can I help you get the dinner out, Lucy? Set the table or make a salad?" She turned to Dana, who was emptying the dishwasher. "Should we wait for Jack?"

"Jack is in Chicago by now. He's being honored by some law association, and he's the keynote speaker. He offered to skip it, but I told him to go," Dana explained. "I'll be fine here with Rose. There's nothing to worry about. Especially since Holly is coming along."

"Of course not," Maggie replied with a halting smile. She wasn't sure that was true. The arsonist who had attacked Holly was still out there somewhere—possibly watching TV and drinking beer in the apartment above the garage. But she didn't want to air her anxiety and frighten Rose.

"I'll stay with you." Lucy turned from the stove, where she was carefully sprinkling grated cheese over the pan of pasta. "The dogs are having a fine time. Tink even asked if there was going to be a sleepover."

Rose laughed. "She asked me, too. Can they stay, Aunt Dana?"

Dana rolled her eyes a bit. "As long as all the dogs are getting along and they go to sleep at a decent time." Maggie knew she was teasing, but she wasn't sure Rose did. "We'd love to have you, Lucy. And Tink and Wally."

Lucy carried the pasta to the table. "Great. That's settled, then. I don't mind some alone time this weekend, but I'd much rather hang out here with all of you tonight."

Rose had set the table, and Maggie had put together a quick salad. Lucy was a very good cook, though she was modest about her efforts. She'd gotten more practice after Matt moved in. In her single days she was likely to exist on scrambled eggs and toast, her go-to meal for breakfast, lunch, and dinner. That, and cottage cheese and sliced apples and cinnamon.

The day had been overloaded with difficult moments. Maggie noticed Dana making a conscious effort to keep the conversation light, and Maggie did, as well. Their talk circled mostly around dog training and care. Lucy was impressed with Rose's dogs, who were so calm and, obedient even off leash. Rose barely needed to say a word.

Maggie found herself asking a lot of questions about the puppies. *Just to keep the dinner talk light*, she told herself. *It's not as if I'm really interested.*

"The litter is getting more active. But they can't leave Bella for three more weeks."

"Because they need to nurse?" Maggie asked.

"Yes, and learn dog things. Bella is a good mother. She's teaching them how to behave," Rose replied. "I already have a list of people who want to adopt them. There won't be any problem finding good homes."

"I'm sure you do. Especially that pup who kissed Maggie." Lucy glanced Maggie. "Isn't she adorable?"

"Completely," Maggie agreed. "She'll be the first to go." Taken in by a nice family with children, who will have a lot of time for her. Not by a half-retired couple ambivalent about dogs.

What was she thinking? She didn't want a dog. Way too much responsibility and commitment. Charles wanted to go to Egypt, for goodness' sakes. They couldn't be tied down with a dog right now.

Where had this crazy train of thought come from? She looked across the table at Lucy, who met her gaze with a smug smile.

The table was cleared, and Lucy put up water for tea. "I even have dessert. Peanut butter cookies. Should we do some knitting?"

"You know I'd never refuse that suggestion," Maggie said. She had a knitting bag in the car, as usual, and wondered if Dana had brought any projects with her. *Probably*, she reasoned, since she'd been staying at the house this week.

"I'd love that," Dana replied as she finished checking her messages. "I can definitely use the distraction." When she lifted her head, she looked distressed. "Helen Forbes called. She can't dodge Detective Reyes any longer. The detective wants a statement from Rose tomorrow. Helen said we can fend off the request for fingerprints. For now, at least."

Dana's news cast a shadow over the mood. Rose had gone to the front parlor to check the dogs and hadn't heard. Maggie was grateful for that.

"Do you think Detective Reyes would come here to take an official statement? She did an interview at Maggie's shop," Lucy pointed out.

"Helen proposed the idea, but it was rebuffed. Not a good sign. The police obviously want the home-field advantage, the oppressive, frightening atmosphere of an interview room."

Maggie understood that, and it deeply concerned her. "Hate to say it, but I was cornered like that once myself. Even with a sharp attorney present, one is liable to make a totally innocent statement that gets twisted in more directions than a balloon butterfly at a children's birthday party."

Dana met her glance, her expression wary. "I can just

imagine what Rose might say, especially once she's stressed. She's so forthcoming and guileless. She's just not equipped with the usual filters."

"Maybe if you tell Detective Reyes that Holly is improving and might be able to speak to her soon, that will buy more time for Rose." Maggie wasn't sure it would fend her off, but it was worth a try.

Dana seemed to think so, too. "Good idea. Helen doesn't know yet that we hold that card. I'd better call Helen first and see how we should play it."

"Has Detective Reyes talked to Toby yet?" Lucy brought a pile of her home-baked cookies to the table, along with the teapot and some cups. "And what about Thornton? Have they found him or any sign of the man?"

"I don't know. And I don't think the detective will tell me, either. Helen might have squeezed it out of her. I'm going to ask."

"I have a feeling Mr. Thornton has disappeared into thin air. Or maybe a puff of smoke," Maggie said. She recalled the stormy night he'd appeared at the Pipers' front door, as if he'd materialized in a sizzling crack of lightning.

"He didn't show up in an internet search, either," Lucy reported. "Of course, I found people with the same name, but none fit his age and description. The search on Toby, however, was well worth the twenty-nine dollars. He's been arrested for passing bad checks and has a ton of legal problems from an online business that was closed by court order. Looked like a scam to me. He's also declared bankruptcy. I'm sure the police have found all that out, too. I've printed the information, if you want to read it." Lucy had brought her knitting bag into the kitchen and now searched around inside it for the pages.

"I'm not surprised," Maggie said. "But poor character and bad judgment still don't mean he tried to kill Holly.

The police need substantial evidence to make a case against him."

"I assume Detective Reyes called him back for more questions. But I agree, just being in proximity isn't nearly enough. There needs to be physical evidence tying him to the scene. The type of evidence they think they have on Rose." Dana stood in the doorway, about to head to a more private spot for her phone calls. "Which reminds me. I didn't check out that photo of the envelope yet. Let's take a look when I come back."

Dana left the kitchen and headed for Holly's office, and Maggie explained to Lucy about the envelope she'd spotted.

"It could be nothing. A piece of junk mail. But it does seem official. I just have a feeling about it."

"If you have a feeling, I think we should check it out."

"What a nice compliment." The tea had steeped, and Maggie poured herself a cup. Peppermint, her favorite.

When Dana returned to the kitchen a few minutes later, Maggie could tell she had news. She sat at the table and spoke in a low tone. "Rose is coming back in a minute. I'll make this quick. Helen heard that Toby was questioned again. His whereabouts Tuesday night don't rule out the possibility that he came here and set the fire. He checked into a motel in Peabody around six. He claims he stayed in his room all night and has some charges on the pay-per-view."

Maggie could just imagine Toby's taste in films while alone in a motel room. She didn't want to dwell on it. "That doesn't prove anything. He could have easily left the TV on, driven out to the nursery and set the fire, then returned to the motel without anyone noticing."

"That's exactly what I said," Dana replied. "Helen agreed. She said Detective Reyes isn't stupid. She knows how long it takes to get from A to B."

Lucy leaned closer to whisper a reply. "There are probably security cameras in the motel parking lot. The video would show if his car had been driven in and out during the night."

"Helen doesn't know if the police checked that yet, but they have looked at video from that gas station at the crossroads near this house. The one we stopped at for gas today. Toby's car was spotted on Tuesday night's recording, around eight. About two hours before the fire started."

"Have they asked him about that?" Maggie asked.

"Helen doesn't think so. She suggested the police might be gathering more information before they pull him in again. Which is good news for us. It does take attention off of Rose." Dana looked relieved to add that, and Maggie felt the same. "But I don't want Rose to hear about this. I don't want her to feel frightened with Toby in such close proximity."

"What about your proximity?" Maggie asked. "Doesn't that count?"

"I can take care of myself. And I have Lucy to protect me," Dana replied with a grin. Her expression grew suddenly serious. "I am glad you're staying, Lucy. Sometimes at night I feel as if someone is out there watching the house. It's the strangest thing," she added quietly. She rubbed her arms, as if feeling a sudden chill. "Probably just nerves and paranoia."

"Toby, you mean?" Maggie asked.

Dana shook her head. "No, not Toby. He's definitely snoring away over the garage, dreaming up his nasty plans. I feel like someone's just beyond view, watching us. I get up at night and peer out the windows, but I don't see a thing."

"Do the dogs bark?" Lucy asked.

"Not really. But the other night, Rose's big dog, Wolf, followed me from window to window. At one point, he did growl a bit, and the hair went up on the back of his neck." Dana sighed. "He could have heard an animal. Maybe a raccoon or a skunk? Jack thinks I'm crazy, but I can't help it. Totally irrational, right?" she asked with a light laugh.

"Irrational" was Dana's idea of hurling a stinging insult at herself.

Lucy touched her hand. "You've been through so much the past few days, Dana. You're allowed to be a little loopy once in a while. Maybe that's a good thing."

Maggie met Dana's gaze with a fond smile. "We won't tell anybody. Promise." She thought a moment. "Speaking of paranoia, let's check the photo and find out if I'm acting paranoid and irrational, too."

"Right. I nearly forgot." Dana took out her phone and found the photo of the envelope. She stretched the image with her fingertips as far as it would go and moved it around the screen so that the return address was in the middle of the frame. She peered at it through her reading glasses. "I can read it now. At least the first two words on the top line and part of the address. But that's plenty."

"What does it say?"

"McClennan, Hoyt and . . . Can't see the last name, but I know that it's Dooley. It's a law office in Newburyport. Rivals with Jack's firm. They specialize in trusts. And breaking them."

"That blows the junk-mail theory." Lucy glanced at Maggie.

"It does," Maggie agreed. "And it raises more questions than it answers, unfortunately. He's up to something."

"As if there was any doubt about that," Dana noted. "If only we could see what's in there, we'd know his plan. I'd bet anything he keeps his car locked."

"We should check, just to make sure," Lucy said. "But I don't know how we'd break in if it is locked. All kinds of alarms will probably go off. I bet it's not half as easy as they make it look in the movies."

"In the old days, you could open a locked car with a coat hanger. Car locks are impossible to open that way anymore," Maggie mused.

"We need the keys, no question. I can't see how that could ever happen." Dana sounded discouraged.

"We could sneak into the apartment while he's asleep and borrow them for a while," Lucy suggested. "If we could find an extra key to the apartment somewhere. Maybe Rose knows where it is."

"Too risky. He's liable to wake up," Dana said. "He'd probably have us all arrested for breaking and entering."

"That would be his style." Maggie sipped her tea, considering the problem. "We have to talk him into giving us the car keys."

"Why would he do that?" Lucy looked doubtful.

Maggie shrugged. "There must be some reason we can think of."

"Maybe it's enough that we saw the name of the law firm he's dealing with," Dana said. "He's obviously trying to worm his way into the estate Holly and Rose have inherited from their father."

"Obviously. But how? Did his attorneys find some loophole in the will finally? Does it have to do with Holly being in the hospital? To be forewarned is to be forearmed," Maggie reminded Dana. "And I do have an idea."

Rose walked into the kitchen and found them huddled at the table. Maggie could see from her expression it was an odd sight.

"What are you doing?" she asked.

"We're going to play a joke on Toby," Maggie replied in a cheerful tone. "You and the dogs can help."

Chapter 11

"It's a simple plan," Maggie explained. "I've parked on the border of grass along the drive, and I noticed that it slopes down into some tall grass and bushes. It's very muddy down there, too, with all the rain lately. I'm going to let my car roll down the slope, until it looks as if it's stuck. Then I'll tell Toby I'm such a silly woman driver, I thought I had the car in reverse, and it was in drive, and my, my, it's stuck in the mud." Maggie fluttered her lashes and shook her head, her brown and gray curls bouncing. "I'll tell him a tow truck is coming, and we need to move his car out of the way so that the tow truck can maneuver . . . How's that sound?"

"Brilliant. But I hope your car doesn't really get stuck," Lucy replied.

"I hope not, too. It does well in the snow. I'm counting on that." Maggie thought the odds of needing a tow for real after this stunt seemed about fifty-fifty, but it was worth the gamble.

"I think it's a good plan. But what if he doesn't trust us and wants to move it himself?" Dana said.

"I thought of that. Which is where Rose comes in." Maggie turned to her. "You need to take a bunch of dogs outside, your best barkers, and let them make enough of a racket to scare Toby into staying inside. I'm sure he'll look outside to check my story. When you see the blinds move, can you start them howling?"

"Very easily." Rose smiled, looking eager to do her part.

"Good."

Toby was afraid of the dogs, their ace in the hole. He felt vulnerable around them, Maggie had decided, though he tried to hide his fear with anger and aggression.

"What should Dana and I do?" Lucy asked. "Do you want me to ask him for the keys, while you stay in the driveway and keep things on track?"

Maggie zipped up her jacket and looked at Dana. "Grab some flashlights from the mudroom and act upset on my behalf about the car," Maggie instructed. "I think Dana should speed-read whatever's in that envelope. She's the most fluent in legalese."

Dana met her glance and nodded. "It's a better scheme than I could cook up. We have nothing to lose by trying."

"Nothing at all. Except for Maggie's front axle," Lucy said quietly.

Maggie gritted her teeth. "I hadn't thought of that. I'll drive very slowly and make sure the slope is clear of rocks."

Just before they left the kitchen, Maggie slipped a dull-edged knife off the table and into her pocket.

"What's that for? Self-defense?" Dana asked with a smile.

"Heavens no. This is for you, to use as a letter opener if the envelope is sealed shut. Maybe you should look for some glue in the mudroom. If you need to break the seal, you can glue it shut again."

"Good point. He might notice anyway," Dana said. "We'll have to deal with the consequences when they come, I guess."

"Let's hope the envelope is open," Lucy said. "Positive thinking, everyone."

They found their jackets in the hall, while Rose gath-

ered a group of her most vocal hounds from the dog parlor, then headed outside. Maggie carefully guided her car
over the shoulder of the gravel drive and then bumped
along down a short slope of grass and into a muddy patch
of weeds and bushes.

She hit the accelerator to test if the car was really stuck,
and the wheels spun. She turned to Lucy, who had jumped
into the passenger seat at the last minute to offer moral
support.

"No offense, but your perfectionist tendencies aren't always a good thing," Lucy reminded her.

"No offense taken. And we can't worry about that now."

Maggie climbed out of the car and stepped carefully on
the soft earth as Lucy did the same.

"On to step two. Wish me luck," she whispered.

"Maybe I should come with you?" Lucy said.

"Heaven's no. You're much too . . . cute. He's liable to
get all manly and try to rescue a damsel in distress. Older
women like me are practically invisible. He'll be annoyed
to simply acknowledge my existence."

Lucy looked hurt. "I hope that's not a dumb blonde
joke."

"Hardly. No one would ever slight your IQ . . . And
you're not really that blond, either. More of a tawny shade?"

"I agree," Dana said. "Too risky. And by the way, you're
still plenty cute, Maggie," she quickly added.

Maggie smiled. "In my own market, I guess."

Rose stood by Toby's car, a large group of dogs circling
around her. Quiet now, though Maggie didn't doubt
they'd do their part. "If you don't come back quickly, we'll
go up and look for you."

"I'll be right down. No worries." Maggie hoped there
would be no need for an intervention, but it was comforting to know she had backup.

The beam from Dana's flashlight guided her to the

garage, but it was dark inside and she used her cell phone light to find a narrow staircase with rough, unfinished walls. She walked up the stairs and stood before the door at the top. She could hear the TV on inside. It sounded like another basketball game. She heard Toby talking on the phone, though she couldn't make out his words.

She took a deep breath and knocked, making a rapid, sharp sound.

Moments later the door swung open. Toby stared down at her. He'd changed out of his suit and into jeans and a sweatshirt and was wearing only socks, no shoes. Maggie was happy to see that.

His phone was squeezed between his shoulder and his left ear. He held a dumbbell in his other hand and was pumping up his bicep.

"What do you want?" His tone was suspicious.

She felt a wave of anxiety and tried not to show it. She wasn't a very good liar but tried not think of that.

"Sorry to bother you, Toby. I had some car trouble. It's sort of embarrassing. I was just about to head home and thought I'd shifted into reverse, but the stupid car went forward instead, and I drove right down into a patch of mud. Now it's stuck," she said sadly.

"I'll call you right back. Something came up," Toby said into his phone. Then turned his back and spoke in a softer voice before he ended the conversation.

He put his phone in his back pocket and squinted down at Maggie. "What do you expect me to do about it? I can't pull your car out. I'm not a mechanic."

"Oh, I've already called for help. A tow truck is coming. But your car is in the way. If you give me the keys, we'll move it to a safe spot."

"I'll move it. I need to find some shoes." He sounded annoyed but also afraid of letting her anywhere near his car. Maggie decided she'd done too good a job pretending she was an addlepated female driver.

"Oh, I hate to bother you. Dana or Lucy can move it, if you don't trust my driving . . . and I can well understand why," she went on as she peered into the apartment.

He'd been in the space only a few days, but it looked like a group of college boys had been living there for several semesters. Dirty clothes, pizza boxes, and beer bottles were scattered in all directions. There were piles of newspapers on the coffee table, along with a notebook computer that stood open, a stack of official-looking documents, and a yellow legal pad covered with scrawled notes. Maggie yearned to get a peek at what he was working on, but didn't dare step too far into the dragon's lair.

There was a row of coat hooks near the door, and she spotted the keys dangling there. She could grab them and run, but she doubted that would work out very well.

"We need to move your car only a few yards. Take a look for yourself," she urged him, remembering Rose's cue to set off the dogs.

With one jogging shoe in hand and the other on his foot, he lifted a shade and peered down at the driveway. Maggie didn't hear anything and worried that her ploy to keep him inside wouldn't work.

Suddenly, a chorus of barking and howling dogs easily drowned out the sound of the TV, even the loud cheers of a basketball stadium. The sound grew louder and louder, daring him to come down.

Toby turned to her, the worn-out jogging shoe now dangling from his hand. "What the heck are all those dogs doing out there?"

Maggie feigned an innocent stare. "Doesn't Rose usually give them a little air at night?"

"You'd think that one was raised in a wolf pack," he

muttered. "Things are going to change around here . . . fast. Mark my words." He waved the shoe at Maggie.

She tilted her head back, waiting to see what he'd do.

His phone rang, and he stared at the number, then fumbled to answer it. "Yeah, I'm here. Hold on . . ."

In a few quick steps he was at the door, where he grabbed the keys and handed them to her. "Be careful with that car, or you and your friends will have to buy me a new one. It's a BMW, you know."

That it was, at least fifteen years old, dented and dusty, with tears in the upholstery. But obviously a source of pride for him.

"I understand." Maggie gripped her prize and started down the stairs, struggling to hide a smile.

His door slammed shut, and she heard him continue the phone call. She paused and strained to hear his side of the conversation.

"Yeah, well . . . I just need a little longer than expected. A day or so . . ."

He moved away from the door, and she couldn't make out any more words. But his tone seemed serious and urgent, and even fearful, she thought.

She was tempted to sneak back up a step or two and listen more. But if he opened the door and found her there, she didn't even want to guess what his reaction would be.

She turned and softly tread the rest of the way down the staircase, through the garage, and outside to her friends.

Rose had settled the dogs. They had sounded like a pack of one hundred from upstairs, but there were fewer than ten.

"Did you get the keys?" Lucy's tone was hushed as she rushed to meet Maggie.

Maggie dangled the ring. "I described my car mishap so well, he nearly wouldn't hand them over. But the dog tactic worked like a charm. And I promised that one of you would move it."

"Great. Let's move his car. Don't look at his window. He's probably watching," Dana said.

Maggie handed the keys to Dana. "Oh, he definitely is. Count on that. An important phone call came through in the nick of time. That helped to keep him there, too. He's up to something. I can feel it. Maybe we can find out what it is."

"How are we going to read what's in that envelope without him knowing?" Lucy said. "He can probably see everything we're doing from the window."

"I was worried about that, too. Then I noticed most of the garage is empty. Holly has only her tractor in there. Dana can park his car in the garage, open the envelope, and read the documents. Even take photos if she needs to. Then I'll take the keys back up. Easy as . . ." Maggie was going to say, "Pie," but she recalled Phoebe's objection to the motto. "As toast."

Lucy caught her gaze and smiled. "Brilliant. Even the evil Toby can't see through walls."

Dana gave Maggie a quick thumbs-up. "We hope. And we hope he doesn't finish his call and come down to investigate before we're done, either."

Dana got into Toby's car and started the engine. Maggie and Lucy walked over to the garage, and each took hold of one of the old-fashioned doors. The type that slid open, Maggie noticed. Or should have. As Dana drove the car into position to pull inside the garage, they tugged on the doors. But couldn't make them budge.

"Are they nailed shut or something?" Lucy examined the doorframe.

Maggie did, too. "I don't think so."

"Maybe glued? There's a reason most of this garage is empty," Lucy said.

"I think they're just stuck. We can't give up that easily," Maggie whispered back. She walked into the garage and scanned a workbench. In the headlights of Toby's car, she spotted a can of WD-40 and sighed with relief. She knew there would be one here. No one who owned machinery would be without the stuff.

She ran back to the doors with the can of lubricant spray and quickly coated the metal rail above each one. "Let's try it now. I'll help you."

They both grabbed hold of Lucy's door and pulled. It wouldn't move at first, then suddenly slid open in jerking starts and stops.

"One down, one to go," Lucy said.

They ran to Maggie's door and did the same. Then stepped aside right before Dana pulled Toby's car into the space.

Maggie followed Lucy out to the drive. "While Dana's checking the envelope, let's stand near my car and pretend to be waiting for help."

"Good idea. If he's still watching, a little more acting won't hurt."

They walked down the grassy slope to the Subaru, and Maggie checked the front wheels, which had sunk even farther into the soft ground.

"Hate to say it, but I think I really do need a tow truck. I'll either have to give Charles the ditzy woman driver story, too, or tell him the truth. I'm not sure which choice would be worse."

Maggie's attempts to help clear Suzanne's name when she was accused of murdering her office rival had been a serious point of contention between her and Charles. They had even broken up over it for a time. Charles had been the lead detective on the investigation, and she had certainly understood his objections to what he called her meddling.

But she couldn't help it then, and she couldn't help it now, she realized. She'd been compelled to do all she could for her dear friend Suzanne, and now she was called to lend a hand to Dana and the Piper sisters. How could she turn her back if she could discover who had really attacked Holly and had set the fire Tuesday night? She felt certain it wasn't Rose, though the police still did not agree.

"Charles isn't a detective anymore. Do you think he still feels so strongly about us getting mixed up in these situations?"

Maggie laughed. "Charles doesn't think police investigations are mere 'situations.' He left the force only a few months ago. Let's put it this way. You can take the man out of the squad room. But you can't take the squad room out of the man."

"You're probably right," Lucy agreed. "I think you should stick with 'ditzy woman driver.' "

The contentious issue of Maggie's habit of getting involved in police business had not come up again between them since they'd become engaged and started living together. Maggie didn't really know what his feelings would be about her attempts to help Dana and the Piper sisters figure out who was behind the brutal actions of Tuesday night, but she didn't want to take that chance.

"I think you're right. For better or worse, even a not so sexist guy like Charles will easily believe that cover."

Maggie pulled her phone out and called Charles. He picked up on the first ring. He was concerned to hear about the car and offered to pick up her up and deal with the tow-truck driver tonight or even the next day. She appreciated his concern but didn't want him to come out so late to fetch her. And she did think there was safety in numbers here this evening, though she didn't tell him that was another reason she wanted to stay.

"I'll be fine. I'll call a truck tomorrow first thing. I have the road service card, so they'll come quickly."

"All right, if you say so. Call me in the morning and let me know how it goes."

A note in his voice caught her attention. She wondered if he was mad at her for spending so much time with her friends. When he'd been working all hours on investigations, it had rarely been an issue. But tonight it seemed more apparent that he had expected her to be home by now and to spend time together on a Friday night, the start of the weekend.

"Are you upset with me for getting stuck here?"

"Of course not," he said quickly. "I just miss you, that's all."

"I miss you, too," she said sincerely. Tomorrow she'd be in the shop, but she wanted to remind him they would have all day Sunday together. But the truth was she didn't know what would happen next with Holly and Rose. Dana might need her help more than ever.

Before she could decide what to say, Charles said good night. She did the same and ended the call.

"Is everything okay?" Lucy asked.

Maggie shrugged and flipped up her collar. "He's fine. A little lonely tonight, I think. He did expect me home for dinner and to spend some time together." Maggie glanced at her. "I guess I'm still not fully adjusted to being accountable that way. I hate to let him down, but I'm used to doing whatever I want when I want to do it."

"I understand." Lucy nodded. "There is a simple solution."

From her expression, Maggie could guess what it was, too.

"You just won't get off the dog thing, will you?"

"Stop fighting it, Mag. I saw you cuddling that puppy. I should have taken a picture and sent it to Charles."

Maggie was glad that she had not, and didn't want to encourage her with any more repartee on the subject.

"What's taking Dana so long? It's getting cold out here."

Maggie rubbed her hands together and turned to check the garage.

Dana finally emerged and trotted toward them. "Sorry for the wait. There was a lot to read. Let's go inside. I'll tell you what I found."

They headed for the back door, and Dana suddenly stopped. "Oh, blast . . . We forgot to return the keys."

"That means you don't want to see Toby . . . and Freud knows, too," Lucy said. "Let me go. I'm younger, faster and, as you all pointed out a few minutes ago, blonder."

"No argument there. You go, girl." Dana fished the keys from her pocket and passed them to Lucy.

"Just whistle if you have any trouble," Maggie whispered.

"Whistle? I'll scream my head off," Lucy promised.

She jogged back to the garage and slipped into the shadows. Maggie and Dana waited silently. Maggie was dying to hear what Dana had found in the envelope, but Lucy's quick return was more important at the moment.

Was Toby dangerous? Had he attacked Holly and set the fire?

Maggie felt the answer to that last question was still rising, like a message in a fortune-teller's ball.

If the answer was yes, no one here was safe tonight.

Lucy returned, and they quickly went inside the house. "I just handed him the keys at the doorway. He was talking on the phone and barely acknowledged me," she reported.

"The less said, the better. Good job." Maggie entered the kitchen, where Rose was pouring hot water from the kettle into the teapot. She'd set out a plate of cookies on the counter and Maggie brought it to the table, then rubbed her cold hands together, eager for another cup of tea.

Before they'd gone outside to move the car, Dana had

explained to Rose, in the least alarming way possible, that they needed to look at some papers in Toby's car without him knowing about it.

Rose had not asked any questions. She was obviously suspicious of her half brother's sudden appearance, too. Though Maggie couldn't say if she connected him with Holly's attack and the fire. She sat next to Maggie with a mug of tea, her three favorite dogs lying peacefully under the table, at her feet.

Lucy filled her mug and sat across from Dana at the table. "So . . . the envelope, please, as they say. Or just tell us what it was you found in it."

"Legal documents, as we expected. There was a simple letter that acknowledged Holly had loaned him fifty thousand dollars and he was going to pay her back over the next forty-eight months, with interest. The payment schedule was all worked out, with a blank line on the bottom for her signature." Dana frowned, looking puzzled by this discovery. "She did loan him money just a few years after George died. I know that. And I doubt he ever repaid her. She considered it more of an extra gift from the estate, since he'd blown through the sum George had left him."

Maggie recalled Dana telling them that the other night.

"From what I've seen of Toby, I'm guessing she kissed that cash good-bye when she gave it to him," Lucy said.

"I'd tend to agree. Though I don't understand why he's coming up with that letter now, setting terms to repay the debt," Maggie said. "Unless she asked him to pay her back after all this time?"

"I don't think so. She knows that well is dry. But perhaps it fits in somehow with the other documents." Dana glanced at Rose. "I don't want you to worry, Rose. I'm just talking about pieces of paper. They don't change anything."

"All right." Rose nodded, trying to tamp down her distress. But Oreo immediately noticed a change in Rose's mood. Perhaps by the pitch of her voice or her posture. The lithe border collie leaned close to Rose's leg and rested her head in her owner's lap.

"But what did you see? What is he trying to do?" Rose asked, fear rising in her eyes.

Maggie could see Dana weighing her words carefully, and also weighing how much Rose should know against how much she could handle.

"There are forms that would make Toby the medical proxy for you and Holly."

"No . . . he can't do that. It's not right. Holly won't let him."

"Of course she won't. I said before, they are only pieces of paper. Now we know what he's trying to do, and we're going to stop him. You'll see." Dana put her hands on Rose's shoulders and held her gaze. "You'll see. I promise."

Rose nodded, her chin trembling. Maggie reached over and took her hand.

"I can't imagine how he thought he'd pull that off," Maggie turned to Dana. "You have that position now. How does he think he can take it over?"

"If Holly signed the forms, he would be named her and Rose's proxy, and my status would be nullified. He obviously took those forms into the hospital, hoping to persuade—or pressure—Holly into signing them. Which I'm sure she'd never do," Dana replied.

"Unless he planned to trick her into signing them?" Maggie offered. Though she wasn't sure how he'd do that, either.

"And doesn't a notary need to witness the signature for an agreement like that to be valid?" Lucy asked.

"Maybe Toby had a notary tucked in another pocket," Maggie quipped.

"Or he knows one willing to cheat on that part?" Lucy glanced at Maggie and Dana. "He'd get the signature by making her think she was signing something else. Like the agreement to pay back his loan. Who would refuse to have fifty thousand dollars paid back in timely installments? He probably has some shady notary lined up, who will stamp it, claiming they had been present and had been a valid witness."

"I know that happens," Dana replied. "It could have been his plan."

Maggie took a warming sip of tea. "I guess it was a blessing in disguise that Holly had a setback. It saved her from his visit." She would have been alone with him, Maggie realized. At his mercy.

"It saved her this time," Dana murmured. "We know what he's up to now, and we know she needs protection."

"You have to tell Detective Reyes about all this. The pages we found in that envelope are like a huge neon sign pointing right at Toby," Lucy told Dana.

"Don't worry. I'm on it." Dana checked her phone. "I'll call Helen and have her pass on the information to the detective. Otherwise I'll be stuck explaining how we happened to get our hands on it. Helen is good at fudging the details."

She picked up her cell phone and searched for the attorney's number. "And I'll call the hospital and check on Holly again. Did you figure out if you really need a tow truck, Maggie?"

"Looks like I do. But I decided to leave it until tomorrow. I already told Charles. I hope you don't mind that I invited myself to stay over?"

"Of course not," Dana said. "I'm relieved that you're not going to wait for a tow to get out here. You wouldn't get home until midnight."

"It seemed the wiser course," Maggie said.

Lucy took a cookie and dipped the edge of it into her tea. "The only problem now is Suzanne. You both know she'll never forgive us for having a sleepover party without her."

Maggie laughed. "I didn't think of that, but you're right. We'd better not tell her."

There was still time do some knitting, and Lucy ran outside to fetch their tote bags. Maggie actually craved it and knew it was the perfect way to unwind after their challenging day.

She exchanged a few text messages with Phoebe, just to check on how store had done during the day. Everything was running smoothly, Phoebe reported. No emergencies. Maggie thanked her for taking over and promised to be in the next morning. She made a confession in her next text message.

We've had a very draining day. We're going to do a little knitting now. Sorry you're not with us.

I am, too. But I bet you're surrounded by dogs. So it's sort of okay. I'm knitting here, too, with Van Gogh in my lap. He likes to hide under the sections of sweater.

Maggie smiled at the picture Phoebe's words summoned. **It all works, then. Have fun. See you tomorrow.**

She found her way to the dog parlor, where Rose and Lucy were already knitting. Rose helped her find a canine-free zone, which was no small task.

The dogs were at that snoozy stage of the night. Maggie wondered if the barking assignment had worn them out. They dozed on dog beds or curled on couch and chair cushions. There was barely room for the humans, but no one had the heart to disturb any of the sleepy canines.

"Your dogs have the right idea," Maggie observed. "The day is done, and it's time to just be." It was relaxing to be around them in this state, she had to admit.

"Dogs know when to work, play, and rest. Except for border collies, like Oreo." Lucy glanced at Rose.

"They like to be productive," Rose said.

"I can relate." Maggie pulled a length of yarn from the ball and turned her work over. She had finished the front of Charles's sweater and was working on the back.

She glanced at Rose's work, which had not advanced much the past few days. Was there any wonder about that? Maggie certainly didn't want to pressure her. That was the complete antithesis of why she'd been asked to teach Rose to knit in the first place.

Rose seemed to sense Maggie's thoughts. "I'm only on my second collar, for Wolf. Oreo's went faster."

"Wolf is a bigger dog. His needs more stitches. I think you can go three fingers wide on that one. I try not to judge my progress or compare myself with others. Each project finds its own pace. Knitting is not a race," she said with a smile.

Rose smiled. "I know what you mean. I like to just do the stitches. It doesn't even matter if I even make anything."

Maggie lifted her head, pleased by Rose's insight. "You'll get far with that attitude. Taking joy in the activity for its own right."

Dana came in and took in the peaceful scene. She looked pleased and found a place to sit on one of the love seats by coaxing a long-haired dachshund to one side. "I spoke to a nurse. Holly is doing very well. They're going to leave the oxygen on tonight, but the nurse is fairly certain she'll be breathing on her own again tomorrow. She said it was just a coughing spasm, and Holly shouldn't speak that much, even if she's able. But she'll be wide awake, and we can communicate with a pad and pencil."

"Great news." Lucy looked up from her knitting and smiled.

"Can we go early to see her?" Rose asked. "I won't talk at all. I just want to be with her."

"Of course, Rose. We'll get up early and go first thing." Dana cast a warm smile in Rose's direction. "I sent Detective Reyes a text and told her that Holly should be able to answer a few questions tomorrow. Not that I want Holly worn out by the police. But a few words might clear up everything, and this entire nightmare could be over. The police may not even need you to sit for an official interview."

"I told Detective Reyes everything I could remember the other day, at the shop."

"I'm sure you did," Dana said. "Let's not worry about it right now. It might not even happen."

Maggie could tell that her strong and capable friend was feeling drained by this ordeal. Had only three days passed since Tuesday, when the greenhouse had gone up in flames? It seemed like three weeks, Maggie reflected.

Rose had answered all the detective's questions the other day, as best as she was able. Maggie had been there. She knew that was so. But if what Dr. Riley had told Dana was true, Rose's memory might offer a solid detail or two of the events. Along with whatever Holly would say, the police would finally have a clear lead to follow.

Had the drifter, Carl Thornton, been here Tuesday night? Or was it Toby? Or someone else entirely? Every time Maggie thought she knew the answer, it slipped like smoke back into the shadows. Like a lost memory.

"Did you tell Helen Forbes what you found in the envelope?" Lucy asked.

"Yes, I did. She's going to call Detective Reyes tonight, even though it's late."

Maggie found that reassuring. "I guess we should all get a good night's sleep. Tomorrow will be a big day." Maggie smoothed her knitting on her lap and checked the stitches. "In a good way, I mean," she added quickly.

"Yes, in a good way, I hope, too," Rose agreed. She got

up and stretched. "I'll sleep on one of the couches in here. Lucy or Maggie can have my room."

"And there's the guest room, too," Dana added.

The sleeping arrangements were quickly sorted out. Maggie was in the guest room, and Lucy took Rose's room. They all said good night to Rose, and she closed the pocket doors of the parlor. Maggie put her knitting bag on the bench in the foyer and started to follow her friends up the staircase.

"I have half my house here," Dana said. "I'll find pj's and necessities for both of you. And clean clothes for tomorrow."

Maggie paused on the steps. "I'll be right up. I forgot something in the kitchen."

She walked to the back of the house and checked the locks on the back door and also on the windows. The room was dark except for a low light over the stove. Bella was snuggled in the puppy den with her brood, all fast asleep, Maggie thought. Until the vigilant mother opened her eyes a crack to check out the visitor.

Deciding Maggie was harmless, Bella sighed and closed her eyes.

"Sleep tight, Bella," Maggie whispered. "And babies."

She headed back to the foyer and checked that the front door was locked, too. There was a chain, and she fastened it, as well.

No great defense if Toby decided to come in the house tonight. He did have a key. But at least they would hear him. The dogs certainly would.

Satisfied that she'd done her best to secure the house, Maggie climbed the steps. At the top of the staircase, there was a wide, square center hall with four doors, one on each of the four walls. Lights were on in all the rooms, and the doors were open. She found Dana and Lucy in the largest room, opposite the steps.

Several duffel bags were scattered around on the floor. Dana knelt next to one and tugged out clothing.

"Oh, Maggie . . . there you are. Were you looking for your reading glasses? I think you left them in the parlor," Lucy said.

"I was checking the locks," Maggie admitted. "I didn't want to frighten Rose, in case she was listening. Toby has keys, but there's a dead bolt on the back door and a chain on the front."

"Do you really think he'd break in here tonight? What would he try to do?" Lucy asked. Dana had handed her a tank top and yoga pants to use for nightwear. She clutched the clothing in her lap and sat on the edge of the bed.

"For one thing, he may have remembered his envelope in his car, retrieved it, and noticed that someone had opened it. Some ditzy women drivers. I'm sure even he will figure that out."

Dana looked up and paused her search. "I tried to leave everything as he had left it. But it's still possible. There was more in the envelope. I didn't want to tell you about it in front of Rose."

Maggie and Lucy stared at her.

"What was it?" Lucy asked.

"Forms that would make Toby the trustee of the estate and Rose's guardian, if anything were to happen to Holly. Even in a medical emergency where she couldn't communicate."

"Like . . . what's going on right now, you mean?" Lucy asked.

"Yes. Though, with any luck, that phase of her recovery is finally over," Dana answered, her voice quivering. She stood up and dropped some clothes on a chair. "It scares me to contemplate what he might be planning, drawing up papers like that. But at least we found them, and Helen has told Detective Reyes by now."

"Let's hope so." Lucy's voice was shaky, too. She glanced at Maggie. "Hate to sound like a chicken, but can we all sleep with our doors open tonight?"

"Cluck, cluck . . . agreed," Maggie said. "And we have the faithful hounds to stand guard while we sleep. That's something."

"I think mine deserted me for their new friends," Lucy said. "They looked so comfortable in Rose's dog pack, I didn't have the heart to call them up here."

"I'm for open doors. And a few lights on," Dana announced. "But I am tired. Guess I'll say good night."

Maggie felt the same. She bade good night to her friends and found her room, which was across the hall from Lucy's. Dana had already laid fresh sheets, towels, and other necessaries on the dresser.

Maggie picked up a new toothbrush and slipped it from the box. She glanced at herself in the mirror. She looked tired . . . and shaken.

Didn't this latest disclosure put Dana in danger, as well? As things stood, she was the only person standing between Toby and all that he so desperately wanted.

Chapter 12

"Maggie? I'm so sorry . . . Can you wake up?"
Maggie rolled over and opened her eyes. A narrow beam of light from the hallway slanted into the room. Dana stood next to the bed. Her voice was low and urgent.

"What is it . . . ? Is something wrong?" Maggie sat up, a frisson of alarm streaking through her body like an electric shock.

Dana sat on the edge of the bed and pulled on a short boot. She was otherwise dressed, including her jacket. "It's Holly. The hospital just called. She's had another setback. It's serious. They caught her just in time . . ." Her voice was shaking with emotion, and Maggie gripped her arm.

"What happened? Will she be all right?"

Dana swallowed. "I couldn't get much information on the phone, but it sounds like the oxygen machine failed. A nurse came in by chance and saw the light was off and a line was disconnected. An alarm on the machine should have gone off, but that failed, too."

"Oh my goodness. That is grave. Was it off for very long?" she asked, fearing the answer.

"I don't know," Dana said honestly. "The doctor I spoke to said that Holly was responsive, so I'm hopeful there's no serious damage. I'm going there right now." Dana came to her feet and zipped up her jacket. "Can you stay with Rose?"

"Of course. I'll stay as long as you need me to."

Maggie rose and wrapped a light blanket around her shoulders. She faced Dana and could see that she'd been crying.

"Maybe I should come with you. Lucy can stay with Rose . . . You don't even have your car," she reminded Dana "And mine is stuck in the mud. That doesn't help."

"I'll take Holly's truck. I already found the keys. I'll be fine. I doubt the doctor will let me see her for long. I know she can't speak." She looked down at Maggie. "You should go back to sleep. I was just going to leave you a note."

"I'm so glad that you didn't," Maggie said honestly. "I'll walk you downstairs. I couldn't sleep a wink now anyway."

Maggie stood at the front door and watched Dana head over to the truck. It was five in the morning, with the merest sign of the new day seeping into the darkness.

A fog had settled in around the house and the cars. It would burn off by daylight. Maggie hoped so anyway. She'd never seen Dana as the type of person who would drive a truck, but she looked very comfortable behind the wheel.

She started the engine and slowly backed out.

"Drive safely," Maggie called.

Dana waved as she passed the house. Maggie watched the taillights disappear into the fog. As she turned to shut the door, she noticed Toby's car. It had not been visible before, but there it sat. How had it moved out of the garage? She wondered if Dana had noticed it, too.

Maggie felt as if she'd slept with one eye open, but she had not heard a car start up or drive away. Or come back.

But it seemed that Toby had gone out sometime during the night.

Had he noticed anything awry with the envelope? She hoped not, but here she was. No place to hide if he decided to confront someone.

The doors to the parlor were firmly closed, and Maggie was careful not to wake Rose. She slipped into the kitchen and put on a pot of coffee. She could hear the puppies rousing. They were early risers, weren't they?

She glanced into the mudroom and saw Bella in her usual pose, stretched out on her side, feeding her babies. Maggie found her water bowl and filled it. She decided not to offer food. That was Rose's territory. She didn't want to do anything wrong.

Maggie felt a soft, furry touch on her bare foot and found the brown ball of fur she'd held the other night nuzzling her ankle. "Good morning to you, too, little one. No breakfast there, sorry to say. You belong with your brothers and sisters."

Maggie lifted the puppy. Its little body hung slack in the air, and it stared back at Maggie while airborne, as if to say, "Where are you taking me?"

"Here's your mom. See?" Maggie set the puppy down next to Bella, who seemed to offer a grateful smile, then watched the pup scramble over siblings to find a good spot for breakfast.

Back the kitchen, she poured herself a cup of coffee and stared out the window. The printout of Toby's background search and the old newspaper articles about the accident that Lucy had found online had been left on the table.

Maggie had forgotten to look at them the night before. She slipped on her reading glasses, and glanced through the pages. She already knew more than she wanted to know about Toby and put those pages aside.

There were newspaper clippings about the accident, the

initial report, and an obituary of Chip Lynch, the young motorcycle driver who had lost his life. The photo alongside looked like one taken for a high school yearbook, which touched Maggie's heart. He'd been about the same age as Holly and her boyfriend, maybe a few years older? Certainly too young to die in such a senseless way.

The article said he'd grown up in nearby Newburyport. Maggie wondered if his family still lived in the area. As it often happened when a young person passed, the article was quite short. Chip Lynch had been an aspiring musician who played the guitar and sang in a band. He'd worked days in construction. He had been a good friend to all and had helped coach his younger sister Tabetha's softball team. His parents, neighbors, and former teachers all had had kind words about him and noted that he would be greatly missed.

There were also two articles about the trial and the sentencing. There had been no close family to fight for Jeremy, Maggie noticed. Just a single mother, who looked careworn and deeply ashamed in the photos. There was a picture of Jeremy from his senior yearbook, a handsome young man in a formal shirt and tie. Another, of him in handcuffs as he stared down at the ground as he was being led from a police car into a courthouse and jail.

Maggie had taught art at Plum Harbor High School for over twenty-five years. Had Jeremy been one of her students? She studied his photo. She didn't think so. Though something about his face in profile in the blurry newspaper photo looked vaguely familiar.

She must have seen him in the school hallways and filed his face somewhere back in her memory. She put the newspaper articles aside. There were no surprises or insights there, she decided. Nothing she did not expect. It was a tragedy, a true accident. Nobody's fault and yet so many young lives were damaged forever in the blink of an eye that night. *In a heartbeat*, Maggie thought.

She took another sip of coffee and felt sufficiently awake to do some knitting. She hoped Dana would call as soon as she heard any news, but knew it might take several hours.

"Maggie? What are you doing down here? Couldn't sleep?"

Maggie's eyes fluttered open, her deep sleep broken by a familiar voice for the second time that day.

Lucy stared down at her, her face in shadow as sunlight streamed in through the kitchen curtains behind her. How long had she been sitting there?

"I got up very early. I must have dozed off in the chair." Maggie sat up and took a deep breath. "Dana had to go out about five. The hospital called. Something happened to Holly. They say she's out of danger, but Dana wanted to see her."

Maggie checked her phone and saw that it was half past seven and then looked at her messages. "I hope I didn't miss her call." She checked the incoming calls on her phone.

Lucy looked upset. "What was it? More trouble breathing?" Lucy asked with concern. She poured herself coffee and sat at the table across from Maggie.

"Not exactly. Something went wrong with the oxygen machine. A nurse found a line disconnected. And the alarm didn't go off, either." Maggie released a shaky breath. "Very disturbing. And it will be hard to find out how it happened."

"If the machine was knocked out by accident, you mean, or on purpose." Lucy took a seat across from her at the table. "I hate to sound paranoid, but whoever attacked Holly on Tuesday could have tried again."

"That's what I've been thinking. But why?"

"Do you think it's because she was coming around and ready to talk to the police? Who knew that except us?" Lucy asked.

"Toby," Maggie replied. "His car wasn't in the garage this morning. It was parked in front of the house. He must have moved it sometime last night. I know that doesn't prove anything at all," she said quickly. "I just found it curious."

"All things considered, I was wishing his car wasn't here at all. I keep expecting him to barge in here, ranting about that envelope."

"I do, too," Maggie admitted. "I'm starting to regret that I dreamed up that scheme."

"No regrets, Maggie. I thought that was your favorite song?" Everyone knew that the famous ballad sung by Edith Piaf was Maggie's rallying cry. "Besides, the information we found in it was very important. It can help the police and keep Rose and Holly safe. Toby may not want to face us after he finds out we saw what was in there."

"I hope that's true." Maggie stood up and stretched. "We should tell Rose together about Holly. Try to keep her calm. Dana was concerned that she wouldn't be here to explain it and handle any reaction, but I'm hoping Rose knows and trusts us enough by now."

"I understand," Lucy said. "The most important thing is to make sure Rose knows Holly is out of danger and will be back on track, given a little more time."

"That's it exactly." Maggie's phone rang. She saw Dana's name on the screen. "It's Dana. I'll put her on speaker so we can both hear." Lucy drew closer, and Maggie answered the call.

"How's Holly? Is she doing any better?"

"She's bounced back. They've given her tests, and it

seems there was no lasting damage, thank goodness. Apparently, a nurse got the oxygen back on in time to avoid a crisis."

An easy way of saying, "Before Holly died of asphyxiation. Or had any lasting damage to her brain or other organs." But Maggie did not interrupt with that comment. There was nothing to gain but worrying about "what ifs."

"Do they know how it happened? Is someone on the staff to blame?" Lucy asked.

Dana's voice lowered. "That's the thing. It was a very light staff last night, and everyone on the floor is accounted for between the time the machine was checked and functioning perfectly and when the disconnect was discovered," she replied. "They have a video of the hallway. The hospital security department is checking it, along with the police."

"Is Detective Reyes there?" Lucy asked.

"She's in the building, but I haven't seen her yet."

Maggie leaned closer to the phone. "I think you should tell her that Toby's car was moved sometime during the night. Did you notice? We left it in the garage, and this morning it's in front of the house."

"I was in such a panic, I didn't notice that." Dana paused. "If he did come here and did this to Holly, wouldn't he be smart enough to park in the same spot again?"

"That would be the smart thing to do. But there's such a thing, I've heard, as 'dumb crook syndrome,'" Lucy explained. "Bank robbers who write the teller a note on the back of an envelope with their full name and address. A form of self-sabotage. I can easily see Toby in that category."

"Me too. Come to think of it, he is the only one who knew that Holly was improving and could soon speak to the police." She paused. "And I mentioned it to Tim Riley when we were on the way to the hospital yesterday. But I don't think he'd ever hurt her."

Maggie still didn't know what to think of Dr. Riley. "When did you tell him that?"

"He sent me a text and asked if I had one of Rose's files. He's looking back to see if she had any instances of her memory coming back while she was working with Emily that he wasn't aware of. I didn't have the file, but I did tell him where we were going and the good news about Holly."

"I see," Maggie said.

"Is Rose up yet? Have you told her what happened?" Dana sounded worried.

"The doors to the parlor are still closed. I'm glad you called. We can give her some good news. Holly is doing much better and is almost back to where she was yesterday. Isn't that so?"

"That's a good way to put it. It's the truth, too. I don't want to hide the event from her. That doesn't seem right. Have her call me if she gets too distressed. I can reassure her that Holly is back on track."

Maggie had the feeling Rose would call Dana immediately after she heard this latest news. "Lucy or I will bring Rose to the hospital. I'm sure she'll want to see Holly right away."

While Dana spoke, Maggie glanced at Lucy, who stood at the counter, filling a small bowl with cereal.

Lucy nodded. "No problem, Dana," she called out. "We're on it."

"Thank you, guys. That will be a huge help." Maggie heard someone speaking to Dana. It sounded like one of Holly's nurses was asking Dana a question. "I have to go. Let's touch base in a little while."

Dana hung up, and Maggie heard the parlor doors slide open. She looked out the kitchen doorway. Rose was leading a stream of dogs out of the big room, toward the front

door, some on leads and some, like Tink and Wally, following along without constraint, looking happy to be in
the parade.

"I'm taking the dogs out. I'll be right back. Is Aunt
Dana up yet?" Rose called from just outside the door.

Maggie walked as far as the foyer. She wasn't sure how
to answer. "She is . . . but she had to go out this morning,
very early. Don't worry. I'll explain everything when you
come back inside."

Rose's placid expression quickly tightened with worry.
But the dogs were on the march, and she had to follow.
One of her favorites, Wolf, stood in the portico, waiting
for her. "All right. I'll put them in the pen and be back in a
minute."

Maggie nodded and returned to the kitchen. Lucy was
quickly spooning up her cereal.

"We have to tell her in the calmest way possible," Maggie said.

"She'll be upset. We all are," Lucy said between bites.
"But Holly's condition is totally under control. The sooner
we get ready, the sooner we can get Rose to the hospital to
be with Holly. Rose will understand that."

Maggie had no time to answer. Rose came through the
back door, her eyes shining and her cheeks bright from the
chilly morning air.

"Is Aunt Dana coming back soon? She said we were
going to see Holly this morning."

Maggie approached her and stopped a few steps away.
"We are going to see Holly this morning. Aunt Dana is already with her. There was a problem with one of Holly's
medical machines last night. She had a problem breathing.
But everything is . . . ."

Maggie had nearly reached the reassuring part of her little speech when Rose started trembling. She squeezed her
eyes closed and put her hands over her ears. "No . . . How

can that be? She was fine yesterday. She talked to me. She was coming home soon . . ."

"She will come soon. In a few more days," Maggie tried to explain. "It's just a little setback. She's going to be fine, Rose."

Rose wasn't listening. She was lost in a cloud of panic. She began to take deep, ragged breaths, her brow glistening with sweat. "I have to see her. She might die in there, and I can't even say good-bye to her . . . Will you take me there, Maggie? Can you take me right away?"

She was crying and fell to her knees on the kitchen floor. Maggie ran to her side and stroked her back in gentle circles.

"Rose, please . . . take a deep breath and listen. Holly is going to be fine. Aunt Dana is with her. You can call her if you want to. There was a problem last night, but Holly is totally out of danger now."

Lucy had crouched down on Rose's other side. "We'll take you to the hospital, Rose. Right away. Let's all get dressed, and we'll go. Holly is going to be fine. You'll see for yourself."

Rose finally lifted her head, and Maggie handed her a bunch of tissues. She wiped her eyes and let out a long, shaky breath.

"I just need to bring in the dogs and feed them," she said, coming to her feet.

"I can help you," Lucy offered.

"All right. You can set up the food and the water bowls in the parlor. I'll bring the dogs back in." Rose dashed out the back door.

As Lucy headed for the parlor, she called, "I'll do the dog bowls, then run up for a fast shower."

"I'll clear up in here. I think there's a shower in the bathroom down here, too. I'll duck in there," Maggie replied.

Maggie checked her phone. It was half past eight; with any luck, they could be at the hospital by ten. She called Dana in the hope that Rose would speak to her for a minute when she came back inside. *That should help*, she thought.

The back door opened, and the pack ran in, the lucky off-leash dogs leading the way. They skittered through the kitchen, nails clicking on the slippery floor, as they raced each other to their bowls. Maggie was caught in the canine stream of paws, snouts, and tails and quickly stepped to the side to keep from being knocked over.

At the rear of the herd, Rose appeared with several dogs on leashes. Once inside, she let go, and they galloped across the kitchen to follow the leaders.

Rose stood in the doorway, only half in the house. Maggie caught her gaze and knew something was terribly wrong. Something more than her anxiety about Holly.

"Rose . . . what is it? Close the door. It's cold out there. We need to get dressed to see Holly."

"Oreo is missing. She wasn't in the dog yard. I have to find her."

"Oreo?" Maggie found that hard to believe. The border collie was Rose's favorite comfort dog. She followed Rose like a shadow, barely letting her out of her sight. "Are you sure? Maybe she's in the yard somewhere? Chasing a bird or a squirrel?"

"She's gone. I looked all over, and I called for her. She always comes to me when I call, even if she runs off to chase something. I have to find her before she gets too far away . . ."

"Of course you do. We'll help you. I'll get Lucy. Wait right there, Rose. Please? Don't run off by yourself. Promise me?"

Rose nodded, but her eyes flashed with impatience. She bit down on her lip, and Maggie felt the risk of taking her eyes off of the young woman. But she had to. She backed toward the kitchen door and called for Lucy. Then ran to the staircase and shouted up to the second floor.

Lucy is in the shower. She'll never hear me.

Maggie grabbed her jacket and ran back to the kitchen, wondering where she could find a pair of shoes. She couldn't run out barefoot in this cold, could she?

As she had feared, when she glanced at the doorway, Rose was gone.

She saw a pair of rubber boots in the mudroom, grabbed them, and stumbled out the door. Rose stood at the edge of the woods and looked back at her.

"Rose . . . please . . . wait for me . . . I'm here. I'm coming . . ."

"Go back. Don't follow me. Please . . . I can find her. I know where she is now."

Rose held her phone in one hand, then stuck it in her pocket. Had someone called or sent her a text?

A chill coursed through Maggie's body. Was someone luring Rose away from the house? Did they know she had started to remember what happened Tuesday night?

Maggie suddenly realized who was behind all this. Rose was in danger, terrible danger. She had to catch up to her before it was too late.

Maggie ran forward, tugging on one boot and then the next. She fell in the grass and scrambled up. Then started running again, her side aching.

"Maggie . . . what's going on? Where's Rose?"

Maggie turned and saw Lucy running toward her, long, wet hair flying. Rose's dog Wolf loped alongside.

"I saw you from the window. Did Rose run away?" Lucy called.

"Oreo disappeared, and Rose ran off to look for her. She told me not to follow. I think someone is trying to trap her."

"Oh no! We have to catch her." Lucy picked up speed, and Maggie did, too.

Wolf seemed to sense the urgency and ran ahead.

"She took this trail," Maggie said. "I'd hate to lose another dog. But there's no time to bring Wolf back."

"He ran out when I opened the door. Maybe he'll lead us to Rose."

The sleek, powerful dog crashed through the trees and brush, a pale streak in the shadowy woods. Maggie heard her own labored breath and heavy steps crunching on the twigs and leaves.

"Rose . . . Rose! Wait for us . . . please!" she shouted as she ran, her voice growing hoarse.

"Let me have a turn," Lucy said, then repeated the chant between ragged breaths.

Maggie pushed herself to keep up and not fall on her face again. They were coming to a fork in the trail. She staggered to a stop and leaned over, with her hands on her knees, drawing in deep breaths of the chilly air. The big dog had disappeared.

"Which way? Right or left?" she asked Lucy. "Did you see which way Wolf ran?"

"No, I didn't. Unfortunately. Let's be very quiet," Lucy said. "Maybe we'll hear something."

They listened for a moment. All Maggie could hear were her gulps for air and her pounding heart. Should they split up? she wondered.

A fragment of color on the trail to the left caught her eye, a color that didn't belong on the mulchy path. She ran toward it and picked it up.

"Oreo's collar, the one Rose made. Let's go this way."

Maggie took off, and Lucy followed. They ran side by side.

"We're headed to the river. See the water through the trees?" Maggie said.

"We're high up. I didn't realize," Lucy replied.

"There are cliffs along the river around here. Looks like we'll reach them a little farther down on the trail." Maggie looked in all directions as she ran. "I don't see any sign of Rose. Or Wolf. Maybe we went the wrong way?"

Lucy jogged to a stop and put her hands on her hips. She took in a long breath, then pointed. "Look! Someone's over there. I see Wolf running in that direction."

Maggie followed her gaze. Through the trees she spotted two figures wrestling and falling to the ground. One was a man, but she couldn't tell about the other at their distance.

Was it Rose? Had someone lured Rose out here to assault her?

"We're coming, Rose! Don't worry..." Maggie called out.

Lucy swooped down and grabbed a large branch, barely missing a step. They burst through the trees and reached the battleground.

Maggie instantly recognized the assailant. Carl Thornton! She knew it. She looked for Wolf. Why hadn't the dog attacked him to protect Rose? Had he hurt the dog in some way?

She ran toward him and flung herself on his back. She tried to poke his eyes, as she had learned in a self-defense class, but he easily shook off her. She stumbled and bumped into a long flight of rickety wooden stairs that led to the rocky riverside at least a hundred feet below.

"Let go of her, you monster!" Lucy screamed, taking aim with her branch.

Thornton turned, his eyes wild with surprise. He raised his arm in self-defense. "Slow down ... You've got this all wrong ..."

Maggie was breathless. She couldn't answer. Her gaze

swept down to the ground. She was expecting to see Rose cowering there.

It was a woman and Thornton had a strong grasp on both of her arms. But when Thornton's captive turned to face them, Maggie saw Beth Duncan. The blood rushed out of her head.

"I knew it . . ." Maggie looked back at Thornton. "Where's Rose? Have you seen her?"

"I'm over here." Rose stepped out from behind a tree, with Wolf at her side.

"Oh, Rose. Thank goodness you're all right." Maggie ran to her. "Why didn't you stop when we called you?"

"Someone sent a text. They said they found Oreo on the riverbank, but she was hurt and I had to come alone if I wanted her back."

"Here's the someone! She did it all. Attacked Holly. Set the fire. Who knows what else she was up to." Thornton grabbed Beth by the arm and pulled her to her feet.

He'd used his red bandana to gag her, and she stared at them, her eyes bulging with outrage. She tried to pull free of his grasp, but it was no use. She couldn't move or speak.

Thornton sneered at her. "I came along just in time. She was about to push Rose into the river."

Maggie heard barking and looked down the wooden stairs. Oreo was tied to a post at the bottom. The border collie looked unharmed but confused; she was obviously wondering why no one had come down yet to claim her.

Rose headed for the steps, and Wolf started to follow. "Stay, Wolf. I'll be right back. All these steps are bad for your hips."

Wolf whined but lay down and stared after her.

"I'll call the police." Lucy pulled her phone out.

"Good idea." Maggie saw Thornton flinch, his jaw set,

but he didn't let go of Beth. "Why are you here?" Maggie asked him. "How did you know Rose was in danger?"

Dana's words came back to her. *Sometimes at night I feel as if someone's out there, watching the house.*

"Who are you, really?" Maggie said finally.

He met her gaze, then stared past her, his expression blank, his lips pressed in a tight line.

With one hand, he tugged on the edge of his beard, just under his earlobe, and pulled it off. In his hand was a stretchy, gooey skin-like substance with long gray hairs attached. Then he stripped off his eyebrows, which were like two gray caterpillars, and tossed them on the ground. Next, he slipped off a gray wig and a tight flesh-colored cap. Last but not least, he pulled out fake, yellowed teeth. Thick brown hair sprung up in place of the silver locks, and a smooth-skinned, handsome young man stared back at her.

"My name is Jeremy Carlson," he said slowly in what Maggie realized was his real voice. "Holly and I were friends a long time ago—"

"I know who you are," Maggie interrupted. "Why did you disguise yourself?"

"I always regretted the way I spurned Holly. I thought about her a lot. When I got out of prison, I spent some time moving around the country. I became a professional actor, just the way Holly and I had once talked about. A few years went by, and I still wanted to see her. Just to find out how Holly and Rose were getting on. I knew that their parents died a long time ago. I was concerned about her. But I didn't want to upset her life, if she was happy."

"So that's why you talked her into a job and worked at the nursery a few days," Maggie mused. "Why did you quit so abruptly?"

"I thought she was involved with that doctor. I didn't want to mess that up by telling her my real identity. But after I left on Tuesday, I had regrets. I didn't get very far." He looked down and shrugged. "I took off my disguise and came back to face her. The fire had just started, and I saw this woman running away." He pointed at the gagged Beth Duncan. "She's Tabetha Lynch, Chip's sister. I didn't have time to chase her. I pulled Holly out and saw Rose wandering, in one of her states. Then she collapsed, too. I pulled her body clear of the flames and smoke and put her next to Holly. But I was afraid of the police. I knew they wouldn't believe my story and might think I did it, out of anger for the jail time I served."

"You can face them now," Lucy said. "It's clear that Beth—or whatever her real name is—was behind all of it."

"And it's quite a long list," Maggie added. Blackmailing Holly, attacking her and setting the fire. And probably the second attempt on Holly's life last night in the hospital, when her oxygen supply mysteriously failed.

Beth Duncan—or should she call her Tabetha Lynch now?—sat on the ground next to Jeremy, her head bowed and her clothes covered in mud. She'd obviously realized there was no use trying to get away. Maggie knew she could hear every word they said, but was unable to deny or defend herself.

"I know it sounds odd, but I feel sorry for her," Jeremy said. "She was never able to move on after losing her brother. So many lives were damaged that night, in just an instant. She's a victim here, too."

Maggie thought that was true and also a very wise observation. There was little she could say. Perhaps now some of that damage could be repaired. She hoped so.

She heard sirens in the distance. The sounds was coming closer. There was much more to this story than could be explained here, and she could barely wait to hear the rest. And hash it all over with her friends.

*   *   *

It had taken over four weeks for Maggie to keep her promise of the "dogs welcome" knitting night. Finally, on the last Thursday night in April, the back room was set up for the meeting, and dinner was heating in the storeroom kitchen. She was going to teach the basket stitch tonight to the more advanced knitters. Rose and Holly were ready to advance to needles and learn the basic knit and purl stitches.

Maggie was ready with all the supplies and patterns, and hoped the dogs would behave long enough for the lesson portion of the evening to be completed. She hadn't thought of any appropriate entertainment for them, but Rose was going to bring some toys, including puzzles that hid treats. She promised they would keep the dogs amused for hours. Maggie only hoped for long enough to get through her lesson.

She was carrying a plate of crudité and dip from the storeroom when, her friends seemed to arrive all at once, bustling in the shop with their knitting bags and contributions to the meal.

"Yum! I'd know that smell anywhere," Suzanne tilted her head back and let her nose lead her to the back of the shop. "Maggie's famous pasta and meatballs!"

Maggie smiled. "Exactly, for the humans. Along with garlic bread and Dana's salad. For the dogs, bone-shaped meat treats. My first attempt was a flop but Lucy loaned me a bone-shaped cookie cutter."

Dana and Lucy followed Suzanne to the back of the shop. "Of course," Dana said. "I should have guessed. Did you make the dogs cookies for dessert, Lucy?"

"I made them pup cakes, carrot and peanut butter flavor." Lucy was balancing a plastic container and her knitting bag on one arm and holding onto Tink and Wally's leads with the other.

She set the bag and container on the oak table, then

dropped the leads and instructed the dogs to lay under the oak table, which they instantly and miraculously did.

Maggie could see her own surprise reflected in Suzanne's expression. "Do those pup cakes have doggie tranquilizers in them? Tink and Wally look suspiciously chill tonight, Lucy."

Lucy laughed, but Maggie could see she was pleased by the compliment. "Rose gave me some tips and I've been working with them."

"And doing an excellent job," Maggie noted. "Let's see how they do when Rose arrives with her dogs. That's the real test. Holly just sent me a text. They're running a little late but they will be here soon," she told the others.

"Where's Phoebe?" Dana asked. "Isn't she joining us tonight?"

"Maybe she's protesting, as a dedicated fan of felines," Suzanne said.

Maggie laughed. "Nothing like that. Phoebe loves all furred and feathered creatures. You know that. She was in Boston today, scouting out new sources for the shop. She'll be a little late as well. But it will be interesting to see the samples that she brings back. I'll welcome your opinions."

It was convenient to have a handy focus group for the shop and Maggie often called in her friends for suggestions on the yarn she should stock and other improvements. She had not set the table yet, but the plates, napkins and cutlery, as well as wineglasses, were set out on the sideboard and her friends quickly got to work on the task.

Dana took the stack of plates and set one at each place on the table. "I'm so glad Holly feels well enough to come. Her doctor said she's almost recovered and there won't be any lasting damage to lungs or heart. He's very pleased with her progress. A night out is a real milestone."

Maggie was happy to hear that news, too. "I think healing has a lot to do with a person's state of mind. Holly has been carrying a terrible burden all these years. She must have been so relieved when this ordeal ended."

"She was," Dana replied. "But of course, she had mixed emotions about her secret being out. She still feels responsible for Chip Lynch's death and Rose's injury. And Jeremy's prison sentence. Though at least she knows now that his feelings for her never changed and he has no regrets about claiming that he was the driver."

Suzanne sighed, nearly swooning. "Wow, if that's not romantic, I don't know what is."

"Romantic or not, what about the issue of false testimony?" Maggie asked. "Will there by any consequences for Holly and Jeremy?"

Maggie certainly hoped not. After all Holly had been through, the last thing she needed was legal charges and lawsuits.

Dana was setting out the wineglasses with care and suddenly looked up. "I thought I updated everyone on that question. The time period for bringing charges has expired, thank goodness. Holly and Jeremy are both free and clear."

Lucy placed a linen napkin, knife and fork beside each plate. "I'm sure she felt relieved but she must have also felt embarrassed, And even afraid of what you and Jack would think."

"She was worried that we'd judge her, but we assured her that we didn't. And assured her that we loved her, no matter what. We're just happy that's she's safe now, and getting stronger every day. Everyone makes mistakes and Holly does feel sincere remorse about what happened. She told me that, at the time, she felt there was no other way than to let Jeremy take the blame. Though she knows now she would have acted differently if she had to decide again."

Suzanne had brought two bottles of wine, one red and one white. She stood at the oak server and started to open them. "No one's perfect and she was very, very young when it happened. She has to give herself a break for that reason alone. All these years, Holly has taken such good care of Rose. That should be some comfort to her."

"A great comfort, I'd think," Maggie said. "And I'm sure that being reunited with Jeremy has made Holly's whole world much brighter."

Maggie had set out a plate of crudité on the server and Dana picked up a few celery sticks "Yes, they're together again. For good this time, it looks like. Their reunion was like a romance novel." She rolled her eyes a bit and smiled. "Rose is delighted, too. She always liked Jeremy and is so grateful for the way he saved both of them from the fire and saved her from Beth Duncan's ploy."

"Everyone is grateful for that," Lucy agreed. "I still don't know how we missed the connection between Beth and the Pipers. But there was no picture of Chip Lynch's family in the newspaper articles, which reported his sister's name as Tabetha. That didn't help."

Dana cast Lucy a sympathetic look. Maggie did, too. Lucy obviously felt bad that her research had not yielded the important link between Beth Duncan and the Pipers.

"It was a tricky one, Lucy," Dana replied. "Beth told the police she's always despised the name Tabetha and went by the nickname Beth whenever possible. Except for formal documents, like a driver's license or passport, and her employment records. But I'll get to that later," Dana noted. "Duncan was her married name. She was divorced a few years ago, but never changed her last name back to Lynch. She told the police she wasn't intentionally trying to hide her identity, but the name change had been amazingly convenient once Rose turned up as a patient at the clinic."

Lucy wasn't convinced. "I still think I should have dug a little deeper. I should have smelled a bone buried down there. I guess it was just a fluke that she was working at the center when Rose came in as a patient. And as Dr. Curtis's assistant, Beth was privy to all kinds of confidential information about Rose and everything Rose said in her sessions."

"Including a recollection of Holly behind the wheel the night of the accident," Dana noted. "Which Dr. Riley didn't know about or had missed when reviewing Dr. Curtis's notes."

"It's a pity about Dr. Curtis," Maggie said. "Did Beth confess to her murder as well?"

Dana stepped over to the oak server and poured herself a glass of wine. "She resisted at first, but finally told the police everything. It seems that Dr. Curtis discovered the connection between Beth and the Pipers, but she never realized how dangerous Beth actually was. Beth told the police that when Rose's memory started to come back, Dr. Curtis began looking through information about the accident. Maybe the same newspaper articles Lucy found were also in the file at the clinic? Dr. Curtis put that information together with Beth's employment records, where her full and formal name was listed—Tabetha Lynch Duncan. So Dr. Curtis realized that Beth's older brother, Chip was killed in the car crash that had injured Rose. She spoke to Beth about it, in a kind and concerned way and asked Beth to follow professional ethics and drop out of Rose's care team. Beth readily agreed, then quickly managed to stage Emily Curtis's suicide before anyone else found out about the connection."

Maggie sipped her wine, recalling the day she'd been waiting in the hallway for Dana and had overheard the two doctors arguing. "What a tragedy. How is Dr. Riley doing? Will he be able to keep the clinic open without Dr. Curtis?"

"He may bring in a new partner, but he hasn't made any

big changes yet. He's still reeling from the loss," Dana's tone was somber. "I'm sure he has some deep regrets."

Suzanne had poured herself a glass of red wine and sat at the table in her usual place. "I don't know about the rest of you, but my money was on Toby Nash. I still think that guy belongs behind bars for something. Did we ever find out if he was the one who snuck into the hospital and disconnected Holly's oxygen?"

"I thought he might have been responsible for that, too," Dana replied. "But the video from security cameras at the hospital showed a woman. She was wearing a lab coat and looked like a member of the medical staff. She walked into Holly's room, disabled the alarm and disconnected the oxygen supply. The facial image wasn't clear due to the low light, but Beth eventually confessed to that, too. She'd overheard the Holly was waking up and was ready to talk to answer questions about her attack. And was liable to tell the police that she was being black-mailed, too."

Lucy was peering under the table, checking on her dogs, who were both so perfectly calm and well behaved Maggie had almost forgotten they were there. She suddenly looked up. "What about dear, old Toby? Where is he now?

Dana smiled and sipped her wine. "Thanks to Maggie's clever scheme, which allowed us to look inside that mysterious envelope, Toby had to explain to the police why he was trying to obtain Holly's signature on a health proxy and power of attorney document under such suspicious circumstances. Jack isn't sure if Toby can be charged with any actual crime, since he didn't carry through with his plan, but the questioning put a good scare into him. He's already left town."

"I doubt Holly and Rose will see him anytime soon. Or even get a Christmas card," Suzanne said. "That's one good thing to come out of all of this drama. The second good thing, when you count Holly and Jeremy's reunion."

"And Rose has made real progress with her memory and her stress issues the past few weeks," Dana added. "It's as if a great cloud that has been hanging over Holly and Rose for years has finally lifted."

"That's a lovely way to put it," Maggie agreed. "I think that's very true."

"Aside from the Pipers, how about the new member of your family, Maggie? The one who has brought so much love, laughter, and licks?" Lucy gave Maggie an "I told you so" look. "That's another good thing if you ask me. A big one, too."

Maggie smiled despite herself. Then glanced over at the plush puppy-size bed tucked under the counter. "She's still napping, the little sprite. I thought Tink and Wally would wake her, but she sleeps like a baby sometimes."

"She *is* a baby, " Lucy pointed out. "She'll be a big dog in no time."

"I know." Maggie walked over to her new puppy's basket. She picked up the little dog and cradled her in her arms. "But not too soon, I hope."

Maggie tried not to smile too widely as she brought the puppy out to show her friends. But she did feel a secret thrill, a little like being a new mother, she realized, though she'd never admit it.

"She's still sleepy but she'll wake up soon." she said. Her friends huddled closer, oohing and ahhing.

"Look at her yawn. She's impossibly cute," Dana said. "I'm not even a dog lover."

"She's adorable. Her fur is so soft, too. Like velvet." Suzanne stroked the puppy's head with one finger and sighed. "I wonder if Barkley would like a little friend? I had to leave him home tonight. He was all set to watch the

Red Sox with Kevin. Once he saw the popcorn bowl come out, he wasn't going anywhere with me. I could use a little pal of my own, don't you think?"

"At one time, I might not have agreed," Maggie admitted. "But I'm all for the idea now. I think Bella has another pup or two left in her litter. Though I do think we picked the cutest one."

Charles had been thrilled with the idea of taking in a dog, and Maggie had had no trouble choosing the one she wanted. As Rose had told her, the puppy had already chosen her. Luckily, it had been love at first sight for Charles, too. Their puppy was too young for real walks, but Charles was a sight, leading the little dog around the backyard on her leash, tossing her toys and already teaching her basic dog manners. He did enjoy the dog's company when Maggie was at the shop and Maggie felt the pup's arrival had made their new home complete.

Lucy took a turn, admring the pup and stroking her fur "I know you chose the right one and I love the name you chose, too."

"That was easy. Since she came from a nursery, Charles and I agreed it should be something botanical. We considered the name Lily, since that was George Piper's favorite flower. But it seemed too serious for her. Charles came up with Daisy. It's such a bright, cheerful flower and she always make us smile."

"That's the perfect name," Dana agreed.

"It's very cute, just like her," Suzanne said.

"She's definitely a Daisy and I'm glad it's working out so well." Lucy took a step back and folded her arms over her chest. "Isn't there something you want to say to me, Maggie?"

Lucy met her gaze with an expression that made Maggie

laugh. Dasiy rested her head on Maggie's arm, and closed her eyes, sighing with contentment. Maggie sighed, too.

"You were right. We needed a dog. Thank you for . . . hounding me?"

Lucy smiled, looking satisfied, "That's all you had to say. I really don't know why it took you so long."

Maggie had to laugh. She hugged her puppy even closer. "I don't know why either, Lucy. Honestly."

Notes from the Black Sheep & Company Bulletin Board

Dear Knitting Friends,

I have a big announcement! There's a new member of our staff, and my little family as well—Daisy, our new puppy. She's a beautiful mix of Portugese Waterdog and Labrador Retriever, and who knows what else. Charles and I are totally enthralled with her. I know that not all my customers are dog lovers, but I hope you won't mind Daisy being about some of the time? If you give her half a chance, I think you'll find she's a little charmer. She loves to just sit quietly at my feet when I knit, and I didn't even need to train her to do that!

I suppose you're thinking now that my shop has gone to the dogs. (If you can excuse the awful pun . . .) But I recently learned so much about canines that I'd never imagined, and saw firsthand *their intelligence, loyalty, loving, and brave natures, in action. What can I say? I was completely won over, and little Daisy hooked me at "Woof."*

My conversion to a canine devotee started with a simple lesson on finger knitting I prepared for Holly and Rose Piper, who own Piper Nursery.

As you may know, Rose also rescues dogs and trains some to be companions that help the disabled. Her work is simply amazing, especially when you consider her own challenges.

But as Rose often says, her success is simply proof that dogs are not only our best friends, they're our best therapists, too. I don't know if our friend, Dana would agree. But in Rose's case, I have to say it's true.

Here are links to the finger-knitting lesson that started the Pipers off. And by popular demand, I'm posting my recipe for flatbread with various toppings.

And, a more recent discovery, a recipe for homemade dog biscuits. Daisy loves them and they're much healthier for her than the store-bought kind. Only the best for our new pup.

Happy finger knitting!

Love & Licks—

Maggie & Daisy

FINGER KNITTING LINKS:

A simple search on Google of the term "finger knitting" will produce a dirth of instructive videos and project ideas. This technique is so easy, you'll only need to watch once or twice before you catch on.

Here are a few you can try. Enjoy!

HOW TO FINGER KNIT FOR BEGINNERS /
Bean Creative
https://www.youtube.com/watch?v=h3BEgP5s9Pg
Finger knit basics with clear, visual demonstration and captioned instructions.

3 SIMPLE WAYS TO FINGER KNIT—wikiHow
https://www.wikihow.com/Finger-Knit
This Wiki-How video has instructions on finishing off and a Q&A section that is very helpful.

20 GORGEOUS FINGER KNITTING PROJECTS & HOW TO FINGER KNIT VIDEO
Flax & Twine
https://www.flaxandtwine.com/2017/05/new-finger-knit-video
This link includes a finger knitting demonstration video and instructions for 20 fabulous finger knitting projects, from area rugs to hair ornaments.

MAGGIE'S FLATBREAD

This is an amazingly versatile and forgiving recipe. In fact, it's hardly a recipe at all. I've noted ingredients for a mushroom, goat cheese and fresh herb topping, but also listed a few variations below. Which are truly endless. Just check your leftovers and figure out a tasty combination.

You can serve these flatbreads for lunch or dinner with a big salad, or serve them as an appetizer at your next party. Everyone will call it "pizza" but it tastes delicious by any name.

Regarding the dough, I rarely make my own, though it's not very difficult, just time consuming. I buy raw dough from our local pizza shop. They are happy to sell it to you, packed in flour or oil. I find flour is best, so ask for that. Or, you can find frozen dough in most supermarkets. That works fine, too.

Instructions:
Preheat the oven to 375 degrees
Grease two cookie sheets. Rimless is easiest to use if you have them.

Ingredients:
1 lb. pizza dough
Quality olive oil
1 or 2 cloves of garlic, minced
1 medium-sized onion, diced to small pieces
1 lb mushrooms, sliced (white are alright if that's all you can find; mini-portabello or even large portabello or shitake are tastier)
2-3 tablespoons finely diced fresh rosemary
2-3 tablespoons finely diced fresh thyme

2-3 tablespoons oregano
8 ounces goat cheese (more if you like it very cheesy)
Sea salt
Fresh ground pepper
Red pepper flakes (optional)

If the dough is cold, let it rest at room temperature about 15-30 minutes, until it is soft. It might bubble up a bit.

Set the dough on a flat, lightly floured surface (like a clean cutting board or counter top), and push it down with your hands to make a flat disk. Cut the disk in two equal parts. Set each piece of dough on an oiled cookie sheet and stretch it out to a rectangular shape, about half the width of the sheet.

In a medium to large sauté pan, heat 2-3 tablespoons of oil. Add the diced onions and garlic. Cook on medium heat until soft and translucent.

Add the sliced mushrooms until softened and almost cooked through. Season the mixture with a dash of salt, fresh pepper (a dash of red pepper flakes if you like) and one tablespoon of each of the herbs.

Let the mushroom mixture cool while you smooth about tablespoon or less of olive oil on the two squares of dough. Pinch the edges all around to shape a crust.

If the mushroom mixture has released liquid, spill that out of the pan or remove with a large spoon. (You don't want a soggy flatbread, believe me.)

Spoon half the mushroom mixture on each of the dough squares and put them in the oven on separate racks.

Cook for about 20-30 minutes, until the dough is golden on the edges. You can poke it a bit to make sure it's done.

Remove from the oven a minute and add dollops of goat cheese. Put the pans back in the oven for a few more minutes, until the cheese melts a bit.

Remove from the oven and serve hot, if you can. Sprinkle on the rest of the fresh herbs before serving and a touch more sea salt, if you like. Voila!

Variations on the toppings:

Mini-tomatoes, sautéed with onions and garlic as noted above. Add shredded, fresh mozzarella towards the end of baking and top with fresh, raw basil and a dash of parmigiana cheese.

Start with sautéed onions and garlic again, add diced prosciutto or cooked sausage meat without the casing. Add in sautéed mushrooms and fresh parsley. Top the flatbread with Swiss, or blue cheese partway through baking.

Top the dough with grilled chicken chunks, and cheddar cheese and top with a mix of raw diced, red onions and mini tomatoes.

Go vegetarian, with sautéed broccoli, zucchini, tomatoes, cauliflower, mushrooms, or whatever vegetables you please. Top with fresh herbs and cheddar, Muenster, mozzarella, Swiss, or goat cheese. Or any mixture of cheeses. A dash of pesto on this one couldn't hurt either.

I'm sure you will come up with a few new combinations of your own. Let me know. I'd love to try them, too.

DAISY'S FAVORITE BISCUITS

As novice dog owners, we've been reading a lot about pet care and nutrition. It's so important to give your dog a high quality diet and healthy treats. Daisy loves raw carrots, string beans, and even romaine lettuce leaves, especially the crunchy white part at the bottom of the head. Of course, she loves peanut butter. Who doesn't?

Dogs are not grain eaters. We look for grain-free dog food and treats with no meat "by-products"—that could be anything—grains, corn, soy, or preservatives. These biscuits are gluten free and made with ingredients that are healthy for your beloved furry friend.

GRAIN-FREE PEANUT BUTTER DOG TREATS

Ingredients
2 eggs
½ cup peanut butter
¼ cup melted coconut oil
¾ cup pumpkin puree
1 teaspoon baking soda
1 tablespoon honey
¾ cups coconut flour (or another gluten free flour such as chickpea or almond.)
1¼ cups oat flour (make it at home by chopping oatmeal in the blender)

Instructions
Preheat the oven to 350 degrees F.

In a large bowl, whisk together the eggs, peanut butter, melted coconut oil, honey, and pumpkin until smooth.

In a separate bowl, whisk the baking soda, oat flour, and coconut flour until incorporated.

Stir the flour mixture into the peanut butter mixture until thoroughly combined and a dough forms.

Divide the dough into two disks and wrap the dough in plastic wrap. Refrigerate for at least an hour.

On a floured surface, roll the dough out to about $\frac{1}{4}$ inches thick. Cut out cookies using any small cutter of choice.

Place on parchment-lined baking sheets and bake until golden and firm, about 20 minutes (this will vary on the size of your cutter).

Let the cookies cool. Store in the fridge.

(Adapted from www.parsnipsandpastries.com)

Look for Anne Canadeo's previous book in the
Black Sheep & Company mystery series:

PURLS AND POISON

At your local bookstore or at your favorite e-retailer!

It is out now!

Turn the page for a sneak peek of

PURLS AND POISON.

Chapter 1

That scheming little minx! The woman has no conscience. No soul! She's a bald-faced liar and a coldblooded thief.

Suzanne knew she was speeding, edging fifty in a twenty-m.p.h. zone, but she couldn't help it. Luckily, the ride from her office to Maggie's knitting shop was barely a mile down Main Street and the Plum Harbor police were not the most vigilant group in uniform.

Her foot pressed the gas pedal, her brain churning with murderous scenarios.

I've always just sucked it up. Doing a tap dance to stay ahead of her schemes. This time, she's pushed me too far.

Lost in a silent diatribe, she nearly flew right by the Black Sheep & Company shop. The sight of familiar cars parked along the street told her she was the last to arrive. She usually warned her friends when she'd be late for their weekly get together, but the thoughtful touch had slipped her mind entirely. She knew everyone would understand when they heard her story.

A parking spot came into view; Suzanne hit the brakes and aimed the huge SUV. As the vehicle came to a jerking stop, the rear fender jutted into the street and a front tire was wedged against the curb. Suzanne barely noticed and didn't care.

Without pausing for her requisite hair and lipstick check, she hopped to the sidewalk and headed for the shop, trailing her huge leather purse and knitting tote behind her.

The Victorian house, turned into a retail space, had been neglected when Lucy's friend Maggie had rescued it years ago. As usual, Maggie's artistic eye had spotted the possibilities—the ample wraparound porch that was a perfect perch for knitters in the warmer months, the faded shutters and gingerbread trim that needed only a dash of paint to restore their former glory. It was "a jewel box" now, or so Suzanne might say in a real estate listing. Not that Maggie was likely to retire and sell anytime soon.

Maggie had left her position as an art teacher at Plum Harbor High School to follow her bliss and turn her passion for needlework into a full-time career. She had recently lost her husband and needed a complete change to pull her from her well of grief.

Using her retirement nest egg, she'd bought the building and set up a knitting shop as cozy and inviting as her living room. Comfy love seats and armchairs were carefully arranged among displays of yarn and stitching supplies. A knitting nook near the front door provided another, quiet working space, and a large room in the back served as the perfect spot for classes and demonstrations.

The apartment above was soon rented to Phoebe Meyers, who worked in the shop and was sort of a surrogate daughter for Maggie, whose own daughter Julie was away at college most of the year. Phoebe had recently graduated from a local college with a degree in fine art and Maggie had promoted her to assistant manager.

Suzanne marched up the brick walk, barely noticing the flower beds on either side, freshened for fall with bright mums and purple cabbage plants, and more autumn flowers that spilled from boxes along the porch rail.

In the shop's front window, a grinning scarecrow in a hand-stitched vest stood guard over a field of pumpkins and skeins of yarn. Just above, scarves, socks, and baby sweaters hung from a tree branch, and a few curious blackbirds looked on.

She noticed none of it. Even the sign above the door, BLACK SHEEP & COMPANY, had no effect. The sight usually elicited a wave of pure calm in expectation of chatting and stitching all evening with her very best friends.

All she wanted to do tonight was vent her heart out and soak up some sisterhood sympathy. And sip some wine. Not necessarily in that order.

She stepped inside and saw the group in the back room, seated around the big oak table. It looked like they were just about to start dinner. An appetizing scent greeted her and she remembered she'd skipped a real lunch, resorting to the dwindling stash of diet drinks she kept in the office fridge. She could have sworn she'd left a full pack there just the other day, but her co-workers were not above food pilfering. That was the least of her problems today.

Maggie walked out of the storeroom that doubled as a kitchen, a bowl of green salad in her hands.

"There you are. We weren't sure if you were coming. We just sat down to eat. Everyone was so hungry. Come, take a seat."

"Working late on a hot deal?" Lucy's tone was teasing but also admiring, Suzanne thought.

She glanced at Lucy and felt fixed to the spot. Maggie and the others—Lucy, Dana, and Phoebe—stared back, waiting for her reply.

"Not exactly . . . More like having a nervous breakdown."

"Are you all right?" Maggie drew closer and touched her arm. "Did something happen at work?"

Suzanne nodded, chin trembling. She thought she might cry, but valiantly fought the urge. "Not something. *Some-one*. You know who I mean. The name that shall not be spoken?"

Everyone knew the famous quote from the Harry Potter novels about the evil Lord Voldemort, didn't they? Even so, Suzanne was sure the meaning was clear.

Dana smiled and shook her head. "Liza Devereaux again? Or should I say the Dark Lord-ess . . . ? Is that even a word?"

"Any way you say it, that woman is pure poison. She was put on this earth to drive me mad. And she finally suc-ceeded." Suzanne felt her blood pressure shoot up all over again. "I'd like to string her up by the strap of that Prada handbag. I'd like to wrap that strand of pearls around her scrawny little throat. . . ."

"Suzanne, calm down." Maggie put an arm around Suz-anne's shoulder and gently guided her into a chair. "What in the world has gotten you in such a state?"

Suzanne took a breath and glanced around at the group. They looked back at her with surprise and concern. As if she'd lost her mind.

"I sound crazy, right? Maybe I am. Dana, tell me hon-estly. I can take it." She turned to Dana Haeger, the group's resident psychologist, half asking, half dreading a profes-sional diagnosis. "How would you rate my sanity, on a scale of one to ten?"

Dana's expression was pure sympathy. "I'd say you were extremely distressed. Just slow down and take a breath. How can we help you?"

She did take a breath, as Dana advised. But she felt tears well up on the exhale. Lucy sat the closest; she leaned over and patted Suzanne's hand. Then handed her a glass of Chardonnay.

"Here you go. I'll get your dinner. Calm down and tell us what your mortal foe did now."

Not good to drink on an empty stomach, Suzanne reminded herself. But she took a healthy sip anyway and tried to focus.

"Stole another sale right out from under my nose, that's what. It would have been my biggest commission this year. Maybe of my entire career!"

Dana sat at the far end of the table, most of her dish filled with salad, Suzanne noticed. "Liza is that supersharp salesperson at your office, right? Your big rival?"

"To put it mildly. A rival is another mom in your kid's grade school class who bakes cuter cupcakes. Liza is a vicious predator, ready to pounce at any moment. A deeply despised nemesis. A painful thorn in my backside . . ."

"I think the expression is simply a thorn in one's side," Maggie corrected in a mild tone.

"I just call 'em the way I see 'em." Suzanne shrugged.

Lucy returned with a dish of pasta that smelled and looked very tasty. She set it down in front of Suzanne along with a fork and napkin.

"Bless you." Suzanne spread the paper napkin across her lap, then tucked another under her chin to protect her black cashmere poncho. She'd been careful all day not to drag the fringe through things. Not the most practical garment she'd ever purchased, though it did hide a myriad of figure flaws, and quite stylishly. Style was way more important than convenience, or even comfort, she'd always thought.

"Carbs are calming. Nature's tranquilizer," Lucy advised.

"Dig in and tell us what went down," Phoebe urged.

Suzanne took a small, fortifying bite. "It started Sunday. I was running an open house in Harbor Hills, the two-acre zone near the country club? A jaw-dropping colonial— five bedrooms, three and a half baths, gourmet kitchen, stadium-sized family room, and a gorgeous stone fireplace that—"

"—A highly saleable property, with a high price tag to match?" Maggie selected a piece of garlic bread and passed the basket to Suzanne.

"Yes, and yes. And mine, mine, mine. Exclusively. That is, until *she* showed up." Suzanne felt the pressure in her head build. She knew what people meant about seeing red, and it wasn't just the sauce on the pasta. Which was delicious. She had to compliment the chef. Maggie, she suspected.

"Liza Devereaux is a killer shark hiding behind Chanel sunglasses. She can smell a juicy listing from one hundred miles away. I should have expected a sneak attack. But everything was going so smoothly, I dropped my guard."

"So Liza crashed your open house?" Phoebe prodded her.

"More like wiggled in, wearing one of her little pencil skirts and super high heels. And all that bouncy, fake hair. A great look . . . if you're a size zero."

Just picturing her mortal enemy on the fatal day made Suzanne's breath catch. Suzanne was a fashionista to her friends, but Liza had a certain classic, country club look that always won first prize on the office runway. Her rival's sleek figure—practically skeletal, Suzanne thought—just made it worse. She'd often heard it said, "You can't be too thin or too rich." Liza definitely had the former down and was very close to achieving the latter.

Suzanne paused for a crunchy bite of garlic bread as her friends waited to hear more.

"She claimed that Harry, our boss, heard there was a lot of traffic and sent her to help. As if *I* ever need help. And certainly, not hers. It was so obvious. She wasn't getting any action on her listings that day and slunk around to poach." Suzanne took another sip of wine and continued. "Before I could check the story, Liza comes waltzing into the kitchen with Juanita and Bob Briggs. I've been cultivating those two for months. I showed them every pricey house for sale within fifty miles. A few weeks ago, they told me that they needed a break from looking. They promised to get in touch once they knew what was going on."

"That sounds reasonable," Dana said.

"Sure, I get it. But I never heard back and didn't want to be pushy. It's a fine line. Anyway, there they are. As large as life and prequalified over a million. The hunt was obviously on again, but I missed the memo."

She sighed and sipped her wine. "We all say hello, nice and polite. I could see they really liked the house. I knew they would. I'd even sent Juanita an e-mail last week about the property. Maybe she missed it? I don't know." Suzanne shrugged. "I talked them up a little, but Liza had covered the sales points and they had to go." She paused and sighed. "Looking back, I should have chased them out the door, tackled them on the lawn, thrown myself on the hood of their Land Rover. . . ."

"Do you really do that?" Phoebe didn't look surprised, just curious. She'd recently started her own business, a sideline to her job at the shop, and often asked Suzanne for sales and marketing tips.

"Whatever it takes, Phoebe. Never hesitate to make a total fool of yourself if it will close a deal. Did I follow my own Golden Rule? No. Oh golly, do I regret it now."

"Don't be so hard on yourself. They'd already signaled they didn't want to be pressured," Dana pointed out.

"That's what I thought. On Monday, I checked to see if they were interested, but they never called back. On Tuesday, I sent an e-mail. Again, no reply."

Lucy helped herself to some salad. "Uh-oh. I think I know where this is going."

"No place good," Suzanne replied. "This afternoon we had our weekly status meeting. The sales team reports on progress with clients, new listings and closings. That sort of thing. I always dread when it's Liza's turn. I never know what she's got up her sleeve. Today, with this big phony smile, she announced she just got an offer on the Harbor Hills property. *She* got an offer."

"—From your clients, Juanita and Bob," Maggie filled in.

"That is so unfair! Classic pickle jar syndrome. Just classic." Lucy tossed her hands in the air while everyone else exchanged confused glances.

"Classic . . . what?" Dana looked the most confused.

"It's like a pickle jar with a tight lid?" Lucy explained. "Suzanne twisted and banged, ran it under hot water. Did everything she could to pry it loose. But it didn't budge. Then Liza gives it one tiny turn and it pops right off. And Liza gets the credit, while poor Suzanne did all the work. It's a law of physics or something."

"I know what you mean. Though I doubt you'd find that one in a textbook," Maggie murmured.

"That happens all the time. I just never knew what to call it before," Phoebe said. "Ever notice when a woman is dating some guy for years, and no matter what she does, he won't commit? The next girlfriend comes along and that slacker is running down to the mall, shopping for diamond rings. Pickle jar syndrome, definitely."

"I don't know about physics, or slacker boyfriends, but in real life, pickle jar syndrome stinks," Suzanne said.

Dana had put her dish aside and opened up her knitting tote. "I hope you brought this to the attention of your boss."

"Of course I did. I put in months on these people, gallons of gas and so much smiling, I sprained a dimple."

Maggie started to say something, then caught herself. "Sounds painful," she said finally.

"Tell me about it. Liza, as phony as her stick-on eye lashes, chats them up for five seconds and waltzes off with my commission? No way, babe." Suzanne shook her head. "Over my dead body. Or *hers.*"

As Suzanne left the shop with Lucy and Dana, a chilly wind greeted them, tossing tree branches and scuttling dry leaves down Plum Harbor's quiet Main Street. Up above, a silver sliver of moon glowed in a deep blue sky. Suzanne pulled her poncho close and waved good night to her friends as they each ran in a different direction to their cars.

She climbed into her SUV and headed down the street. Knitting night had definitely brought some peace and perspective.

But alone again, worries crept in. Was Kevin still up? It was only a quarter to eleven, but her husband worked hard at his construction jobs. "Early to bed, early to rise" was his motto. He really did need his sleep and Suzanne knew she wouldn't have the heart to wake him when she got in, even to share her awful day. Or warn him that she might get fired tomorrow. *At least one of us should get some rest,* she reasoned.

Right before the turn for her usual route home, the sign for Prestige Properties came into view. Suzanne noticed lights on inside. She expected to see the van for the office cleaning service. They came every Thursday night, without fail. A reason she preferred to invite clients to meet there on a Friday.

But only a white Mercedes SUV stood parked in front of the building tonight. The personalized plates on the back—

AMEYMOXI—told Suzanne all she needed to know. Liza was burning the midnight oil.

Probably making her case for getting me fired. Or trying to figure out what other deals she can steal.

Now, now . . . you have to summon up a better attitude, pronto. Remember what your friends said? Good advice. Get yourself resigned to some heavy duty groveling. Or you might be very sorry. You can catch more black widow spiders with honey than vinegar, right? You've got to sweeten her up, before she talks Harry into giving you the boot.

Suzanne slowed down and pulled up behind Liza's vehicle. Time to get this over with. The pep talk from her pals had psyched Suzanne into doing the right thing. But she knew that by tomorrow, she could wake up feeling mad all over again. It had certainly happened before.

Suzanne shut the ignition, then checked her hair and lipstick in the visor mirror. Not going to win any beauty contests, but looking a little ragged might work on Liza's sympathy. If she had any, as Maggie claimed.

Suzanne slipped out of the driver's seat, took a deep breath, and headed for the realty office.

As Mom always said, "No time like the present."

Chapter 2

Large lights illuminated the gold-lettered logo of Prestige Properties, which hung above the storefront window. The glass was covered with glossy photos of houses, apartments, and vacant land for sale. It was a thriving office with lots of juicy listings, and Suzanne would hate to leave it.

The heavy glass door was unlocked and Suzanne swung it open easily. She wondered why Liza wasn't more careful. There was little need to worry in Plum Harbor, but a woman alone, especially at night, needed to be cautious anywhere. Suzanne always told her daughter that.

The reception area was dark and empty. Further back, where the worker bees sat in partitioned cubicles, a soft light glowed, and Suzanne headed toward it.

Suzanne liked to joke about the padded walls in her cubicle. Definitely a plus when things got crazy. Most of the time, she didn't mind not having a "real" office. She did most of her wheeling and dealing in her car, or at home, from her cell phone and tablet, as did the rest of the sales staff. The cubicle was a landing spot, a little nest where she rested and recharged before new adventures. She liked to think of it that way.

She passed her own space, catching a glimpse of the photos that covered one wall. Mostly of her family—

dressed in their best at some holiday party; Alexis, in her lacrosse gear, grubby but victorious; her twin boys, Ryan and Jamie, mugging for the camera as they blew out the candles on matching cakes at their last birthday party.

When she felt drained and unmotivated, the smiling faces of the people she loved most in the world never failed to pump her up again.

That's why I work so hard, she reminded herself as she walked by. Not to "best" Liza Devereaux. Or even for cashmere ponchos and other fine things. *I do it for my family and I'll sweet talk, or even beg this woman, in order to keep my job. I'll do what I have to.*

A thin shaft of light stretched into the hallway from Liza's space. Suzanne's steps slowed as she approached. She listened for keyboard clicks or Liza's voice, talking on the phone. She didn't hear a thing.

Was she in there? Maybe she was back in the staff kitchen, getting a cup of coffee? Or sipping one of those diet shakes she seemed to live on?

Suzanne paused and delivered her opening lines as she stood near the entrance to Liza's cubicle. "Sorry to bother you so late. But I saw your car outside and wondered if we could talk."

Suzanne stepped into the partitioned space, listening for a reply. . . .

But only heard her own scream of panic.

The desk lamp had fallen to one side, the harsh light shining directly in Suzanne's face, casting long shadows around the small space. She raised her hand to shield her eyes and get a better look at Liza, who was sprawled out on the floor.

Suzanne rushed toward her and crouched down. She quickly checked for a pulse and leaned closer. Was Liza breathing? She couldn't tell for sure.

"This can't be . . . Liza? Please! Can you hear me?" Suzanne slapped Liza's cheek, but there was no reaction. She felt for the pulse in her wrist and then her neck. Then pressed her ear to her rival's chest, desperate to hear a heartbeat.

Nothing.

"Oh, Liza . . . Answer me . . . please! Can you hear me? Please wake up. What happened to you?"

Suzanne stared down at Liza's motionless body, the blue-tinged skin of her complexion, her blank, staring eyes. The surprised expression, frozen on her face. Suzanne sat back on her heels and felt the room spin. She staggered to her feet and stumbled backward. The soles of her boots rolled on small, round objects, and nearly made her fall.

She looked down and saw pearls, all over the carpeting. From Liza's favorite necklace, she realized. The string had somehow burst and sent the precious beads flying.

Someone could gather them up and have the necklace restrung. It would be as good as new, Suzanne thought. No such easy repair for its owner. No remedy at all . . .

She turned and ran into the hall, heading for the light in the staff kitchen. "Help! Help, somebody! Is anyone here?"

No one answered. She was all alone. . . .